DRIFTING
CURTAIN

DRIFTING CURTAIN

JAMES S. LEITCH

TATE PUBLISHING
AND ENTERPRISES, LLC

Published by Tate Publishing & Enterprises, LLC
127 E. Trade Center Terrace | Mustang, Oklahoma 73064 USA
1.888.361.9473 | www.tatepublishing.com

Tate Publishing is committed to excellence in the publishing industry. The company reflects the philosophy established by the founders, based on Psalm 68:11,
"The Lord gave the word and great was the company of those who published it."

Book design copyright © 2013 by Tate Publishing, LLC. All rights reserved.
Cover design by Jan Sunday Quilaquil
Interior design by Mary Jean Archival

Published in the United States of America
ISBN: 978-1-62746-693-6
1. Fiction / Thrillers / Military
2. Fiction / War & Military
13.06.21

DEDICATIONS

This novel is dedicated to the family who always said I could, even when I never believed it myself.

PROLOGUE

It seemed like everything was slow, as if he were underwater. Hanson could feel the sweat beading on his forehead, becoming heavier and heavier, until one bead broke free from its place and rolled down his nose. He tried to listen, but all he could hear was a piercing ringing in his ears, a ringing that seemed to dwarf any other noise. He looked around him, straining to see through dust and smoke that filled the air, which created an opaque sheet in front of him. He noticed shadows, some by the light of the sun, others from a fire that erupted and then disappeared into the cloud. He could see the silhouettes of what appeared to be men, sliding on the other side of this drifting curtain of sand and destruction.

Things then began to speed up, and Hanson became more aware of where he was. He noticed he was propped up against a large orange-gray bolder, adjacent to a road. *It was an IED, that's what the explosion was,* he thought to himself, but that is all his mind would give him. He couldn't remember what country he was in or the squad he was with—everything in his head was blank except the letters "IED." It was strange; he felt like there was something important about those letters that was meant for him, something that was just outside of his reach. He started to remember something Sergeant Walker said, but then, all he could think about was who Sergeant Walker was. Then he remembered, Sergeant Walker told him something about the letters. *Where is he? What did he tell me?* His mind just kept repeating those words; he knew he had to find him.

He turned his head; the bead of sweat finally released its grasp and dropped until it landed on a pistol. He looked at the weapon strangely as if he didn't know what it was, and then he realized it was his Beretta 9mm, and he gratefully picked it up from the ground. He began to stand but then collapsed when he felt a crippling pain in his right leg. He looked down and noticed that the padded area around his thigh was torn and soaked in blood, and he could see a piece of metal, broken glass, and what looked to be staples protruding from the wound. Then something caught his attention; it was someone screaming, penetrating the noise, and then he realized it was himself that was screaming. Yet he wasn't crying for help or from pain, he was screaming the letters that now seemed to have voices of their own, and he was simply the medium for the words to travel through. "IED! IED!" he wailed, but the time for that warning had already passed.

He looked up once again, into that drifting curtain, and seeing someone laying a few yards from where he was, he began to crawl, slowly and painfully, to the body in front of him. As he got closer, he could see the symbol on the man's arm; then the word *Sergeant* popped into his mind. The man looked familiar; suddenly he realized it was the Sergeant, and this new knowledge caused him to crawl faster. The ringing in his ears began to subside, and he could hear the sound of machine gun fire somewhere near him, but then it was halted by another explosion. He was just a few feet away when he noticed the sergeant was starting to move, so he screamed the name that he believed he should call. "Sergeant! Sergeant, can you hear me? Sergeant!" He continued to repeat this until the sergeant turned his head and looked at him.

After what seemed to be an hour of sliding beneath the drifting curtain, he finally reached the sergeant, who had pushed himself up into a half-sitting position. The sergeant's right arm was saturated in blood to the point of turning the dirt it touched to red mud; however, it seemed to be functional as he used it to situate himself. As he did, it became clear that there were burned and bloody gashes on the right side of his face and chest. By the time the soldier had reached the place where his sergeant sat, his world had returned to its familiar loud and crisp sounds, and his vision had lost some of the blur that had been clouding it, but the ringing was still there. He was about to ask the sergeant if he was okay, but the sergeant spoke first, "What the hell happened with that bomb, Hanson?!" This question surprised Hanson, who now had positioned himself against the same rock as Sergeant Walker, but he didn't know what had happened with the bomb; he then realized he knew the sergeant's name.

"What do you mean, sir?" Hanson replied. A pit began to form in his stomach, as if he had just swallowed a rock.

"I'm asking what you did to make that thing go off?!" Hanson wasn't sure what to say. He kept looking around him; now the curtain was lifting, and he saw dirt and sand-covered bulges lying near what looked like small hills.

Hanson was searching for an answer to the question he had half-forgotten when he noticed something on his own shoulder. The letters "EOD" were printed in bold just above the symbol of rank. *EOD? What does that...*

Suddenly, all the memories rushed back into his head like a freight train, and as he remembered what had happened, his reaction followed suit. He remembered the platoon he was walking with when one of the point men, whom Sergeant Walker had sent, came from the front and alerted them (he and his Explosive Ordinance Disposal squad) to an obscure pile of trash up the road. He remembered being brought up to the area with his partner, both of them wearing protective gear. He remembered the beep that had broken his concentration on the missile-shaped explosive whose timer still had thirteen seconds on it. He remembered looking up at his partner, whose expression of terror and surprise no doubt mirrored his own. He then remembered yelling for everyone to get back, although most had moved away from the blast area, and he himself running away. Finally, he remembered the feeling: the same way an ocean would lift and carry someone, just amplified to that of title wave proportions. From here, he only remembered the heat and glimpses of his rapid journey into the small quarry of boulders where he lost consciousness.

Hanson's mind snapped back into the now and realized that his partner hadn't gotten far enough away from the blast. He then began to panic; he couldn't breathe, his vision now was blurry from the tears in his eyes. *I killed him!* he thought to himself and then he said it out loud, to give his officer an answer to the question.

"Serge, I killed Billy! I killed Billy!" He was about to stand up to go look for him when his sergeant pulled him back and yelled, "You stand up, and I'll be draggin' your dead body! I'll be draggin' your body along with any more I can find!" This made it clear in Hanson's mind; it was his fault that the bomb went off. If he had only disarmed it sooner, maybe he could have saved them, but it was too late to change what had happened. Sergeant Walker then told him to stay put while he went to look for any survivors.

Hanson began to lose track of time; he saw the sergeant run hunched over toward a dirt pile that turned out to be a dead man, and he moved on. Hanson looked up into the sky, seeing only a few rays of sunlight through the dust and smoke. *I killed them...I killed them...* all he could think about was the men whose lives he must have ended. Things became distant then; he was numb and could hear only a few noises but was too preoccupied to figure out what they were. He turned his head over just a little to see what had become of the sergeant and saw him return with a few men whom Hanson didn't know. His vision then failed as he heard one last thing: "It's not your fault, kid, it's not your fault."

SECTION ONE

FIRE

CARDS

0925 hours, July 8, Camp Bastion
Helmand Province, Afghanistan

The sun had risen just a couple hours ago, the heat beginning to return to its regular oven-on-high feeling, and the sky bright as ever. A rush of sand was blown up from its resting place along the extensive dry banks and hills, and as it crashed against the dehydrated foliage that dotted the landscape, its sound was that of a soft rain. In the distance, vast mountains cast their forms against the sky, like ripples of darkness against an endless canvas. A single road, with little besides tracks left by large vehicles, stretched along the ground as a line drawn in the sand, going in either direction for miles with little more to see than its crossing with other roads. It is along this road, just a few miles south of Kandahar-Herat Highway, that the largest British military base in Afghanistan is located: Camp Bastion.

The base itself is little more than a quadrangular speck on a map, or at least on one large enough to show the landscape and roads that systematically section off the lower part of Helmand Province. From the inside, however, the camp has the feel of a small city; buildings set up for function rather than appearance, vehicles moving at an almost leisurely pace, and the people either upholding a social life while working or just working. Many times it is easier to hitch a ride with an equipment transport than to walk, as most people will move out of the way; but this is not ideal on days when one doesn't feel like mixing with people, as you would have to sit next to someone. Specialist Daniil Brish was having one of those days.

He was heading across camp to eat, either from regular rations or the Pizza Hut on base. Or at least that's what he told the guys back at the poker game. In truth he was fuming, unable to register the loss of money in his mind, and unable to drive away the feeling that he did everything right and still lost. Thus, as he made his way to the mess tents, he ignored any thoughts of transportation; so he baked in the sun while he boiled under his camo.

"Can I get the regular?" He asked, sarcasm apparent and reciprocated when the man who handed him his A-Ration package smirked and asked if he wanted any ice cream with it; Daniil simply sat down and roasted his food with his demeanor.

As he ate he looked around, observing the buildings where a majority of the important offices resided, including the Army Criminal Investigative Command (CID) Offices. Basically the a militarized form of modern detectives, CID agents were well trained, sharp, and astoundingly forward in every advance; either in following a lead, or chasing tail. He was simply jealous of the air conditioning that accompanied the office. To his right sat the barracks tents, aligned in long rows and shimmering slightly against the sun; one a few rows back held his cash and his pride. He couldn't stop thinking about it. With each bite of the well-preserved but poorly flavored apple he replayed hands, tossing ideas around in his mind until he could come up with some answer. So far no solution presented itself. So he stayed thinking, and nearly missed the conversation, which the pair of men sitting behind him were having.

"Bro, Raymond is kickin' tail today. I think I lost more than I did the last time I was in Vegas."

"You've been to Vegas?" the other asked, an obvious Danish accent letting off that he'd only heard stories about the great city of Vegas.

"Yeah, and I thought that trip was bad."

"Well you know," the Dane spoke up again "I was watching Raymond during the game, and he wasn't worried at all. Not once. Seemed like he was ready for anything you or the rest of the table had. Strange, uh?"

"What do you mean, bro, like he was playing us?"

"That I don't know, but he seemed pretty confident. He had a tell though." Brish was listening intently. Full focus on what the man had to say next. "Every time he had a good hand, he was rubbing his forearm, like this." The man showed his friend as he massaged the underside of his wrist.

Brish had turned around by then, seen what the Dane had done, and made his way out of the mess tent; his plate was ravaged within a minute of his leaving.

—*ανα*—

The tent was as comfortable as when he had left it; with little room, lots of heat, and plenty of nervous energy as those in the tent watched the game. Only a few more hands from conclusion, it was obvious already who was going to win; the only question was whether it would be by a full house or a straight flush. It was only Raymond, however, that knew the hands. In front of him a pile of cash from several different countries sat, the dark skinned man on the other side of the table glaring at it with envy. He noticed Raymond was staring at him then looked back to his cards. Raymond checked, the man checked, and the last card turned up.

The dark man across from him looked up at that moment, devilishly grinning, and asked if he was nervous. Raymond simply smiled and said he was just worked up from all the winning he had done. The men around the table laughed, and the hand reached its conclusion, with the tall American winning again. Suddenly the tent door was pushed open, and a stocky individual, no more than five foot ten or so, walked in and removed his sunglasses, ice-cold blue eyes locked on to the tall American. The other men in the room were quiet; Raymond's eyes were now noticeably more nervous than before. But in order to break the silence, the losing player was the first to speak up, "Hey, Daniil, glad to have you back in the game."

"Thank you, Alard." Corporal Daniil Brish said, "But I am not here for the game." His eyes never left the tall one. Daniil then approached him quickly, causing the tall man to stand but not back up; Raymond's pride wouldn't let him and was so forceful in fact he began to reestablish his self-appointed dominance. "Can I help you, bud?" he said mockingly.

"Yes," Daniil said, his generally suppressed Russian accent now obvious in his deep, raspy voice. "I would like to have the money you cheated me out of." As he spoke, his eyes never wavered from Raymond's; the two locked in a tangible but inaudible battle until the tall man averted his gaze.

"Listen, Brish," he said, still avoiding Daniil's gaze, "I didn't cheat you out of any money. You just lost a fair game of cards. These guys have all lost to me, and they're not demanding their money back. Maybe you just need to calm down or go walk it off or something."

"If you didn't cheat me, I wouldn't be here. I want my money back, Corporal Raymond, and I want it now."

"I don't know where your little Russian head is getting this stuff from, but Americans don't call cheat every time they lose."

The guys standing around sighed or shook their heads. "Bad move, Ray," someone said, to whom Ray shot a piercing look. However, when he returned his focus to Brish, his confidence dropped, and he immediately stopped smiling.

Brish's face had rapidly faded into a look of cold, harsh intent; he was done with the conversation. He swiftly jabbed his fist into the side of Ray's neck, just above the clavicle, causing a spasm to run down the man's right side, bringing his arm up and causing him to crimp downward. As soon as his hands came up, Brish grabbed the right elbow with his own right hand, then stepping around to the man's side, he pulled down on the elbow and dipped and hooked the right leg forward and up with his left arm. Raymond attempted to strike back with his free hand, but his balance was lost and he went cascading downward. This action forced the tall man over on to his back, bouncing off the edge of a cot and then slamming onto the floor. Brish grabbed his right thumb and hand, twisting to turn him over. The hold seemed to be relatively painful for the receiver of the strike, who expressed his discontent by scrunching his face like an animal who just found out what a shock collar feels like—it sucks. When he tried to get up, Brish pressed his boot onto the man's shoulder blade, which kept the angry look on his face. Brish reached his fingers into the sleeve, removing a couple high cards from a wristband that had held the cards just out of sight but also in reach. Brish, with a look of not only disgust but also pity coming on his face, threw the man's hand down and proceeded toward the table, taking the money.

Noticing the others in the room and realizing he had taken more than was his, he counted out what was his and then set the rest down on the cot. "About the game, I apologize, I know some of you wanted to finish. But I know you didn't want to play a cheater's game." He turned to leave but then stopped and looked at the man he had just dispatched, who was now leaning against the cot he had so abruptly intercepted on his way to the floor. "You gonna squeal about all this stuff?" the downed man asked, attempting to maintain some of his dignity.

"No, there would be no point. I don't need higher-ups to defend me." He turned to leave, but as he was leaving, he remembered the remark about him being Russian. "Oh, and I am just as American as you are, Raymond, you should know that." Brish looked down and shook his head. *Cast not thy pearls before swine*, he thought then turned away and went outside.

—⟨⟩⟨⟩⟨⟩—

Further away from the barracks, a relatively large building was stationed. As one of the only solid (non-tent) structures on the base, it can, and in fact must house the needs of the main Southern Afghanistan hospital. Due to this great responsibility, the hospital is staffed with several different surgical sectors, and specialized help ranged from orthopedic, if someone were to lose a limb, to thoracic, if a lucky soul were to take one in the chest and be able to make it to surgery. The recovery sector of the hospital, which is both inside and outside the walls of the facility, has many who have made it from the battlefield outside the base to the warzone within the walls of the lifesaving encampment, and then made it out alive. Making it out alive is what every soldier, or at least most, believes is their destiny. But when one is lost, those left behind begin to wonder why they're still around. This is especially true for Damian Hanson, an experienced Explosive Ordinance Disposal (EOD) Technician working with the United States Army, although he himself was a Navy.

Hanson was laying on a medium-sized bed, long, white metal poles serving as the railing, just to make sure that he didn't fall off and break something. He was covered in white: from the wrapping around his head, to keep his brains from pouring out he surmised, to the casting brace around his side and thigh, and to top it all, he was covered in white sheets. He figured that if there were better lighting, he would go snow-blind. His leg was numb, but a slight throbbing was still emanating from where some shrapnel had tore into it, leaving him unable to move it without significant protest. He was sitting halfway up, held in place by the torso wrap that was protecting his bruised ribs. He was staring out the window that was located to the right of his bed, observing the silent motions of the soldiers outside and thinking about how the desert that claimed the lives of so many was still roasting outside his room, completely callous to its insatiable thirst for bodies. He became depressed and angry almost immediately, so much so that, in order to suppress his escalating depression, he needed to eat. He turned over, and by that, he really just turned his head and attempted to reach for the food on the tray. After about a minute of feeling like someone was driving a hammer into his side, his hunger gave way to frustration, which gave way to him deciding to flip the tray off of his bed with the tip of his finger. The decision made sense, and a second later, he had covered the floor with a beautiful arrangement of apple sauce and bread. It was after the tray hit the floor that he realized he shouldn't have done that, mostly because he'd already done that three times before, and the British nurse who came in to clean up before, a starkly unattractive brunette with an increasingly angry look on her face, would probably not appreciate the gesture. And sure enough, the nurse leaned in, gave him one of the meanest looks he'd ever received, and walked away.

The door opened up slightly, giving Hanson a glimpse of the hallway, the path to freedom if only Hanson were capable of getting out of bed. His picture, however, became obscured by a soldier clad in US Army camouflage, seemingly stretched together to fit the masculine form that filled it. Hanson looked up to see Daniil Brish walk into the room and take off his hat, revealing his angry, steel-colored eyes resting beneath a heavy-set brow and short bangs, matted down from their regular military stand-at-attention placement by the hat, which he set at the foot of the bed. He pulled a bench out from around the set of blue curtains separating Hanson's room from the emptiness of the other room and sat down, eying the mess on the floor. Brish paused for a moment, seemingly contemplating whether or not to stay quiet or to try to make Hanson feel better. Hanson was so tired he didn't really care what he had to say: he was simply glad to have some company that could amuse him more than knocking a tray off his bed.

"How you holdin' up?" asked Brish.

"I've had better days, Danny, I've had better days." Hanson turned and looked out the window.

"All right, but you do need to stop buggin' the nurses. I'm pretty sure they're planning on putting you in a mini coma till you're well enough to leave."

Hanson's mood lightened up a little, and when he saw that Brish was half-smiling, like usual, he decided that sulking had taken up enough of his day. "So how did the game go? You win?"

Brish's smile faded a little. Hanson could tell something hadn't gone well, but Hanson knew not to press into it; if Brish wanted to say, he would.

It became quiet, both men simply unable to come up with a conversation that wasn't serious, that didn't mention the incident that had happened a few days before. Eventually, and to Hanson's disappointment, Brish had to bring it up.

"It wasn't your fault, you know, with Billy." Brish had turned his chair to face Hanson, his eyes now stern. "What happened was an accident. It's not like you shot 'em."

"But I was there, right next to him. I was working on that thing when it went—" A nurse walked in, blatantly ignoring the mess that had recently appeared on the floor and went toward a desk. She grabbed a couple gauze rolls and a bag of pins and walked out the door, eying Brish's rugged, masculine features; apparently she was one of those nurses who dig guys in camo. Brish, contrary to his usual attention toward women, ignored her presence. The door closed.

"I didn't stop that bomb, and he died because of it. So no, I didn't shoot him, but I could have stopped him from buying it, and I didn't. Instead, I survived, and what's left of him is flying stateside. What the hell kind of justice is that, huh? What in the *hell* is that!?" Hanson looked for something nearby to throw, but he was all out of trays. Brish had nothing to say; he just wanted to help, and Hanson knew that but he just wasn't feeling right.

Brish got up from his chair and walked slowly toward the windows to his right. He looked at the floor inquisitively, as if his next line were written on its metallic white glimmer. He reached the window, rested his forearms on the windowsill, and proceeded to explain more on how Hanson wasn't to feel responsible for Billy's death and that Billy would want Hanson to move on, and a bunch of other generic help-me-up lines. Hanson listened, not because any of it made him feel better, but because if he didn't, he would just piss Brish off, and he would start to yell at him in Russian. The words weren't pearls of wisdom, in fact, unlike stories and movies, there is rarely ever a nugget of unheard truth that can be pulled out of one's rear to save the day; the point was simply that he tried. Besides, if someone didn't talk to Hanson, he would probably try to get up, hurt himself, and be stuck in this whitewash needle factory for however long the needle people say he has to.

Brish suddenly lit up, as if some wonderful idea had been shot into his brain by the Happy Brigade. Hanson couldn't wait to know what it was.

"Dom?" The name that people call him instead of Damian. "You got to grieve, and then you have to move on. Now I know it's a little premature to start forgetting your bud, but if you keep blaming yourself, you're just going to keep falling. So"—Brish stood—"I'm going to go see what information they have so far from one of the guys at Army CID, and I'll get you a tennis ball so you can throw and not make a mess." Brish smiled as he spoke, and the culmination of the sarcasm and generosity of Brish's disposition brought a real smile to Hanson's face as well.

"Hey, Danny," Hanson called. "Thanks for coming."

"Not a problem, *comrade*," he said in sarcastically thick Russian accent. "I'll be back in a while." Then he left. Hanson resituated and was instantly reminded why he should refrain from doing that. All of a sudden, he didn't feel that interested in staying in this place, but he knew he wasn't going anywhere for now.

HEARTBEAT

He could hear pounding, a deep throb that cascaded through his mind. In the darkness, he could feel pressure, something he had felt before, but couldn't place what it was. And despite his inquiry, all he was given in answer was the pounding. At first it only shook him, moved him, made him aware of its approach. But as it neared, he began to see light, fading in and out with each strike of this drum in his mind. He could see dust, or sand, or smoke…in truth he didn't know what it was; but it was drifting. It moved around him ceaselessly, until finally, a small amount of light breached its hold on his thoughts. He could see the sun, but it changed, became angrier as it transformed into a fire, burning its way toward him. He seemed to be looking up, but slowly, his gaze fell onto the outline of a man. As the fire grew, he could feel its heat, and the pounding still grew ever louder with the pressure around him closing in, until the fire engulfed the silhouette, and finally him. As it did so, the light began to give in to the resurging power of the cloud, and the fire finally faded away into a black smoke. He slipped back into the darkness, but the pounding continued, until by a burst of his own will, Hanson awoke.

His heart was pounding in his chest, and he could tell by its rhythm that it was the source of the tormenting resonance from his dream. He stared up at the bleached ceiling, glazed over by the shadows contrasting the red sliver of light that blazed through the small crack between one door and its partially opened counterpart. He could see movement outside of his room, causing the light to flicker at times, but it never left him, thus passed every night he'd been there. The outside world seemed as though it were restless, agitated, and numb. Then he realized that was him, and that the world was callously moving on without him. He could hear the others in the hospital, following the rest of the world, moving busily from one objective to the next. Hanson thought about where he would be now if he wasn't closed up in this little white bubble of bandages and sheets. It surprised him just how much he would do, or would have done, that before he never even considered. He could walk freely, even when he was on assignment; he was able to work in his own way. It was as though he, now tied into this small bed in this secluded room, was able to see the things he had done and all his plans, and he realized that there was too much. All these thoughts flooded him so quickly he almost shouted, trying to push the world back so he could fix these mistakes, but his yelling would do nothing for him. Just as his strength, his will, or even his courage waivered, so did his consciousness.

He turned over a little, and even with his pain now dulled by either time or the Vicodin, his body still only let him know he wouldn't be moving much more. He sighed, watching the light that passed by his window, created by Humvees or trucks, still working long into the night. He remembered back in Arizona, when he and his friend Bill Tompkey were driving to a local diner a few miles outside of Phoenix, Billy had been his best friend since they met at the University of Phoenix, in the Reserve Officers Training Corps. Hanson believed then he wanted to be a general, the guy who would make the decisions, save the world from a new third Reich kind of thing. Billy, as a major gearhead, just wanted to work on the army's tanks and jeeps; he couldn't keep his hands off of machines, and he was goaded routinely to be a mechanic. It was this night when Hanson and Billy decided to change their plans. Hanson remembered how he proposed the idea that they both enter into the EOD programs after they really got into the swing of the military. Billy didn't think it was a good idea, mostly because even a firecracker he had when he was younger had almost blew his fingers off, so he figured it would be safer for him to just deal with stuff that didn't have a tendency to, well, explode.

"But if we do EOD, Billy, you get to work on the technical stuff, we both get higher pay, and we won't have to do it as long. Besides, neither of us will mess up on something as big as a bomb, that's why they train us anyway." Hanson remembered saying that to Billy, he remembered Billy's protest, but most of all, he remembered Billy giving in. Hanson had come to a conclusion over the last couple days; Billy died because Hanson changed his mind. "It's not your fault," some have said; others say that the crazy bastard who planted the bomb deserves the blame, but Hanson knew better, and if he had just let Billy be, he would be outside working on one of those heavy lifters that continue to pass by his window. What a guilt trip or maybe just guilt.

Despite Hanson's total-recall moment, he was having trouble remembering, to his slight relief, what he did to make that thing go off. He closed his eyes again, thinking back to just before the explosion where he and Billy were approaching the estimated area of effect. He remembered clearing the soldiers who believed they were far enough away from the bomb to be unharmed, and then made their final approach. Just like the others he had seen and worked with, it was surrounded by an assortment of trash, old bottles resting on plastic bags obscuring the shape to be all the more menacing. He remembered feeling cumbersome as he removed a plastic bag atop the suspected explosive, his heavy suit making it hard to even pull through its restricting protection. As he pulled the bag away, Billy was on the other side checking below the bag for any tug wires that would cause the explosive to go off if they were removed; there were none. They pulled the bag away to reveal a couple of broken RPGs with their impact primers removed and wired to a central piece, resembling that of a large pager, a digital timer counting down from just below three minutes. Beneath the timer—linked by strange-looking silver wires—rested a Russian incendiary bomb, around the size of a small person and far too cumbersome for them to remove by themselves. It had been placed inside some old cardboard boxes, and Hanson was unable to get a clear view of the piece; again the worry being trip wires. He disabled the RPGs; they simply were wired to go off when the energy burst from a battery pack was released; however, they wouldn't be the only worry. He remembered handing them to Billy. As he looked through the small gap between the timer rig and the bomb beneath it, he saw only two points of contact with the battery pack, meaning that if he snipped one, the other would go off, so he needed Billy to cut with him simultaneously. They worked to the sides, each with their own wire cutter pressed lightly against the explosive, and the small black wire between the two. They counted down, snipped the wires, and were still breathing after a few moments; both sighed and laughed with relief. It was then when Hanson saw it; so subtle that he barely noticed. The strange wires that he had seen in fact weren't wires at all; they were paperclips. As he gazed at them, he remembered Billy saying that there were more wires leading to the underside of the bomb. He remembered that as they looked underneath, they found a radio transmitter and realized that someone was going to trigger the explosive; the bomb was not disarmed. It was then that Hanson knew that this thing was a trap. He pulled the cutters away, warned Billy not to make any adjustments, and looked around very quickly. About thirty yards away, Hanson remembered a man sitting in an old building, watching whether the explosive was going to explode or not. Then Hanson saw someone to the side of the building walking away from the area, and he had a large walkie-talkie. The man stopped, turned, and looked directly at Hanson, and then he looked over to his right, at a road. All of the sudden, a light-blue car roared out of a hole in a building on that road, and it drove straight into the group of soldiers. Hanson remembered telling Billy they had to move, he remembered hearing the car blow with immense force. Dust kicked up in a wave as he turned toward Billy, only a little ways behind him. Suddenly his body grew very dark, the explosion behind him igniting the air around it and reaching outward, the contrast even made the sun seem dark. That was all he could remember.

He brought his mind back to earlier that day when Brish had told him about the information they had learned from the attack. From what Brish told him, the explosive was simply made up of materials sent straight from Pakistan, where a majority of weapons came through virtually unchecked. However, the setup of the attack, being as elaborate as Hanson described, matches the MO of two other bombings, both almost as devastating as the most recent attack. Yet according to the forensics, trolls that were fitted comfortably in their air-conditioning, the only lead they have is that whoever created the bomb wasn't trained in Afghanistan. This news just became more complicated; however, when Brish had said some of the CIA suits had confiscated a lot of the forensics and files, giving the CID, the Criminal Investigative Command, jive excuses like "it is need to know" and "we're looking into it." For Hanson, this meant that forensics was good, but that the CID would remain uninformed and that he needed to at least talk to them before they handed everything over to the company. He was just hoping they would be interested in being vocal, but chances are, they weren't.

When it comes down to it, though, the explosion went off and killed Billy, and wounded several others. Then, like clockwork, a vehicle ended up blowing right in the middle of the more tightly amassed group of soldiers, killing thirty, wounding fifty, and destroying one of the supply trucks. All in all, it was a blind side, and it woke up the green shirts higher up to the fact that the enemy is still very capable, and ever present.

Hanson, still dissatisfied with his search through his memory, and even more so with what people were telling him, pondered his plan for after his release from the hospital, seeing as he was only temporarily wounded. He thought about what the funeral would be like, and whether Billy's stepdad would show, if Hanson himself even wanted to go; he didn't, he didn't feel it appropriate to mourn someone who still feels so close. He thought of the medals he would get, like the Purple Heart, or some other trinket that only represents a fraction of the real value of what was given; again he wasn't interested. It was then that a thought crossed his mind that shocked even him. It brought to him a feeling of completion, or closure, or maybe just pleasure; he wasn't sure which. What he was sure of was that this is what he wanted to do: to find and kill the one responsible. With the thunder of his own heart shouting its approval, he realized what he wanted: revenge.

WATCHING

A mist had gathered just above the ground outside, covering the grass and low foliage in a cloud as thick as the night itself. The trees were a thick, black drape that sheltered the grateful animals perched inside their protective branches. However, many of the animals, restless and hungry, left the safety of the trees to walk the forest floor and gather fallen seeds. The creatures that hunted them, however, were not coming from hiding but were waiting patiently for the arrival of their prey. However, most of this activity, though occurring throughout the woods of Colorado, went unnoticed, and even unappreciated. Especially at this time of night, when man and all his strengths were most vulnerable, so that man rests behind the walls of their own making. Man, woman, and child would have curled up together all the more tonight, and the water of Manchester Lake cooled to almost that of an autumn nights.

On the north end of the lake, just a small ways back from the rugged, grassy shore, a large, modern-looking white panel house was set motionless, in contrast to the lively night sky. The house, although hard to tell at night, looked majestic from the lake, when the sun refracted off of its marvelously well-kept whitewashed walls. Its two-story roof sat deep below the top of the trees, and at this time of night, the home would remain unnoticed from the road, save for the single light on the west side of the house, overlooking a small clearing just to the left of the house. The room had a blind that had been pulled down, as if to hide what was inside even from the animals who, being too enthralled in their game for food, wouldn't notice its difference compared to the rest of the home or the shadow that glided across and disappeared from view. This shadow was the only motion to be seen of the man inside, who sat down at his computer, and set down a half-finished bottle of water.

On the large computer screen on the gray office desk in front of him, a news article, a couple pictures, and a data analysis report had all been set up in several tabs. Each was being compared to the other, information to information, detail to detail. For all this to be deciphered in its annoyingly complicated state was quite a feat for most people: however, it was nothing more than a leisurely read to the man who now sat slouched in his chair. He was an older man, the facial wrinkles and stress marks resembling those normally prevalent on the faces of presidents, but in truth, he was not over fifty. His hair was gray, lighter and thicker in the back than on the top of his head, due to his habit of wearing tight fitting hats, and creases that suggested a lifetime of scowling through a thin pair of sunglasses. His blue shirt fit tight against his skinny-, but not feeble-looking body, and as he stood back up to get a better look at the screen, which took up a significant part of the wall, his dark khakis shuffled slightly, the sound of which caused him to realize he'd been wearing the pair a little too long, and they had lost their crisp feel they once had; he would have to replace them. His hands were rough but dexterous, and as he gazed at the computer screen, he slowly followed the lines of text, and diagrams that described the type of explosive that was used in the Helmand attack just a few days past.

He currently was the chief CIA liaison officer in charge of operations in the increasingly volatile Helmand Province. In fact, he used to work directly out of Afghanistan, receiving okays and no-go's from Langley, where such orders are thought up by analysts who had never been in the field, and handling whichever asset they had decided would be best handled by his self-affirming genius. His job was to coordinate operations out of UN-sanctioned military camps or "get friendly" with the indigenous living in or around points of political interest. He, in fact, headed most of these operations, especially those pertaining to the co-op between the US and Great Brittan in Helmand during many of the campaigns throughout the War on Terror. He never really believed in the fight, though, and in fact, it was one of the lowest of his priorities at the time; what he did believe in, however, was the abundance of *opportunities* that the land had to offer. So he worked hard and worked efficiently, so hard in fact, that his status with the agency monkey suits allowed him to accomplish much from the comfort of his own home, set in serenity in the woods, using a secure Langley network, of course.

The recent activity in Helmand, however, had been rather unnerving to the aging officer, realizing that the frequency and intensity of attacks has been rising from its regular hellhole status to something near chaotic. Just a year ago, the first real attack had occurred since the initial offensive against the radicals. This was especially clear after a Chinook helicopter was shot down by some Russian advanced anti-air tech, blowing the helo right out of the angry sky, which resided over Sangin. Several soldiers were killed, and their bodies were used in a trap similar to what the Viet Cong had used years earlier, using grenades to kill soldiers who came to collect them. This trap seemed to spark a series of attacks over the ensuing time period, all equally unexpected and surprisingly effective. Yet this most recent attack was different, for this claimed more than three times as many soldiers than any of its predecessors, and left a huge hole in US moral in the province. It was a simple attack, enough so that it wasn't thought of as a major threat, but it did far more damage than most of the thick skulls in Washington were willing to admit. It had bombs set to perfection and insurgents who laid down heavy fire for what seemed to be hours until the US boys were able to get a handle on them; what was needed to answer was more action, but a lot of them just want to stick their heads in the sand and hope for the best, a foolproof way of losing in the mind of this seasoned tactician.

The actual setup of the attack resembled that of a strategist, striking at the heart of the target. It followed a sort of strike, restrike, ambush—forcing the men in the convoy to cluster back, away from the IED that had been placed up front, and then, using a car full of unchecked Pakistani fertilizer, mainly ammonium nitrate–based, a lone insurgent drove right into their center and detonated, inflicting casualties close to eighty, almost half of which were killed.

He wiped the sweat off his forehead, already perspiring from just the thought of that sad, sun-scorched excuse for a military hiking trip; he wanted to avoid returning more than he missed any of the action. He had grown accustomed to his leisure and was extremely hesitant to give it up. However, with a lot of the higher-uppers at Langley breathing a smolder down his back, it was apparent that his expertise was needed just a little more than what his current stand-back position was allowing him to give. So in the interest of national security, and more importantly his own preservation of generous CIA stipend, he knew he would soon be leaving his "shack" in the woods to pay visit to his old friends in the Afghani desert. Maybe then he could work some of the magic he still had left and get a medal or something, just as long as he didn't have to stay more than a year because he had other plans.

He stood, feeling complete in his analysis of the situation from the bird's-eye view of what had transpired. He tossed his near-empty water bottle into a blue plastic bin in the corner of the room near the trash can because he always recycled; he felt it was his way to give back, for he didn't feel like giving much else. He signed out of the CIA message page by signing his name into a digital pad just beside his keyboard "Officer Richard Matthews," which deleted itself from his computer, then he signed out from his desktop, leaving the computer on, and in finality, he turned off the large TV screen that took the place of a traditional monitor. He left the small, dreary room and turned out the lights, feeling his way down a long hallway to the spiral, stained oak wood staircase that led to the large bar and the second floor of the house. He proceeded down the stairs, felt for the double light switch, and pushed both the small levers to the top. As he did this, the lights above the island bar went from dim to bright and a TV, automatically set to CNN for the emergency news readings, sprang to life. He grabbed the remote that he always placed next to his home phone in the corner and turned up the volume; this allowed him to drink and check updates at the same time.

Some suit-and-tie was being grilled by one of the media's hound-of-hell reporters over his stance on some political scandal in Michigan. At the bottom of the screen, some rapid moving text scrolled from right to left, giving informative blurbs on the real news that is so readily looked over by the vampiric mainstream media, always searching through the dumpsters for "juicy scandal" instead of a real story; in truth, these organizations were generally an insult to the intelligence community. In his opinion, which he believed to be the trump card for most discussions, they were a hindrance and cripplingly annoying. The things they said and tried to support with out-of-context statements and twisted facts made him want to drink. It was then that he remembered the real reason for having this channel on right next to the bourbon on the shelf was: encouragement.

He grabbed a glass from the pantry, poured a liberal amount of bourbon, and walked over to his large window seat, which overlooked the lake from a particularly calming viewpoint. He sat, sipping gratefully on the auburn colored drink, and closed his eyes, for there was nothing to see outside this late at night. He reached into his memory, feeling for his Afghanistan mind-set, one he had hoped wouldn't be needed anymore. But now, with the possibility of returning to that sandy oven, he realized this may be when he needed this mind-set more than ever.

FOOTSTEPS

The sun had carried itself above high into the resonant whiteness of the sky around it. As the light ran ceaselessly toward the earth, it seemed to collect itself on the edges and points of the tall buildings that held steadfast against the gusting, winds which brought the staunch heat. Even at a near distance, whole sides of buildings seemed to ripple with the heat waves as water down the side of a sheer cliff; it was a mirage of progress against a backdrop of desert. Windows reverberated with the strong winds that whipped their way from building to building and resounded the sounds of old machines that fought desperately to cool the inside of the gigantic structures, giving off a faint but vivid whirr. It was this sound that had captivated Zahid for the last few moments as he stared out the window of the building at the expanse of Kabul.

Zahid al Khatri was sitting flustered at his desk, writing a small column on his old, barely functioning Windows 2000 computer. He was typing rather slowly, observing all the marks and mistakes in a set of sloppy notes given to him by one of his British coworkers, who had gone to the site of the recent military shooting without him. For each of these mistakes, Zahid became more and more frustrated with the fact that this man has barely any literary understanding of Balochi and was mixing that limited knowledge with Darhi and Pashto. He was giving

Zahid a migraine. Becoming increasingly impatient, he checked the clock at the bottom of his screen, just around ten till eleven.

The column was for the accredited newspaper *The Daily Afghanistan*, which was located in a moderately sized, modern-ish building in Kabul City. His column was discussing a shooting that had occurred at one of the checkpoints that guarded the roads into the city just a couple days past. From the confusing notes, Zahid was able to understand that the shooting occurred when a couple militia soldiers tried to smuggle opium into Kabul. When they were caught, one of them tried to run; he didn't get far. An athletic checkpoint guard chased him into a local diner, where he plastered the runner against a wall with a submachine gun (the Brit forgot to write down the type of gun, so that lead was blown). After the guard finished with the human spray can, he proceeded back to the car where he forced the other man out of the gray sedan at gunpoint and shot him in front of hundreds of people. That man was rushed to a hospital where he ended up passing on after about twenty minutes. The guard was considered a hero by most of the general population, but a lot of the diplomatic community was in a rage. The higher-uppers were going to review his actions on Tuesday, but the guard wasn't going to make the meeting; he was killed a day after the shooting by some militia sympathizers. This is when Zahid decided to defend the guard saying that "Sometimes, evil just needs a couple well-placed bullets to make the streets just a little safer." Also, Zahid wasn't about to ransack the name of a dead "hero-to-the-peopo-," as the guard had been affectionately referred to by a news service in the United States.

Zahid looked at the clock on the wall, it had stopped at around four thirty that morning and hadn't moved since, so Zahid checked his watch; it was now eleven. He sighed and rubbed his head, feeling exasperated with the amount of work he had to do that day. However, he pressed on, being near completion of his important yet draining task, for he would soon have to make a long drive to Sirak, a town around twenty-five miles north of Sangin in Helmand Province; it would be around a twelve-hour drive with stops and checkpoints. Frankly, Zahid would rather just call the people he had to see, but there were three very important reasons why he shouldn't, or couldn't. First was the fact that phone service out there was near nonexistent, with barely enough communication lines for maintenance crews even to consider fixing them. Second, Zahid was not about to call *them* because he didn't want any known connections with them. This is where the third reason comes in; if he were to call, he would be killed. One for possibly allowing NATO forces to catch wind of an extremely dedicated Afghani liberation organization, or terrorist cell as the Westerners call it, and two for making such a mistake, which would lack an unbelievable amount of vision on his part. *They* do not accept failure, and mistakes are met with the edge of *their* sword, or the callous meeting of bullet to head. Point of conversation: mistakes are unacceptable.

Zahid typed away, finally able to get the ball rolling with such a daunting task of deciphering stupidity; he had almost reached his limit with this guy and was ready to show him his "friends" mistake policy. After a few more painful lines, he tossed the notepad aside, and finished probing for its usable information. He eventually came across a blog called *Flawed or Freedom*. Scrolling to the bottom of the page, he checked its upload date; the site had only been there for two days and was already filled with the words of emotional citizens. He began to read through some of the blogs, most of which were just different people venting their view of the story in reverent respect or blatant condemnation of the gun-slinging checkpoint guard. Zahid was almost finished with the site when he came across a string of very eloquent, focused, and powerful ideas, written by a user who called himself "Word-Warrior 83G"—a fitting name. Zahid printed the page.

He looked around for a red pen, and grabbed the case he believed it was in. He pulled it out of the bag while he was looking at his computer screen, realizing that he had copied a mistake in Balochi when it was to be done in Pashto. He was about to change it when he noticed the unnatural weight of the container in his hand; he had grabbed the wrong one. The pen case he was looking for was a gray transparent plastic; this one, however, was a hard, opaquely black container. It had a grainy feel to it, plus heavy-duty snaps and the letters "DSM" in bold on the top. He looked around to make sure no one saw it and then quickly returned it to its nestling place beneath his clothes. When satisfied with his privacy, he returned to work, using a light blue pen, instead of the preferred red, and he highlighted the important info from Word-Warrior 83G on the blog This would be very useful, maybe even politically provocative. In any case, Zahid's journalistic side of his personality was buzzing with excitement.

When he finished info-fishing, he added in the final touches to his article, sighting the blog site as a significant contribution to his column. As he pressed the save button, one of his coworkers came up and asked him if he wanted to go to lunch with them. He returned the kind gesture with a smile and a "no, thank you," telling them he had to go west to Jalalabad, a one-hundred-sixty-kilometer drive, which would last around two and a half hours. The short white man just smiled back and said it was fine, in English. The use of the Outsider's language was insulting to Zahid, as it was, to many who found the Western civilization, in its entirety, insulting. In fact, the real reason for his decline of the invitation was that he was going to drive to Sirak, which was just over eight hundred kilometers in the opposite direction from where he told the others his destination was. Now, witnesses in Jalalabad would attest to him being with them, following a lead on a story about local gang activity along the Kabul River, near the town of Bashud, and its ties to the bicycle bombing in Mazar-E-Sharif, which had been set off several months ago—a very believable story. In reality, his meeting was one of a more cunning nature, and he was well aware of the required secrecy of the whole trip.

Zahid grabbed his duffel bag up from beneath his desk and placed it on a small stool stationed to his right, which he usually used for a lunch table. He unzipped an outside pocket and placed his pen and his notepad inside, being careful to keep the pen facing upward in a cylindrical, flexi-grip nylon tube, to prevent any spilling. He reached over to his computer with his right hand, while zipping up his bag with his left, knowingly avoiding speed where the zipper may stick. He clicked on the save button at the top of his screen, and then exited out of the text software. Pulling up the paper's intranet system, he entered in his pass code, selected his newly saved column file, and placed into the editor's "Finals" folder. Zahid then red-ex'd his way to the blank, blue desktop and then shut down the computer; he wouldn't be returning for a while.

Zahid exited the elevator, waving good-bye to the small send-off party that had congregated inside. As the door closed, his smile was maintained, aware of the camera that was placed directly above the elevator door. He turned and walked a ways down a gray hallway, dirty windows obstructing his view of the street. He always hated when he lost visibility of an area, it always made him uncomfortable to know he was vulnerable. To compensate for this, he placed his hand in his brown leather-coat pocket, which had its inner lining torn away, to give him unobstructed access to a seven-inch boot knife, which was sewn to the inside of his coat; he was readily prepared for unwelcome occurrences. As he exited the building, he abruptly stopped and turned to his right, looking down the embankment that had been previously obscured from his view. Reassured, he continued walking, still eyeing his right side, however. Zahid wasn't sure why he always was so cautious, especially if his plans had been protected as they were supposed to have been, but he still was more comfortable with being, as some would say, "paranoid."

He walked to his jeep, a dark-blue rig, skirted in a translucent layer of dust. It was well taken care of in comparison to many of the other vehicles in the country and, in fact, was a relatively new model as well, only around twelve years old. Zahid opened the door, tossed his bag over onto the floor in front of the passenger seat, and was just about to get in when he heard footsteps. The steps were rapid, and louder than most, suggesting a heavy person was running toward him. He also noticed a shadow move just beneath his feet; the sun was giving away the position of a second man on the other side of his jeep. Zahid could almost feel his mind change, as though he were asleep and suddenly was called awake. He made himself ready, and when the steps came close enough, he reacted.

He ducked down to his right, as he avoided the strike of a crowbar that missed its intended target and landed forcefully on his front seat. As he dropped, he removed the knife with deadly fluidity slashed just behind the knee of the surprisingly large individual. The man fell, his own weight causing the pain in his leg to be all the more excruciating, and as he fell, Zahid leaped forward and seized him on his mouth with his left hand and supported the heavy man's weight with his hip, ensuring he wouldn't accidentally snap his own spine in Zahid's iron grip. Zahid then placed the knife's razor sharp edge just below the earlobe, outside the jaw. His attacker, who had been screaming in pain, abruptly silenced himself as he felt the cold steel press against his neck, and willingly stopped his squirming.

The other man came around the car enthusiastically with another crowbar but suddenly became less brave when he saw his larger partner now in the lethal hands of the former Quds Force Captain, Iranian Special Forces.

"Put the bar down, boy, or I'll give this man a brand new smile." Zahid pressed the knife a little, causing the man to whimper, making his intentions clear. The other man, apparently not feeling brave, dropped the bar and backed away.

"Now come around front, face me the whole time, and reach into the side pocket of the door. Grab the small bag that you find there." The man readily complied, walking around with his back toward the jeep. He reached down, shifting his gaze from the knife to the pocket, and then to Zahid's eyes, which had grown even darker from their regular deep-brown color. He removed the plastic baggie and started walking toward Zahid.

"Stay!" Zahid said, stepping back. The young man, or rather an older boy, stopped and held up the bag. "Now remove the Flexi-Ties from the bag and bind your hands."

"What about Nahir?" the boy asked, gesturing toward his large friend with a nod of his head.

"I will take care of that, now tie."

The boy did as told and then sat down with his back against the tire. Zahid then kicked the man who he was holding in the knee, forcing him to the ground. From there, he removed the knife and reached his left arm around the man's neck and squeezed, having his well-formed bicep and forearm press against the arteries that run upward in the neck. The man squirmed silently until he eventually passed out. Zahid then tied him, wrapped his leg to control the bleeding, and then laid him in the back of the jeep.

"Get in the other side and sit. Do nothing or you die." Zahid followed the man around and put him in the jeep, and then he reached down and grabbed a longer Flexi-Tie from the bag and anchored the man's hands to the rigged grip of the door, then he closed it. He got into the driver's seat, making sure that no one was around the back of the building grabbing a smoke or anything who may have seen the rapid sequence of fighting. Finally, he started the car, and it lurched forward as he shifted from park to drive. The boy asked where they were headed, but Zahid kept silent.

They turned left onto a narrow street. Both sides were loomed over by the walls of the surrounding buildings, fences also running along the expanse of the street. A couple of people moved across the street heading toward the market district. They were women, covered by long, light-blue burkas, which covered the head and draped down the back, but were open in the front to show more modern attire. The children walking with them were oblivious to their surroundings, their mothers herding them while they attempted a game of tag. They were rushed off the road, however, when Zahid's jeep came steadily toward them.

He turned right when the road ended, heading toward a building that was still heavily under construction. He passed the construction site and turned into an old parking structure on the other side of the street. He reached and grabbed his cell phone from the inside of his jacket, pressed the redial button, and waited. A voice on the other side spoke quickly and sternly asked for a verification word. "Saben," Zahid said into the phone and then said "hamsa," meaning "five," and then hung up the phone.

He parked the car on the second floor and turned the ignition off, and then he turned and looked at the boy. He was no more than fourteen but seemed to act older, sitting with his legs facing Zahid and his hands over his knees; he seemed calm. Zahid turned and looked at the man in the back, who was clearly *not* the boy's father, for the age difference was too small and the facial construction wasn't close enough. He turned back to the boy.

"What were you trying to do? Do you know who I am?" Zahid's serious gaze tore into the boy's eyes, forcing him to look away. Realizing it was too much, Zahid looked out of the car, trying to make the boy calm down a little. Even after the boy started talking, he continued to stare away.

"My family needed jeep to go to the North, where my uncle, him"—the boy gestured to the unconscious man in the back—"has some friends who own a farm. My father died, and we can't live in the city anymore, so we tried to take the car. If we don't leave, we won't last another month here."

"You almost died yourselves, you understand? You chose to take someone else's property, for your own use."

"No I—"

"Yes, the answer is yes. You did try to steal, and you should be killed for it." Zahid turned toward him, his eyes now passionately strong. "But if I were to punish you, your family would suffer, and that is something I am not willing to allow."

Just then, an old, white SUV pulled in, several men exited and walked toward Zahid's car. He got out and walked toward them, out of earshot for the boy.

"What's the problem, Zahid?" a deep-voiced man asked. He was holding an American Colt .45 in his right hand.

"The boy in the front seat and the man in the back tried to take my jeep so they could get their family to a friend's farm in the North. I need you to take them and their family to that place. Don't hurt them and don't get caught. If you do, termination is necessary, understand?"

"Yes, sir," the man answered, unwavering in his allegiance to his commanding officer. He returned his pistol to his gray jacket and went with his men over to the jeep, helping the boy and his unconscious uncle out and into their SUV. The rest of the men who had been watching out for onlookers returned to the vehicle, and it revved back to life.

Zahid walked away, his back to the exit of the small structure, and returned to his jeep. He sat down, staring blankly at the dashboard in front of him and wondering if he made the right decision. He understood that letting them go would risk them talking about him, and it would be over for him and his... aspirations. But he couldn't kill them because he couldn't take life from the family that needed help so badly. The thought then crossed his mind about the bomb he had set off the day before, on a patrol of US soldiers who had been on their way back toward

Camp Bastion. He thought about the men he killed there, about what he took from their families. Then a picture flashed into his mind's eye. It was old, weathered, a little bit of color had been washed away by the years that had passed since its creation. There was a woman, wearing a white burka, some of her long, black hair visible from the side. She was holding the hand of a young boy, no more than ten, as he walked beside her. He was smiling up at her, and she down at him.

Zahid opened his eyes, wet with emotions that had been inside him for so long. He thought about those American soldiers, and a wave of satisfaction rolled over him. He didn't kill that boy because he had done nothing as bad as what those Americans, those Outsiders, had done to him. He had reason for their destruction, and he was going to carry it out on those who have stayed to witness his vengeance. He started the car.

GLARE

**1122 hours, July 9, Camp Bastion
Helmand Province, Afghanistan**

Hanson removed the covers from his legs and stared for a moment, surprised at the amount of color he had lost over the last couple of days. He looked around, taking in the light that came through the window, cleansing his mind from all the clouds that had formed overnight. With the lightness of the pain, he could tell he was already getting better, although he had yet to move very far; things had always healed fast for him. Even the bad injuries he'd received from fights when he was in high school or his car crash in college had only taken him out for a few days, and he knew this was nowhere near as serious. Still, as he sat up, he still felt the aftereffects of stopping one's flight with a large rock. The warmth of the sun felt good on his legs and provoked him into moving just a little more. With one arm he grabbed the frame of the bed and pushed himself upward. As he stood, his ribs complained even more, but he persisted, and they slowly began to silence. He could see fairly well out the window, but there was a truck that had pulled up and blocked the light from his part of the room, so he slowly began to walk. He moved in a lame-duck fashion, each step with its own cost to his comfort but steadily got easier as he moved to the other side of the room.

There was a blue curtain that had been used to split his room in two, and he hadn't seen the other side since he had moved in. So when he reached the beam of light that had splashed onto the floor, he turned and pulled the edge of the curtain back. Just then, a loud beeping noise emanated from the bed, followed by an immense commotion as several nurses rushed into the room. Hanson watched as they brought in the crash cart, apparently the patient had gone into cardiac arrest, and a doctor began shouting orders to give some amount of epinephrine to him and to start assisted breathing.

As they moved, he caught a glimpse of the patient's face and realized he recognized him. The memory of the explosion came back to him in that room, and he could see in his mind's eye the soldier who had informed him and Billy of the IED. He had been the message carrier for the soldiers to move to the center of the convoy and most likely had been hit by the second bomb. Now he's lying in a gurney, fighting for all he's got left. They wheeled the man out of the room, most likely headed for the cardiovascular wing of the hospital where he may or may not have surgery, Hanson didn't know much more than that, seeing as how he only knew the names of this stuff from watching doctor shows back in Phoenix. They moved swiftly and rounded a corner, eliminating Hanson's line of sight.

It was here that Hanson remembered last night what he had decided, so he began to move. He sat down carefully and removed the constricting brace around his ribs. As he did so, and his own weight was once again supported unassisted, he immediately knew he couldn't handle this for very long. What's more is that as he moved out of the room, he realized he had only thirty minutes before the nurses came to check on him, so he at least needed to be back in the same wing of the hospital as his room before then; he could explain that away. He moved out of the hall the same way the nurses had gone with his roommate but then made a left instead of continuing straight where the emergency room was. He walked the expanse of the hallway, making sure to nod at those who made eye contact and to avoid the others who were too busy to pay attention. Commotion picked up as a couple people ran past him, pagers blaring in his ears. Then a group of MPs entered the area and started toward Hanson. He realized he was still wearing patient garb, so he slowed down and then entered a room just off the hall. It was here where he found a line of camouflage clothing, most of which were uniforms that the doctors would wear outside of the hospital. He grabbed one of the uniforms and pressed it up to his chest and replaced it because it was too small. He repeated that a few times until he found one just a little wider than the rest. He held it up to his chest; it fit. He locked the door and began putting the pants on quickly but then slowed down when he tipped into the wall and felt a sharp pain shoot through his side; he just couldn't avoid hitting it. He finally finished his dressing but then could only button the top up to his midchest due to the gauze wrapping around his cavity, so he grabbed a checkered-style black-green turban and wrapped around his neck and let it drape down the front. He then took a deep breath, unlocked the door, and realized that wearing a doctor's uniform as an unfamiliar face in a hospital would most likely get him caught; so he undressed. He then wrapped the uniform into a white towel and exited the room, still wearing his patient's gown.

Hanson walked all the way to the end of the hall he had entered before he made a turn into one of the side rooms near the exit. As he closed the door, he made sure to look back, seeing if anyone had noticed him, but all were still oblivious; it made him wonder just how much he could get away with, but he reeled his thoughts in for the task at hand. He put on each piece of clothing as carefully as he had done before but rushed himself just enough to snag his side into the corner of a small desk. Angrily, he quietly exclaimed his disdain for the obtrusive piece of furniture, making a few statements about firewood as he grudgingly tied his green turban around his neck. A few moments later, after regaining his composure, he pressed his military cap tightly to his head to cover his eyes, figuring that every little bit that concealed him was worth it. He checked for a mirror but then quickly remembered that he was in Afghanistan, where hat style was less attractive than body armor, and just went with what he had.

The door rushed open as he pushed on its low-positioned wooden brace, lingering outward for a moment as Hanson walked through. As he moved, he could feel the immense heat burning through his clothing, causing him to instantly perspire, surprising him mostly because he had hoped the time in the hospital wouldn't make him soft. He paused, his eyes grazing the view in front of him as they searched beneath his low-brimmed hat for a small building. Then he saw it, and the inscription above the door told him all: "Army Criminal Investigative Command" and then, in lowercased letters below the title "Camp Barber Post," Hanson never really understood why the US had to have a different name for their base that resides within Camp Bastion. He guessed it had something to do with the presence of a Danish base, but other than that, it just made everything a little confusing. Although he had to say "Barber" sounded a whole lot better than "Bastion 2," he remembered that the new building adjacent to one of the large gymnasiums was being fitted for an army CID command center. The CID is the army's Criminal Investigative Command, which basically is an effective military version of the NYPD, talented at most levels, but sometimes just a little rough. Usually they're the guys who watch over more technical matters in comparison to MPs, who are the enforcers of the rules. Thus, Hanson knew that if he were going to get anything more than a condolence and a hug, they were the people to see. Now he knew he shouldn't be caught prodding around simply because they may assume he has gotten too attached and is a danger, which they are probably right about; he was attached and dangerous, but only to whoever the evidence set his sights. So he wore his disguise, and he prepared himself for finding answers that part of him did not want to see; he owed Billy that much at least.

———◦◦◦———

The lines on the paper began to blur, as if they no longer needed to keep themselves firmly planted on the page. Letters and words repeated one after another until the whole sentence seemed to be one constant remake of the movie *The Shining*. Frustrated and tired, Agent Celia tossed the file over her shoulder onto the wooden desk on which she had been resting her head. She swiveled her chair around and leaned back, stared blankly up at the ceiling, and counted the tiles row by row. She already knew the number, mostly because she had counted them what seemed like hundreds of times before. Yet as if it were her very first time, she reached the number thirty-eight and felt a small sense of accomplishment. She closed her eyes for a moment and attempted to relax, but just as she is when trying to sleep, her mind just wouldn't let go of her surroundings. She could hear the indecent noise of several people working in the room behind her, stirring to such an excitement by the recent flow of both enemy chatter and allied agencies messages about the ambush the week before. Ever since the attack, the men and women of CID Bastion have been ferociously investigating the possibilities of who may be responsible; even some groups in the West have been feeling the waves from their prodding. In the room in front of her office, analysts typed like machine guns as they probed the data bases dedicated to investigation, messaging with analysts on the other side of the world who work deep into the night while trying to bring some sense of order to the ever confusing and volatile world of anti-terrorism. But they were working, and even if it took them all day they were making real headway, despite what so many who have never even taken a look at evidence said about their lack of progress. Celia longed for the chance to give them her job for a day and then see if they really wanted to keep poking the bear.

After a moment, she realized that she was, in fact, angry at other people. This didn't come as a surprise, per se, but it still made her feel like she was still in high school, where just the smallest thing could send someone right off their rocker. What's more, she noticed she was hungry and decided that, for the good of her subordinates and her own conscious health she would have to eat. She took her backpack out from beneath her desk and removed her military-issued cap and a second hairpin and set her hair in a bun. Every time she put the hat on, it seemed that her hair would find some odd way of scrounging out of order, and she would get talked at for what seemed like thirty minutes of why she should be less flamboyant. What this meant to her is that she needed to be just a little more manly. She stood, making a mental note of where she had placed her most recent file and left the room, passing by several work stations too deeply enthralled in their current mission to even notice the commanding officer checking on them as they toiled away. She was proud of them, and she knew that eventually all this mechanical, methodical, and ultimately painstaking work would soon pay off; and they would get to go home.

She left the computer room and entered the front "lobby," which was basically just a small room that separated the air-conditioned insides to the inferno like temperatures of the outside world, and walked toward the exit. She was in a very inquisitive mood, only just realizing the strangeness of the investigation. Usually CID agents leave it up to command and their partners to work on combat-oriented cases, but this one was different. Not only was her group fully engaged in all the work they had going on, but Langley now had their analysts at every step with the investigation, with a CIA liaison officer right there to make sure everything they need to know is given to them without delay. It was like having two bosses, where one can, in some ways, just completely out step the other. Celia noticed she was getting a little too curious, but more importantly angry, so she decided to drop it and pick up her personal questioner at a later date, which, with all the work they were doing, would be a very long time away. She was so enthralled in her thoughts, in fact, that she failed to look up to stop herself from running directly into another soldier.

Hanson barely knew what hit him. He had simply been walking, worrying himself to the point of hysteria about how he was going to get into the building, and what on earth he would do once he got in there. He was getting ready to open the front door to the building when it opened and somebody slammed right into him, knocking him off his feet. Disoriented and in a surprising amount of pain, he turned himself onto his back, squinting his eyes against the incredibly bright sunlight. He tried to pull himself up by grabbing onto the grill of a Humvee that had been parked next to him, but reaching out hurt just a little too much for his now very tender right side. It was then that a shadow came and saved him from the intense sunlight, and he looked up gratefully to see who had come to help.

"Are you all right, sir?" the voice asked in a worried tone. "I am *so* sorry, I didn't even see you there." Hanson noticed the voice was that of a woman, and immediately he decided to man up and be just a little less of a shrimp.

"Yeah, I'm allright, don't worry about it," he replied, doing his best to avoid sounding like an old man bending over. She extended her hand and helped him off the ground. As he stood, he winced a little in an attempt to regain his balance, but he did and finally was able to get a good look at her. "Thank you," he said then paused. "Was that you I ran into?" He realized that he was just floored by a woman, and an attractive one at that, so he wasn't sure what to think; he just moaned. He sighed in disappointment with himself, his cheeks smoldering in a light red, and she smiled a little. He walked over to the wall adjacent to the entrance to the CID building and put his hand against it, taking off his hat to make it seem he was only getting out of the sun rather than making sure he wouldn't fall over again.

"What's your name, Corporal?" she asked, and without hesitation "Rick" spurted out.

"Okay, Rick, I am sorry for running into you." She smiled kindly as she spoke, although he caught just a little bit of pride.

"No, my bad, miss…" he prodded for her name.

"Agent Salviana."

"Agent, huh, CSI-style or something?"

"Yup."

"Sounds exciting."

"Well, believe it or not, the whole CSI is kind of boring, but it's a good job." Celia shrugged her shoulders and tried to sound convincing.

"You sound so enthused." He smirked sarcastically. "Well, you seem to be heading somewhere pretty urgently. So if you don't mind, I'll walk you there, try to regain at least some of my manhood." Of course he was thinking he might be able to learn something from her, but the fact that he hadn't had a conversation with a girl for a while didn't take a backseat to his request either.

"No, I'm just going to the post, I'm fine," she insisted, though she wouldn't mind the company.

"No, no it's the least I can do for running you over."

"Well, if anything I ran you over, Doc." He was bewildered, first because she called him doc, until he remembered that he was wearing an army doctor's camouflage uniform. Then his mind caught the "I ran over you," and all of a sudden it was a competition. He looked at her in disbelief. He smiled, she smiled; he almost said bingo.

Hanson walked with her back to the CID building, both talking nearly without pausing, save for one another. He had never had a talk with a woman like this; she just carried herself as if she were talking with a friend she had known for years. She didn't try to please him with her beliefs but instead took a stand and he listened; he guessed that was typical behavior for agents, or at least the "special" ones. They reached the door, their walk having already taken a good thirty minutes, and stood talking for a just a little more.

"Well, that was fun," he began to conclude, realizing that he had to get back to the hospital.

"Yeah, and it took up just enough time to put me behind, Corporal." She smiled and handed him the bag full of snacks. She turned and opened a keypad's sliding door. He focused intently on her fingers, as they swiftly flowed over the keypad on the left hand side of the door. She pressed enter and the door unlocked itself then swung open as she pulled on the handle. Hanson looked to his right, down at his feet, and in any other direction that at the door to make her think he hadn't seen the code, or at least wasn't interested in it. He walked forward and she allowed him in, and instantly he was greeted with the forceful affection of cool air. He looked around as the door to swing itself closed, and he realized that he would have trouble doing much of anything in the way of searching, seeing how there was a second door, and a second keypad on the other side of the room. She walked around him, and when he saw her approaching, he immediately forced a smile. Yet when she turned toward him and smiled, her dark black eyes shimmering against her sun-kissed skin, his smile cemented itself in place; he didn't have to force it, she made it easy. He handed her back her bag and she thanked him.

"No, thank you for letting me come, I got a free bag of chips out of it so I can't complain."

"Yeah, a free bag of chips and a bruised rib," she joked as she sat atop her desk.

"Well," he breathed the word out heavily, "I guess I'll talk to you later, ma'am." He stood up straight and pushed his shoulders back, accentuating his chin and acting as though he were standing at ceremony. She smiled and shook her head; he laughed and let his shoulders drop back to a regular position.

"Yeah, I'll see you later, Corporal." She paused for a second, "Rick." She ended, showing that she indeed remembered his name. He backed out through the door and waved; it closed behind him. As he walked back to the hospital, he recited the code he had seen her put in but also berated himself. Mainly because he told one of the best-looking women he'd met that his name was "Rick"—*what a dumb name,* he thought, then he remembered his own name was Damian, and how many times he's been made fun of for that, and decided "Rick" wasn't so bad.

CONTACT

1306 hours, July 9, Kandahar-Herat Highway
Helmand Province, Afghanistan

The road had Jakub in a sort of trance, as if it were pulling him along rather than him choosing to take it. He stared through the windshield at the asphalt that ran persistently through the blistering heat that was oh so common in these desert flatlands. He had been driving since sunrise, heading back to his small town shop on the eastern outskirts of Kandahar; now he was tired enough to wish he could just pull over, but he had a date to keep. It occurred to him that even though the road represented much of the "progress" that Westerners on the news kept calling what was happening here, what stood in effortless defiance to what they were trying to create was a desert and a people both too doggedly accustomed to the scorching heat than they were willing to allow more "progress." Now, many of the city dwellers, including his "friend" Zahid understood the good the road was doing, but for those who live and breathe the sand and clay, and usually enjoyed unchecked freedom from any government or agency, find themselves stuck on one side of "progress" and wishing to their god that they could get past it or just make it go away. Not that the other side of the road brought anything much more than maybe another small village forgotten by the world, or even a small desert oasis, but it was the principle of the land that they have had for so long and traveled so many times before being their own and not having to wait for it to change again or push back on the very forceful hand of progress.

Jakub had been driving for what seemed all day. His hands were moist with sweat, giving the steering wheel a feel of damp leather. He wished to close his eyes for a moment, just rest them from their constant battle for sight against the ever-oppressive sunlight that created such a contrast before him. What's more, there was just enough dust in the air to prevent him from opening his window, so it felt as though he were simply rolling around in a very mobile oven. Frustrated, he attempted to relieve some of the heat by turning on the air-condition and was unsurprised when he heard a gritty, sputtering noise that informed him that his cold air wasn't going to be available today. He looked out his passenger window, a vehicle passing him on that side, grabbing his attention. The driver of the passing car didn't even turn his head; he just kept looking up from his phone for a few moments and then back down until he was far enough in front of Jakub to switch lanes; the man was going somewhere around thirty kilometers faster than him and was paying far less attention. Jakub wanted to honk or get right up behind the man then honk—not because the man past him but rather because he was texting while driving, and he couldn't stand the idea of someone paying so little attention to what he was doing. As he stewed, he hardly noticed himself pushing harder and harder on the accelerator until he tapped the back bumper of the man in front of him. Shocked, he pressed on his brakes and pulled into the other lane, his heart pounding heavily in his chest as he realized what he had done. Angered at himself and seeing the man whom he had just nudged with his front bumper begin to slow down, he frantically reached for his GPS and began to fiddle with it, as though he had no idea what had transpired only moments ago. Out of the corner of his eye, he could see the man shouting at him, raising his arms and gesturing not so nice signs toward him.

He tried not to look, but then something happened that he didn't expect. A heavy jolt forced him out of his lane and nearly off the road onto the shoulder. Shocked, he turned and faced the man directly. Still shouting, the man went to turn the vehicle again, but Jakub was prepared. He broke hard, causing the man to shoot directly in front of him at a hard angle. With an aggressive motion, he turned his car hard into the rear of the man's car in front of him, and that was the end. The car spun, screeching all the way off the road until it slammed into the concrete guarding that ran alongside. Jakub was now sweating more than ever, and he could hardly focus on the road. He had the pedal touching the floor, and even despite his better judgment, he couldn't bring himself to calm down or to slow down for that matter. He checked his rearview mirror then both sides; no one seemed to be following him from what he could see. He stared intently forward again, taking deep slow breaths as his heart rate began to slow and his mind gradually with it. He wiped the sweat away from his eyes and face, which beaded and fell from his hand onto the floor. A scene from an old eighties movie popped into his mind, in which there was a whole lot of car scenes. He smiled, feeling almost dominant with his car skills and he began to think as such; the thought crossed his mind that he was someone who people shouldn't mess with. Suddenly a poignant ringing permeated the silence with a sharp jolt, sending his moment of indomitability away in a start.

"Good God!" he spurted, fumbling roughly through the pockets of his jacket that sat in a crumpled pile in the passenger seat. The jacket fell to the floor. "Damn!" He leaned over just enough to begin to pull the car off of the road. He jerked forcefully on the wheel as he slammed on the brakes, back into the middle of the road. Only then did he decide it was finally time to pull over. Once parked on the shoulder, he let loose a slur of curses, snaking almost inaudibly through a set of rigid teeth as he pulled his jacket back onto the passenger seat. Then he felt vibrations in his left chest pocket on the gray shirt he was wearing, and hurriedly he reached in: cell phone.

"What!?" he inquired forcibly, angered that he had to pull over after all that he'd gone through and was fully prepared to ream into the unfortunately timed caller.

"*Ahlahn wa sahlahn*, Pesek. Are you upset?" the chillingly calm voice was like ice water over a warm back—even his heart waited in apprehension.

"Zahid?"

"Good guess. I trust you have my package ready at the store. I'm stopping by in a little while."

"How long is a little while?" Jakub asked, trying to sound unworried.

"Well, does that mean you're not ready, or maybe not even there?" The sarcasm did little to soften the vivid condemnation pouring through the phone line.

"No, no, I'm there, I mean, here. Holding your package right here behind my counter."

"Well, when you actually arrive at your shop, which I would expect to be *before* I arrive, I will need you to move the package from behind the counter to where we agreed to meet the last time I called. I trust I have been clear."

Jakub sighed. "Yes, I'll be ready."

"Good, enjoy your drive." Then a click and the call ended.

Jakub started the car again. "Good Lord, if this drive doesn't kill me, this guy will." He muttered sarcastically as he checked his side-view mirrors and then merged into traffic.

The street would have been only a short drive, nothing more than a minute or so, if it weren't for the sheer number of goat herders, salesmen, and families bustling about through a crowd that took up the whole of the street. Jakub was used to the busy and generally impenetrable crowd around his store, for most of the time it brought him good business. But today was different. He pressed down on the horn, urging the people and animals to part, but it was to no avail. To his right there were several buildings, a couple streets that appeared less crowded than his own, but impossible for him to reach without rolling over several curbs and people to get to them. He looked at his watch, a little plastic piece with a small digital screen; he had less than ten minutes to get to his store and have the package ready and waiting in a small basket just behind the store, and in his car he just wasn't going to be able to get through the crowd. In a final, desperate attempt, he let his horn ring out, but no one paid attention, save for a small coupe full of chickens, which jumped and cackled with the loud, startling sound.

Jakub turned the ignition off and got out of the car, leaving it parked in the middle of the street. He pushed himself through the crowd, moving people out of the way while shouting at others in front to move as well. A few gave him looks of anger, others simply ignored him, but all in all, he was moving, and he would have to be ready within the next five minutes. He rounded a corner, now able to see the front of the small building in which he lived and worked. From what he could see, there was no vehicle there yet. He reached the back door, threw it open, and charged down the hall way, making a sharp left when he reached a small, open entrance room at the far end of the hall. The wall adjacent to the door had several windows on it, all shuttered up so that the only light that could enter the room poured through the cracks above the planks of wood and cardboard that had been hammered into the frame. The room had several long, rugged carpets that lined the floor, along with one or two wooden pallets beneath a small dresser, some tables, and one large cabinet. The cabinet had three large swinging doors, two of which were bound together by a padlock and chain, the other guarded by three large latches, all held together in a similar fashion to that of the first two doors. He approached quickly, reached into his pocket and grabbed a set of keys. He unlocked the door, pulled down several pieces of electronics and clothing, and a box full of low-level jewelry, setting them all alongside the cabinet on the ground. On the floor of the cabinet, a large steel plate rested above what seemed to be a hollow compartment, this was again held in place by a small padlock with a combination. He input the three-number code, lifted the latch and plate, and stepped back. He was in shock.

Inside the compartment, where there should have been a medium-sized cardboard box wrapped in brown paper, instead sat a large stack of American twenties and a note that read in Arabic "money deducted for loss of time." Jakub clasped his hands behind his head. He wasn't more than a few minutes late and just getting in with all the right keys and codes took him an extra minute.

"Leena!" he called and waited impatiently for his wife. A few moments later and no answer, he called again but more forcefully. He then heard footsteps down the hallway, and she entered the room.

"Yes?" she asked mildly, perceiving his bad temper and, in turn, trying to cool it down.

"Did you let anyone into the house today?" He stared piercingly into her eyes.

"Just one or two of the regulars. No one else."

"No one?"

"No one."

"You're sure you didn't see any extras or anything?"

"Yes." She approached him and took his hand. "Do you need me to do something for you?" She walked over to the cabinet and tried to put some of the clothing and things back inside. But he moved her away from it, closed the compartment, and returned everything to its place and turned to see her again. She had left the room.

He sat down on a small couch on the edge of the room, facing the cabinet and rubbing his face with his palms when he saw a second note, taped to the on the wall just to the left of a small table. He scooted over, just barely lifting himself from the couch to do so, and took the piece of paper down from its perch. On it was written a series of numbers, five series in all, and each had a letter on both ends. He stood quickly, searching his pockets for a pencil while walking into the study, which was the room opposite the one he was in. Inside sat a short, collapsible table, on top of which were several boxes and packages, along with a calculator and an old typewriter. He sat down, facing the windows that allowed him to look out into the street and also just over the homes and buildings to get a substantial view of the mountains. However, his eyes still hadn't left the encrypted page. He opened a small drawer in a makeshift file cabinet and removed a plastic pen from a cup full of others. He switched on a light on his desk and began to decipher the code. After what seemed to be around five minutes, he held the note in front of him and read the new lines that he had written in below the coded ones. He stood, sighed, and then took the page over to a small, cast-iron oven with a chimney attached. He put the page in, doused it with lighter fluid, and set it ablaze. He grabbed his cell phone from his pocket and pressed three, then call. After one or two rings, a voice on the other side answered in Czechoslovakian.

"I would like to buy a switch."

"Is there a brand you would like?"

"Victor Fagan. Third series."

"What do you need?"

"Two sparks and twelve pounds of the heavy clay."

"Three days."

"Fine. Parcel, confirm?"

"Sending, confirmed." Then the line went dead. Jakub exited the room and closed the door, was about to sit down at a table, but stopped himself when he remembered that he owned a vehicle, and right then it was sitting in the middle of a street. So he turned and exited into a dusky evening.

IN SECRETS IT LIES

1800 hours, July 9, Sirak,
Helmand Province, Afghanistan

Zahid pulled his jeep to the side of the road and grabbed his blue duffel bag from behind his seat. Setting it next to him, he pulled the small, brown paper wrapped package from the far side of the dashboard to just behind his steering wheel. Several cars passed his side, their lights fading in and out, but providing him enough light to see as he removed his black, hard-covered case from his duffel bag, set it atop, and opened it. Inside rested a Makarov 9mm pistol, two full clips, and several extra bullets wrapped in a plastic bag. Anxiously he removed the pistol and fluidly began to strip it down, first removing the large slide and then the bore itself and set both on the bag next to the case. He took the package off of the dash and pulled a medium-sized flick-knife from his jacket pocket. He dug the edge of the blade into the top left corner of the box and slowly dragged the razor to the adjacent corner. He removed the knife, closed it once again, and then ripped the top off. The package jerked as he did so, and a second black tube lurched out of its place and landed on his lap. A car passed and poured in a copious amount of light, and so quickly, he took up the piece before it fell to the floor and scanned its surface. It carried no industrial oil on it, no powder preserving, and no fingerprints. It had rifling down the inside of the barrel, and he compared it to his current bore. They were slightly different, and seeing as his current barrel had come from the same company, he was sure that this new piece had a design that wouldn't be tracked back to them and, most importantly, him.

After another car passed, he looked out of the passenger window. A few lights twinkled off in the distance, not very bright, but they gave just enough of an interference to hide the town that sat beneath the hill on which the road ran across. It was down there, hidden inside the harsh landscape and a misleadingly unimportant town, where a people of ideals had grown to a number that many had only dreamed of. Zahid knew how well-protected that secret was, and that each day its arm of influence grew ever stronger and ever closer to the Outsiders' bases, where they assume safety and immunity from their actions. Soon, when they were ready, that arm would reach out and strike. At least, that was what his drive was for: to see when their strike would be made.

The road worsened as Zahid neared the house. It seemed that within a single kilometer, the road could disappear and return as if it were doing it all on its own. Alongside several large craters dotted the landscape, all of which came to be when an Outsider column was moving into the town when several Taliban mortar teams ambushed them; it was a perfect trap, and it was just a little too good for the now fanatically clouded Taliban leadership to pull off. Yet the craters did little to stop his advance as he winded his way through to the small, nomadic homes that made up the outskirts of Sirak. The road split off in several directions in small tributaries, not large enough for his car, but for a camel or a goat herd, it was passable. The houses became more and more frequent, slowly changing from an empty, sand-covered rural setting to the empty, sand-covered urban town that was common in Afghanistan. The town was guarded by an eerie blackness that covered the surroundings, enough to make it too hard to see anything that was not illuminated by the headlights, and this, for most, would be rather foreboding. However, for those who understood this land as a warzone, and the movement of vehicles generally being a harbinger for violence, it was all too common to drive through an area and see it as just another desert ghost town. In fact, it was so empty it seemed that had Zahid not known its usual routine, he would have believed it vacant and himself alone on his path to the Brotherhood. Yet none of this offered the slightest deterrent for him, and so he pressed on.

Eventually, toward the edge of "Main Street," Zahid came to a curve in the road, which headed off east when he came to a crawl. It was here, just inside the turn, where the house resided. It stood alone, or at least separated, from the other homes by a good ten meters or so. Outside the house sat a man, of unknown age due to his obscuring head dress, and behind him rested an assault rifle, which seemed to be some strange, larger variant of the AK-47. Zahid pulled to the side, in between the house and a small shack, beneath a cloth overhead canopy. He parked the vehicle, turned off lights, and cracked the window open; and instantly he was greeted by the chill of the desert night. He uttered a phrase, something irrelevant and unknown to many who would hear it, but to the man sitting in the chair, it meant "turn on your flashlight, see who I am, and let me pass." The man did like so, and seeing who it was, he stood and his large .44 caliber revolver suddenly became apparent under the glare of the flashlight, which now pointed to the door the man had been guarding. Zahid exited his vehicle, made a small gesture of thanks to the man for his help, and with that, entered the house.

Inside, three men sat with a low-lit candle and a copy of the Quran, all three seemed to be deeply enthralled, for they barely even stirred upon his entering. Zahid stood, waiting patiently for the men to take notice, and eventually, someone did. One of them, who wore only a pair of glasses to cover his face, stood, nodded to Zahid, to which Zahid bowed—a gesture just timid enough to understand who he was. Zahid sensed a smile on the man's face, for normally one of higher social stature wouldn't bow, but it was just for that reason that this was the confirmation of his true affiliation with the group. The man, now satisfied with Zahid's intentions, turned and signaled to the men at his sides, who immediately stood and joined him in front of a large wooden crate. They positioned around it and lifted the crate in synch with one another. Beneath it was a carpet, which was rolled over once they had set the crate down on the table to reveal a hole just large enough for a man to fit through, with a wood stepladder at the bottom to offer assistance in getting to the tunnel below. Zahid thanked the man to his right, who was wearing a covering similar to that of the man outside, and then entered the hole, which led down to a tunnel large enough to crouch in while he walked. As he moved, he could hear some of the sand beneath him slide as it fell through a grate and into a small hole, where a man was most likely stationed to kill anyone moving above who hadn't been cleared by the regular silence of the happenings above. Eventually Zahid came to a bifurcation, and he went right, to which he encountered another split where he went right again, until he came to a wooden pallet, with light that poured in through the gaps in the wood. When he reached it, he could hear soft speaking on the other side, coming from several different sources. He spoke abruptly, saying a variation of the same word he had spoken to the man outside. Almost immediately, the wood was pulled away from the entrance, and Zahid passed through the opening into a carved out room, another ladder positioned at the edge of the room.

Zahid stood, now that he was in a room large enough to stand in and he bowed once more, but this time because he was in the presence of Amir, who deserved all respect. Zahid was welcomed by the rest of those in attendance to the meeting, all of whom were brothers, each with their own special contribution to the strength of what many had come to call the Brotherhood of Cleansing Fire. In the center of the room, a table had been set, which was low enough to the ground for them to sit on the pillows, which had been set in a ring about the edge of it. One of the spaces at the table was still open, and Amir motioned gladly for Zahid to take the seat; he did so gratefully.

"Where were we?" asked Amir, now returning his attention to the pictures that lay in front of him on the table.

"The base's population, Amir."

"Ah, thank you, Behnam, population. Observe." He pointed at the small man who had just spoken, whose face lit up with admiration at the attention he was receiving from Amir; he gave him his full attention. "In this small base, there are several times a week when it is most infested with Outsiders, and during one of those times is when we are to strike. What I need from you is to work with Zahid to gather more information on when those times are and how quickly they can change. Do not, in any way, make yourselves known to anyone in or around this camp..." Each man in the room, whether from a school or official position in Kabul, considered themselves of high caliber. What's more, as they spoke in a formal dialect they added respectful portions to words. They listened to the Amir, thought silently and waited to speak at an appropriate time. Were it not for the dirt walls it would have seemed like a literary conference.

When this was said, it was immediately apparent that Behnam was not thrilled, but he dare not express his dislike of the partnership; what was done was done for a reason, and no one wished to question Amir. Zahid was also less inclined to work with the likes of Behnam, but he was better at hiding his emotions than the former scholar, who used to teach at a school in one of the rich suburbs outside of Kabul City and was still not used to the ferocity that was their cause, However, Zahid was far more aggravated with the assignment and decided to speak up.

"Amir?" Zahid spoke, cutting off the tail end if what had turned into a small hate speech against the Outsiders and was, thus, off topic.

"Zahid, silence!" Behnam raged, but a soft raise of Amir's hand quelled the man's poorly controlled temper.

"What is it, Brother?"

"In my opinion, since we have been waiting for such a long time with very little to show, and with those who know what goes on at the Outsider camp already positioned to watch, I believe that it would be better if we were to begin our attack." Zahid had grown tired of the timidity and low frequency of violence done in Helmond. If enough was going to be done to spark a response from the American intelligence agencies, then things were in need of an escalation.

"You have voiced this before. Is your concern that we will run out of Outsiders to send to their afterlife?" The humor did little to lighten Zahid's mood.

"No, I fear that in our light pressing, the Outsiders will simply bolster rather than retreat and if that were to happen…"

"Then we would have to wait a little longer and then strike all the more. You cannot be hasty. Our time for dominance will come. Leave the random violence for the Taliban.

Zahid backed down; they were not ready for the fight that he envisioned, and so he would wait. Both he and Behnam thanked Amir for the opportunity to serve the Brotherhood and left their disgust with one another to be dealt with later. It was in this formal tone that the meeting continued, long into the night. However, aside from Zahid's new objective, the main points discussed during this meeting had already been established in those preceding, and to those in the room it felt like waste of time, but that is not the case. The meeting was instead designed to boost morale of those who weren't even present, to give them a sense of order. Whereas it is dangerous to meet too often, for suspicion from Outsider scouts and traitors would be raised, it would be more dangerous if those who were soon to carry out this elaborate plan would lose faith in the cause that was so vehemently promoted just a short time ago. So they stayed, discussing each point with as much repetitiveness as possible so that they could at least iron out some of the wrinkles that may have accumulated over the last few weeks.

"AMIR"

**0638 hours, July 10, Denver,
Colorado, USA**

"They call him the Amir," a man said, his voice echoing through speakers that lined the ceiling of the blackened room. After a pause, without reply, Agent Windburg's image appeared on a large video screen, and he spoke again. "As his name suggests, he is the leader of a group that we now suspect has been working with one of our mock opium cultivators in the area. That kind of connection is actually common for terrorists to gain a steadier source of revenue. We believe they may be responsible for some of the more violent attacks that have turned up over the last couple months, although there isn't much chatter to go on as they seem to be well off the grid. When it comes to movement and actions, they haven't taken responsibility for anything as of yet."

Officer Richard Matthews, director of the Afghanistan Intelligence Committee, said, "It would seem to me that your time in the desert has only given you a whole lot of suggestions, maybes and not-sure's." He stared at Windburg with an intent gaze; Windburg shifted his away.

"I'm sorry, but that's all these locals are willing to give me. From most of my experience in the area, especially around Sangin, people wouldn't tell you where the bathroom was, let alone give up information about a new terrorist group reaching out around them. They're scared."

"Well, don't take this the wrong way, son, but your experience isn't much to write home about. Now you start tracking this 'Amir' character. Find out where he goes and what he does, if you can see if he has any regular visits to stores, maybe you'll find someone who knows him and wouldn't mind flipping for the extra coin. Get it done, Steven, next time you call I want more than 'maybe'!"

"Yes, sir, I—" was all that made it through before Matthews cut the connection. Matthews turned from his desk, still eyeing the hazy picture that Steven had given him on his touch pad. He was, despite what he lead the boy to believe, impressed with the find, but if someone can make a find, then they can do it just a little better. He set the picture down, opened the heavy wooden door, and exited the room. He stood on a long walkway, overlooking a large field of computers, desks, and cubicles—all of which were manned by analysts and technicians alike. This is where so much of what the CIA's purpose is accomplished. These men and women all did their jobs with staggering proficiency and an immense amount of pride. To many, they were the tool of justice; for him, they were simply tools—very *lucrative* tools in the right hands.

After a couple moments, Matthews turned away, returning his mind to what he had learned from his meeting with Steven. *This "Amir" fellow,* he thought to himself, *what does he wish to accomplish?* In his mind, he compared the most recent heavy attacks that had wailed upon the forces stationed in Helmand province. *They have only connections,* he realized as he saw that their attacks hadn't stretched far according to intelligence. *Not very many followers, but strong connections.* He thought about how they could track anything that they may have used, as if there would be anything to track. Then he remembered that someone had survived that last attack that may have been theirs, and he might be able to tell just a little about what he saw and start him on the right track. *If that happen.* He smiled to himself as he walked into his office. *Then maybe I can let Steven handle it, and I*

won't need to go. The thought of going to the desert again crossed his mind, and he suddenly needed a drink.

VEILED

2013 hours, July 10, Camp Bastion
Helmand Province, Afghanistan

Hanson reached under his pillow and grabbed a small makeshift bag, filled almost to bursting with the items of clothing that he had procured earlier that day. His muscles tensed and his heart sped as he caught a glimpse of the green turban, which now represented another part of him, a part which both he and Celia knew, but he alone felt the connection between it and who he truly was. He felt a little juvenile in the way he was acting, knowing full well that his little escapade that morning amounted to little more than a glimpse at the full measure of the task that lay before him. Yet it reassured him to have that piece that defined his alter ego and allowed him to become something he had never encountered before: a living lie. After a moment, he listened to his own thoughts, realized that he had strayed a little too far into the imagination that called him, and remembered that Daniil had given him a little bit of help—unknowing, of course, on his journey.

When they were eating, Hanson had asked Daniil if he had found anything from the CID guys, as he had said he would. Daniil told him of their suspicions of the attack being orchestrated by a new group, something about the two-stage attack being a little more innovative than something other than a third party group could have come up with. When Hanson pressed further, Daniil explained that they had found the technique and structure of the bomb to point toward Iran and her special forces divisions. What this meant for Hanson is he now knew where to start prodding when he goes to see Celia tonight. So fully cloaked in his disguise, he exited his room and followed the road down to the CID building. He noticed that there were far less people active than had been there that morning, which is strange because usually evenings carry a heavy load for such a large hospital. In any case, he was just happy there weren't many MPs hanging around might catch him, and in fact, those that were there were far too busy talking to nurses to even notice his passage. Finally, though, he made it to the door and exited into the fiery dusk that had laid itself down upon the camp.

As he walked, he felt the turban shift in the wind that gracefully dragged itself along the sand. The warm air cooled as it wrapped around him, and caused his sweat to evaporate, chilling the top of his skin. It was when the turban lifted off him that he felt as though he were standing alone, hurriedly searching the earth around him and deep inside himself for the answers. It seemed as though the wind was pointing him somewhere, and though he couldn't tell where, the green cloth that draped over him guided him along, its long drapes reaching in the wind out, and so he followed their gesture. He knew he was being strange, and maybe it had something to do with the pain killers flowing through his system, but it wasn't like he knew what else to really do. Eventually Hanson reached the CID building and noticed that a majority of the vehicles that had been present before were now absent, with the exception of a couple parked toward the end of the parking lot. Realizing that he may have missed seeing Celia and his chance at learning the second code, he approached the door and knocked. After a few moments of something near desperation, his fears were quenched when the door opened, and Celia smiled as kindly as she had just that morning. Hanson almost forgot why he was there, but he regained his mental composure and proceeded with his reintroduction.

"Hello." He sounded almost robotic, disappointing himself, but her smile diminished in no visible manner.

"Hello," she repeated, attempting to mimic his tone. He apparently had come off as more macho than intended. In any case, he was lacking at the art of enchanting introductions; she forgave his malpractice.

"I was just wondering, you know, if you…" he had almost no idea how to ask about the attack without sounding strange, so he said, "Well, it's just that I have this friend, and he lost a buddy in that big bombing."

"The one on the convoy?"

"Yes. Anyway, he just wanted to know if you got the guy responsible yet."

"Is this the same friend that gave you a beating?" she asked jovially.

"Well, no." The thought of Billy sent a pang through his chest, but he kept his cool. "But he'd probably like to know, too, if that'll help."

"We aren't very far, sadly. We've been going all week pretty steadily on this thing, but the attack was well-orchestrated, and no one has claimed responsibility yet. It's like they're just trying to mess with us, or they don't care about sending a message."

"I heard that you guys think the guy who made the bomb is Iranian, is that true?"

"Yeah"—she looked perplexed—"you know, I just told someone this morning, just after you left, some guy named Dan or something. Is that who told you?"

Realizing his mistake, he searched for an escape. "Well, I think I know who you're talking about. I more or less overheard the Iran bit from a patient today, a little while after I had left here."

"Then that must be him." All of a sudden, she focused intently on him, and he expected a very serious question." So where you from?" Her stern look and tilted head made him feel a little strange, but he realized she was simply spontaneous; he liked that.

Before he could answer, though, the door to the control center opened, and a scraggly looking man, with a very poorly kept beard, walked over to her desk, grabbed a stack of files from beneath her chair, and then walked back to the door, eyeing Hanson jealously as he went. The man apparently had feelings for Celia but was unable, or unwilling, to act on them. In any case, Hanson was unthreatened by the looks and gave a kind nod as the man backed through the door and disappeared into another room on the other side of the computer room. However, Hanson felt like thanking the man because now he had code number two; Hanson felt like should have been a secret agent.

Interested in why the strange-looking man took the files from her desk, Hanson inquired with his hand and a raised eyebrow; she caught the question.

"He's Chris, the file guy." He gave her a look as if to say, "What kind of a title is 'file guy'?" And she clarified, "You know, he makes sure everything gets put where it's supposed to be."

"Are those all case files?"

"Yeah, I've been pounding through 'em all day, trying to make 'em fourth-grade reading level. Apparently most of the reports are too detailed for some of the analysts' liking."

"No doubt due to the file guy, huh?" Hanson joked.

"Yeah, that's why he looks so ornery today. He hates when he is too smart for everyone else, but he loves it too. He's a complicated guy." *That's not the only reason,* Hanson thought to himself.

"What were you asking me?" Hanson asked, now prepared to change the subject and leave.

"Your home, where are you from?"

"Well, I was born in a hospital, there were doctors and nurses, and I had parents…" he rambled through a couple more obvious and generic details until she smiled and shook her head.

"Okay, you don't have to tell me. *I'm* from California and was also born in a hospital."

"Congratulations! I thought I was alone with that one." Hanson felt as though he were ten years old, using lines he'd said to girls when he was in middle school and even before that, but she was laughing, so they had to be working. As they talked, Hanson began to open up more. He told her how he'd grown up in Phoenix, right near the university, and had always wanted to attend there. Eventually, he was able to get in on grades alone, seeing as how his sports ability was simply focused on staying in shape. After he got in, however, he fell in love with the military and decided to enlist. She asked about his medical career, and he remembered he was supposed to be a doctor; he had to explain that he had also worked at the VA hospital for a while, when he was in high school, and he wanted to help those guys out. Though his being a doctor was a flat-out lie, he actually did work at the VA, but only as a janitor. Eventually, though, he was able to return to the truth and told her a little bit about his friend from Meriden, Iowa, a guy named Billy Mack Tompkey. It was here when he felt that pang in his chest again, and when he looked down to see if he'd just been feeling something, he saw his green turban, now motionless against his chest as if protesting his current inaction. He realized he needed to know more, so he decided it was his turn to be spontaneous.

He was sitting on the edge of her desk and she in her chair, which she had pulled out from under her desk and situated left of the control room door. From his spot, he could see some of the unfinished files she had strewn across her desk. He talked, only half-paying attention to her as his eyes grazed over the folders as that wind had done on the sand around him. Then he saw it, just under the top few folders, with the barcode and name tagged on the top left-hand corner of its dull yellow spread: the "Convoy Attack" file. He reached for it, and when he did, his hand was immediately pushed away. So he reached short and quick, luring her to try and stop him again, but he pulled back and reached over her arm, successfully defeating her attempted defense. He held it high, and she giggled as she reached for it but backed away when she realized it was to no avail. He smirked at her small insult at him, acting like a child, and opened the file.

"So this is what you look at all day, huh?" he said, attempting to seem uninterested as he read.

"Yes, now may I have it back?" She reached her hand out pleadingly, but he pulled away and jovially said, "I'll be done in a moment." Then he found a section, just under the description and review of the attack, which gave him something he didn't expect. A picture of a man, no more than forty, was positioned below the description of the detonator. He read for just a moment while desperately trying to keep up a conversation with the now impatient Celia. However, he stopped trying when he read that they knew where the equipment was from—an American company in the Czech Republic, and the man was an Afghani businessman that had just recently bought out the company. However, while he was so enthralled, Celia was able to snatch the file out from his grasp, and thus his reading time was ended.

"Why so interested in this attack? You were pretty spaced out for a minute."

It was her vernacular that brought him back to civilization. "Spaced?" he inquired. "I haven't heard that since I watched a *Saved by the Bell* episode about ten years ago. You a little trapped in the past?"

"Okay, so I have a lot of history to me, and most of it comes out. Don't we all?"

"I guess so, just some a little more than others, huh?" She smiled and rolled her eyes, waving off his remark. "Well I best be headin' out." He stood, walked to the door, and turned around.

"Would you like to…"—then he lost his nerve—"uh…you know, hang out."

"'Hang out.' I wonder what that was supposed to mean before you said it." She smiled kindly and then looked as though she were thinking intently; he awaited her verdict. "When and what did you have in mind?"

"How 'bout tomorrow, after you're done with your rewrites. We'll just get something to eat together?" He nearly kicked himself for what he was doing—not just because he sounded stupid doing it, but because he shouldn't be doing it at all. He hoped she would decline.

"Sure," she said, both disappointing him and completing his daily wish. "We can do that. I'll tell you when I'm done tomorrow."

"How 'bout I just drop by same time tomorrow? Sound good?"

"Sure, see you then." She looked at the clock and finished with "Don't forget!"

"I won't," he said "I'll catch you on the flip side!" he yelled, mocking her old-timey word with a disco reference.

PROPOSITIONS

0900 hours, July 11, Camp Bastion
Helmand Province, Afghanistan

EOD Chief Sergeant Francis Walker adjusted his helmet, the strap pulling just a little too hard on the right side of his cheek. He fumbled with the clasp, trying in vain to loosen it while balancing in the unstable Humvee on his way to the hospital. The Humvee passed a large grouping of tents on their left, several people, in US Desert camo, walking in between the long isles that together with the tents made up the troop barracks for the British troops. Fed up with his safety strap, he decided to ignore it, and he removed his canteen and began to drink. He actually had a camel pack with probably three times as much water, but he knew that after a few hours on patrol in the middle of this desert, he would at least want half of that in reserve; so canteen it was.

A gate in front of the Humvee opened and allowed them to pass through, and thus they entered the American side of the camp. As they did, Hagen picked up a brown file from the seat beside him and reread the portion that described the man's injuries. From what he could surmise, this "Corporal Damian Hanson" should be healed up enough to go and have a meeting with an agent from the CIA, and so the chief wanted to see if he was even up to it. They turned again, this time driving right past the mess tent and into the staging area outside the hospital. He opened the door, dust still catching up to the armored vehicle, its deep purring felt even through the ground. He stood, gave the file one last good look, and then tossed it back into the Humvee. From here, he was able to unsnap his helmet, and he walked into the hospital.

When he entered, he asked one of the nurses at a desk near the door where he could find Hanson. When she asked who that was, he simply asked where the recovery rooms were; she pointed him down a hallway. After what seemed to be a few minutes of turns and dead ends, he came to the recovery area and asked a passing doctor, who turned, gestured to a room at the end of a dimly lighted hallway, and then moved on before the chief could thank him. He walked down the hall, knocked on the door, and entered.

Hanson was sitting up against the wall with his bed pushed closer to the window, the sun pouring in like a blazing set of headlights as it provided light for the book in his hand. Behind him, several pillows were stacked and piled so as to offer just a little more support. The only visible bandage on him was wrapped around his waist, and even that seemed not to be bothering him very much.

"Corporal Hanson?" The Chief leaned over a little to be seen better from that side of the curtain.

"Yes?" He looked up, recognized his rank, and started over. "Yes, sir!?"

"How you holding up? Everything feeling better I hope."

"Oh yes, sir, just starting to get back on my own stance."

"Good." The Chief nodded and looked around the room. Hanson perceived he had something to say besides how are you, and so he helped him out.

"Anything you need, sir?"

"Well, as a matter of fact, looks like the company men would like to talk to you."

"What about, sir?" Hanson racked his mind for why the CIA would want to talk to him.

"Do you remember that explosion?" The Chief winced a little. "Of course you do. Well, what I'm trying to say is that they believe that bomb was part of several other attacks, and it looks like you're the only man alive that was close enough to the bomb to actually know anything about its structure."

"So what? They want me to tell them about it. I already did that. They have the reports, sir." Just talking about the attack made Hanson angry.

"I'm not exactly sure what they want with you specifically, it's not my job to know that stuff, and it's not their preference to tell me. You know how they are, the less collateral information sharing, the better. Anyway, they want you up at the office, and so I'm here to take you there." Hanson sighed, tossing his book aside.

"All right, I'll ask my nurse."

———✦✦✦———

His nurse said no, but that really didn't matter too much to the chief, and so there Hanson sat, his ribs aching with the constant jarring of the Humvee; the driver was just a little too aggressive for his liking. However, the drive didn't last long, and after a few minutes, he was back inside another ventilated building, sitting in a chair next to an MP and waiting for…he couldn't remember the man's name.

A door opened suddenly, several people in camouflage outfits and one or two body vests filed out of the room. At last a man walked out of the room, his longer black hair slicked back and his eyes covered by a pair of dimmed transition-lensed glasses. He looked around a little until his eyes settled on Hanson.

"Corporal Damian Hanson?" he inquired, sticking out his hand forcefully for a handshake.

"Yes, sir." They shook, and as they did, the man said, "Agent Steven Windburg, thanks for coming." *Not much of a choice, Steven, but you're welcome anyhow,* Hanson thought to himself as they entered the room.

Steven gestured to a chair in front of his desk, several others arranged behind it, most likely to accommodate the men who had just vacated moments ago. They sat, and Hanson began the conversation.

"What do you need, sir?"

"What? No preliminary niceties, not even a drink?" Hanson asked for water, and Steven handed him a cold water bottle that had been sitting in a mini-fridge just behind the desk.

"Thanks. Now, what did you need me to do?"

"Okay. Seeing as you are the sole surviving EOD tech from the explosions that we believe are tied together, we realize that you have more experience with this specific type of bomb-making technique. At least from the description you gave, it was specially made. Different than what you were used to?"

"Yes, sir, it was triggered in several different ways, including a radio set from what I saw. And that wasn't even the main attack, as you probably understand it was a two-stage ambush instead of just an IED."

"Yes. We know. What we need from you is not just information, but rather that you would, in a sense, *consult* with the rest of EOD missions that we carry out so that when you encounter an explosive, you will be able to tell whether or not it was like the one you had to deal with, or if it's just a more generic bomb. You may ask, 'Why on earth would we do that? A bomb is a bomb, it kills, and it's gone what more do you want from it.' Well, we are trying to establish a pattern. If we can get the sphere of influence in which this organization works, we may be able to limit their movements and start to dismantle it."

"So you don't think it's just another bomb maker, and you don't know how far they can reach?"

"Exactly, that is why we want you out there. Now, because this is extra added on to your regular duties, and that you will be working hand in hand with my office, we are willing to pay you double your current income for the duration of your assignment. Interested?" Hanson thought for a moment, trying to decide whether or not he wanted to get tied up with this guy when he already had his own plans for finding revenge. Then he realized that his plan would rest on whatever these guys were able to come up with, and reluctantly he agreed.

"Great, you are free to leave. You will start tomorrow when the patrol goes out."

"Will you be attending, sir?" From Hanson's experience, these CIA types rarely ever went along for the ride.

"No, I have some other engagements. Thank you for your time." He stood and opened the door for Hanson. They nodded to each other, and Agent Windburg closed the door. Hanson shook his head as he walked with the MP back to the Humvee; he figured the CIA wouldn't stick it's neck out too far, *but it had no problem sticking mine out.*

OBSERVE AND REPORT

1015 hours, July 11, Outside Foreword Operating Base Edinburgh, North of Sangin, Helmand Province, Afghanistan

The sun beat down upon the small car's roof with a vengeance. For Zahid, the heat was expected, and so he only wished he would have brought a pair of sunglasses to aid him in his surveillance. Rather, the constant barrage of whimpering that was flowing from Behnam was beginning to take its toll. It would have seemed that even after a few hours of sitting in the smoldering vehicle, when accommodation or at least the small fan that blew a light puff of air would have at least allowed Behnam to calm down. Yet all he could do was complain incessantly about how much he missed his comfortable occupation in a school.

"Why must we park directly beneath this boiling sun, Zahid? Do you have any sort of explanation for this inconvenience?" Zahid lowered the binoculars down from his eyes, yet he didn't actually turn to acknowledge Behnam. He simply said yes.

"Well, do tell. I have been sitting patient and quiet for hours now, and all you have done is look through your binoculars at the base into which you can't actually see." He crossed his arms.

"Behnam, you may believe that you were actually quiet and patient. I don't have the energy or the care to argue that with you. However, if we were to go under shade, we wouldn't be able to see anything for sure. What's more, I am not trying to see in the base, I'm watching the helicopters." He returned the binoculars to his eyes as he spotted a Chinook take a large turn around the base and land on the other side of a wall; several crates attached to its underside.

"Well then, what have you learned?" Behnam finally seemed interested.

"The base is simply a stop-and-go. It sends out supplies and brings in more of the same. Also, I see a lot of the faster helicopters heading south, so they're probably sending wounded too."

"What do those things going south have to do with wounded?"

"There is an extremely large camp south of the highway. That is where they send their wounded."

"So then, this place must have a large importance to their men out here." Zahid nodded slowly, only half-listening to Behnam's obvious statement. Zahid, while watching the helicopter's ingress-egress, had also been paying close attention to movement of patrols or land vehicles into the base, and from what he saw, there weren't very much. Thus an attack with a vehicle would be a little harder because anyone who sees their approach would be that much more curious. However, they had only been watching for the last few hours, and thus, their departure was still a long way off. Or so he thought, until he got a call; it was Jakub.

Hanson tossed the book from his lap with a look of accomplishment, but also, disappointment crossed his face. He stared at the ceiling, the happenings of the novel crossing his mind and still none of it making any sense. *The Catcher in the Rye,* he thought to himself, *what an awkward book.* He grabbed a pen from the little desk next to his bed and a pad of paper and began to write.

> Dear Jed,
>
> I thought the novel was really interesting and well-written. Plot didn't make too much sense, but I'm no English major like you, so my judgment is kind of limited. Whenever you want to send me another would be great timing (it gets pretty boring out here in the sandbox).

Sincerely,
Uncle Damian

He folded the letter, stuffed it neatly into an envelope—which he, in turn, laid aside in a drawer beneath his bed. As soon as he did this, the door behind him burst open suddenly. Hanson looked to find a soldier standing at attention. He handed Hanson a piece of typed paper, turned back around, and left out the door, all the while the sound of large, angry engines growled outside. Hanson read the note aloud, each word sounding like gold coins hitting the ground; the sounds of opportunity resonating in his mind. He would finally go after his enemy. Thus he stood and walked around his bed to prepare, roughly throwing open the trunk at the foot of his bed. He let the surprisingly light lid rest lazily upon the strength of the stabilizing arms as he gazed inside. In the trunk, several items were arranged. His new uniform seemed to gleam as he stared at its crisp folds. In a small way, he felt a twinge of nostalgia, although his old uniform had been damaged in the explosion, which he had been trying to forget. Yet despite his best efforts to keep focused, the past pulled ever harder on his psyche. His fall came swiftly, just a glance at the EOD patch that was sewn into the arm of his uniform sent his mind reeling back to a dust-covered desert, blood blotching the sand and on the patch, which was torn slightly off from his arm. He closed his eyes, a deep breath surging through him as he pushed himself to stay focused, but the darkness was only swept away by the brush of fire against his mind's eye. His eyes opened, and he saw it, surging for an escape and finding it at the top of his wooden chest: attached to the lid was a picture, a moment captured, showing a time that he still couldn't fully grasp had passed. He could see himself, standing and smiling as though the only care in the world was to simply ensure the picture turned out all right. To his right he could see his friend, the man he had trusted and worked with and befriended for so long. In fact, he still felt as though he could turn and say, "Hey, Billy, you remember this?"

But Billy was gone. Then his eyes passed to her, a girl no taller than Billy, standing beside him and seemingly doing her best not to laugh as she posed for the camera. He knew that no one would miss Billy more than her; they were nearly inseparable before he and Billy had left, until war finally coursed itself between them. He thought about calling her, saying maybe that he was sorry or that he wished he could take back their enlistment or something, but he couldn't. In a final fit of attempted control, he reached out and took his uniform and laid it on the bed, fully determined to close the chest. He turned back to close it when he saw the tags, and he could hear them in his mind—he could feel them as they landed in his palm at the airport, where he saw the body of his friend for the last time. He couldn't take it; he slammed the lid.

Outside, the wind had grown agitated, lifting and pushing small dunes of sand up and across only a few feet above the ground, bits of glass reflecting glimmers of the immense light of the sun into his eyes. To his right hummed two large armored trucks, each bustling with excitement as they were loaded for the impending trek out to the school where the bombing had been attempted, just a few dozen miles from Camp Bastion. He took a step, his heavy boot shod foot sinking reminiscently into the sand as he had done so many times before. But there was a difference, one that only he noticed as he dropped his bag into the side compartments of the truck and one only he could cherish, staring out from the shadows within the cabin; something he was going to keep quiet.

Zahid pulled up to the house of the Amir, having already let Behnam take on the responsibility of watching the FOB. He angrily muttered the password, exited the car, and went into the house. After a couple minutes more of moving through their defenses, he arrived at the underground room that he had entered the night before. At the edge of the room, just beyond the table was a ladder, which lead directly into a house that was several homes away from the one in which he had entered. He quickly scaled the ladder, pushed aside the mat that covered the hole, and was immediately greeted by the barrel of an AK-47 pointed directly at his head, a set of dark, rigid eyes perched calmly behind it. Suddenly, a deep voice muttered a word, one that Zahid wasn't familiar with, and then the man promptly stood away from Zahid and rested his rifle upon his shoulder.

"Zahid, are you not supposed to be watching the Outsiders with Behnam?" the voice of the Amir came from a man turned away from Zahid, facing out a small window toward town square.

"May I speak, Amir?"

"I would hope you would," the Amir retorted sarcastically.

"I would ask that you not become offended, but I desire an explanation as to why you went behind my back to Jakub, taking what I had asked for."

"Zahid"—the Amir turned to face him—"what I have done was to reach our goal all the more rapid, and I do not need to ask you for that, do I? Besides, I have nothing to say as to more of an explanation."

"Amir, if nothing else, may I at least carry the mission. I will build the bomb, and take it where ever you wish. I am the best at what—"

"I have already used the bomb." He looked into Zahid's eyes, trying to see what the man was feeling, but all he found was a wall rather than a window.

"Why?" finally the words spurted out. "Why didn't you trust me to do this. I heard nothing of a plan or practice, who did you use? Rahim? Cahled?"

"I used Behnam's man and had him carry it out. However, I feel as though I have made a mistake in doing so. The explosive never detonated, and when I questioned him, he simply said that the wiring was off."

"Was Behnam aware of this?'

"Yes."

"So then, his man retrieved the bomb?" Zahid stated in more hope than actual belief.

"No, the local police found it, and he was unable to get near it again."

"Amir." Zahid knelt down and looked into the Amir's eyes, and as the Amir stared into Zahid's, he found the eyes of someone without remorse, a venomous cobra in the grass—a wolf. "The police will share it with the outsiders, the CIA will find it and they can use that to find where it was taken from. Amir, they could find us out."

"Zahid." The Amir stood, attempting to regain some of the dignity that he had lost with this humiliatingly obvious mistake. "Do not worry about any of that. Allah will protect us. You know that no Outsider weapon can harm us when he is on our side. I have had enough of this Zahid." He patted him on the shoulder. "You will be fine. Now go and finish the important task I gave you before." And with that, the Amir left the house, and Zahid was standing in solitude.

TRICK OR TREAT

1407 hours, July 11, Kala Town
East of Camp Bastion, Helmand Province, Afghanistan

The school stood as a diamond in the rough, glimmering as the pinnacle of advancement in the small, nearly nomadic village. Its large, concrete walls stood in stark contrast with the rest of the homes and shacks, which were a dark, sandy orange that reflected light well from the rest of the desert. The school itself was well-placed in relation to the center of town, standing on the western side of the large road that ran uninterrupted through the center of the village; it reminded Hanson of home, or at least Arizona. The school changed, however, when Hanson noticed no power lines, no windows, and with large barbwire fences that ran along the edge of its dirt-covered playgrounds. Also, a gate with several guards was now standing outside, each holding a machine gun and watching the crowds that had gathered with the children; the place now seemed to resemble a prison, and Hanson remembered it was nothing like Arizona.

Hanson's truck pulled up as second to last in the four vehicle convoy that parked along the fence. As he exited, the sound of hundreds of people milling around the area drowned out everything but the engines and of the shouting of the guards who were leading Hanson and his crew through the gate while keeping the people at bay. Once inside on the flat area in front of the school, it was apparent to see that the children had been rushed from lunch, dropping trash and wrappers along the way off the school grounds, much of which was uneaten. Behind him, Agent Windburg was typing rapidly with one hand into his phone while taking a briefcase from the soldier next to him, then the soldier ran up in front of Hanson and opened the door, all the while watching the crowds. Hanson patted him on the shoulder and gave a wink through the visor that was attached to his heavily padded armored suit. To Hanson, this kid was still getting used to the violent nature of people when they are around things like bombs, and Hanson himself used to act the same way. Working with bombs with crowds of people around, however, had become something of an expected environment; Hanson just ignored their shouts.

As soon as they walked through the door, a large Afghan man walked briskly up to them and introduced himself as the headmaster of the small school. Behind him, Agent Windburg spoke up and asked where the explosive was, but Hanson interjected.

"Sir, how many explosives were located on the grounds?"

"Just one bombs in room, no other," the tall Afghan replied, his eyes showing little bits of fear as he spoke about these weapons.

"Well, I am going to take a look around. From what I remember, our bomb maker likes the double placement. You may have only found a decoy."

"Yes, very good, sir." And with that, the tall Afghan took up part of his robe and showed them into a large room to the left of the entrance; it was full of desks. Hanson turned to Agent Windburg and motioned for him to leave the area, and so Windburg removed himself and the others from the room and they exited the building.

Hanson then turned back to face the room, all the while looking for anything that could set off an explosive. As he walked, he felt along the edges of the desks and the legs of the chairs, yet he found no wires and could see no laser trip-beams. He reached the edge of the room, just beneath a large blackboard that reached from the window to nearly half the large wall. It was above the blackboard's wooden frame that Hanson noticed a tile in the ceiling that had been moved, as there was a pile of white dust that had collected near his feet. Hanson reached and grabbed a chair from a stack to his right and stood on top as he prepared to lift the tile. He closed his eyes for a moment; deep, low breaths brought him to a place just outside of his fear. He reached down and grabbed a mirror from his chest pocket and started to push the block up instead of sliding it, trying to fit his mirror just through the crack. He could feel weight on the other side of the block, and so he turned on the flashlight that was attached to his helmet and peered through the mirror. Above the ceiling was essentially empty, with only one or two pipes running along the roof to interrupt his field of view. He turned the mirror, all the while stabilizing himself with his heavy boots on the small surface of the chair. Then he saw something positioned just above him, and he froze. It seemed to be poised on the edge of the block he was holding, and so he lightly brought it back down. He took another deep breath, removed a pair of scissors from the same pocket, and proceeded to lift lightly once again. He could see no wires, but that didn't mean there weren't any, and so he slowly reached the scissors through the crack and prepared to feel for any resistance along the edge of the small black container. He followed the edge, nothing more than hard plastic along the whole of the container-like box. Then he felt it—a little tug against his tool no harder than a piece of twine protruding from its surface. He pushed just a little higher, the chair complaining with the added force. Opening the teeth of the scissors, he pressed them against the wire and started to close them. Then the chair gave way, tipping to one side and pitching downward. He dropped the scissors and, without thinking, pushed up on the tile block and caught himself from falling, then he heard the sound of something falling and hitting the tile overhead; the bomb had fallen. He prepared for the explosion, although he knew full well that he wouldn't survive. He closed his eyes again; time moving slow and his heart rate moving ever faster. He could feel heat pouring over him, and in his mind's eye, he swore he could see fire. Then it disappeared, sand and smoke plunging his mind behind its drifting curtain so that nothing could penetrate its secrets.

Then seconds pass, and he felt nothing, could see nothing, and heard only his heavy breathing above his racing heart. He opened his eyes, his flashlight still shinning as he gazed up at the ceiling above him. The walls were intact, there was nothing destroyed, and he was not dead; the bomb didn't go off. He stood and took a step back up onto the chair and peered into the hole. Sitting there, just off the edge of where the tile had been, sat a plastic Gameboy and a controller attached to it with a wire. Relieved, Hanson took it down from the ceiling and placed it onto a desk, took off his helmet, and put the Gameboy inside it. Sweating, he took himself and his find back out into the main hall and then out the door where he was greeted once again by the tall Afghan, who motioned him toward a table.

"Hanson, what did you find?"

"There is no second device, just the one that your police located." He gestured to the tall man, who gleamed with excitement that his men had done well.

"Have you seen the actual device, sir?" Hanson asked Agent Windburg, who raised his finger to get him to wait as he finished up the message in his phone. He then dropped the phone into his pocket and signaled for the chief to bring the large box in his hand over to the table; the chief immediately complied and brought the box, Hanson opened the top to find the explosive still intact, but the digital timer was off and the electrical primer that rested in a large block of C4 appeared to have shorted out.

"So no one has touched this device?"

"No, Corporal, it was left in the box as we found it, although it was Marzi's men who brought it out to us." The chief gestured to the tall man. Hanson never looked up from the bomb; instead he was focused on the wiring, looking for the same difference that he had seen before. He could hear the chief still rambling about where they found it, but as Hanson looked through each piece carefully, he found that it had no small silver wires; no paper clip like the bomb he had seen before.

"Does that sound like our guy to you, Corporal Hanson?"

"Does what, Chief?"

"The fact that it was placed directly beneath the stage and was set to go right before lunch ended. That took planning and a knowledge of the school itself. So do you think it's him?"

"No." He looked up at the chief. "No, I think it was someone else. But…" he started to pick through the bomb pieces, black streaks of where plastic burnt from the power surge seemed to be collected around just one area; a small bridge between the timer and the primer was held together by a red wire. He closed his eyes and thought back to the bomb on the road, a picture of the connection between the radio receiver and the primer with a gap made the same way, but it had worked, and it was made with a paper clip instead. "I'm not sure about this, so don't jump on anything yet, but this might be some of the same equipment our guy uses, just maybe he made a mistake in building it, or somebody else built it for him."

"How do you figure?" Agent Windburg finally seemed interested.

"From what I remember, the last device had a connection just like this one here"—he pointed at the bridge—"but the connection was made by something other than wire: a paper clip."

"You're basing this off a look and a paper clip, Corporal?"

"Just hear me out, Chief." Hanson picked up the burnt primer in his left hand and pointed with his right. "The only reason this thing never went off was because it shorted out. If you look here, too much power was sent through the wire, and instead of triggering the bomb, it just fried the primer. That means that this power supply was adjusted to work with a different type of connection here, one that doesn't transmit energy as well."

"Like a paper clip." Windburg's face suddenly lit up as he realized they might have something.

"Exactly," Hanson said. "The last one I dealt with had one, this one didn't, so it doesn't work. Most of the same pieces just set up wrong."

"That still leaves us with someone else and not our guy, right?" the chief asked. Hanson thought about it for a second and realized he was right. Then Agent Windburg spoke again.

"Actually, if this stuff is the same materials, then it came from the same place, what I think we can do is just track it to where it came from and see what we find. We can at least get closer to where we might find him." Windburg took out his phone again, nodded to the chief who took the components of the bombs back into the box, and both men walked back to the Humvee. Hanson grabbed his helmet and the Gameboy inside it and turned toward the crowd. As he walked out, he noticed one of the young boys was staring at him, his eyes nearly in sync with his hand as it swung back and forth with the toy. Hanson, knowingly allowing the boy to see it, placed it in a small pile of rocks and trash and then jumped up into the large truck. The convoy pulled out, and Hanson watched as the young boy ran over and grabbed the toy, several of his friends following him around the corner of a house. Hanson smiled.

As the convoy pulled away, hundreds of people were crowded near and around the road. Stark contrast between the light of the walls of the surrounding buildings struck by the sun and the shadowed windows where light seemed to disappear, and where a young man sat watching the trucks pull away. Once the last one had hit the main road and moved on, the man removed a large, military grade radio from a dark green backpack in between his legs and clicked the button.

"Saben," he whispered, and then he waited for a response.

"Go ahead, Furan," a voice from the radio spoke.

"The Outsiders have found the weapon, they are taking it with them."

"You're sure?"

"Marzi told me, he was the one who showed them where it was."

"Give Marzi my regards." Then the radio went quiet.

The young man stood and turned to his right with his bag in hand, facing a small door way with bead strands serving as the door. The young man reached back into his bag and removed an American .45 caliber pistol, a suppressor lingering like a spear off of its tip. He took a deep breath and then walked through the beads. Three hushed taps, and then he left through the door on the other side.

PAST

1045 hours, July 11, Denver, Colorado, USA

Officer Matthews walked into the ops center with swag in his step. He, even at his "advanced" age, hadn't even had to try to hit big with some secretary in the domestic affairs wing, and the best part was she really wanted it; being in great shape probably had something to do with his confidence. He passed by a window that offered a good glance at a mirror, through which he gazed beamingly at his slightly grayed sideburns, wickedly smug grin, and sharp blue eyes. Even through his suit he looked athletic, his upper body sloping perfectly with the strong muscles he had formed in his core over the years. She was a moderately young, tall blond, tanned as if she lived on the beaches in California but serious enough in her posture to put most men off, usually. Her posture changed, however, whenever he wanted it to, and so he didn't mind obliging her. *That's it*, he thought, *I obliged her.* She was serious, always had to be in the CIA, and yet despite all the rules, regulations and chances at getting caught, she just wanted excitement out of an otherwise completely dreary day. *I obliged her.* He smirked again.

He swiped his card against the electronic lock, and with a click, it opened. He walked down a slight incline, all the while snickering at his catch and wondering how he might do it again. He barely noticed that his call was already waiting and that Agent Steven Windburg was up on the high-def screen.

"I've been waiting here for almost twenty minutes, sir, you said for me to call at ten thirty. Where have you been?"

"First of all, it doesn't matter where I've been Agent Windburg, and if it did, I sure as hell wouldn't tell it to you. Second, it has only been fifteen, don't exaggerate, it's not becoming." He sat himself down in one of the gray chairs that lined the wall. "What do you got?"

"All right, so I was working with Corporal Hanson, the EOD tech, and he said that whoever made the explosive wasn't our guy."

"Hold up just a second. Explain to me again why Corporal Hanson can make decisions like this? And which explosive are we talking about?"

"Sir, Hanson is the one that survived the convoy attack last week. He has seen this guy's work in action, and he knows what he is looking for. Now, the bomb we're talking about is the one found in the little school in Kala. I texted you earlier, didn't you get it?"

"I have been predisposed all morning, wasn't able to read it." A smirk cracked on his face, but he suppressed it before it was noticed.

"Well, Hanson went over the device that was found, and he said that there was no way it was the same bomb maker."

"Why?"

"Well, he said that the bomb maker we've been looking for has a habit of using paper clips as the connection between the trigger and the primer. Whoever made this bomb didn't know that the power supply delivered more than the regular kick, and so he used regular wires, so the primer's triggering circuit shorted out. That's why we found it, and that's why it can't be our guy. Also, the last one had a second trigger and a second bomb, this attack just doesn't fit the MO."

"Terrorists and their complexities." Matthews sighed as he crossed his legs, his mind sifting through the info until... He stood. "All right, chances are good that most of this equipment is just going to lead us right back to Pakistan's horribly managed borders, which is like tracking specific drugs to Mexico, you get lost once you get to the edge. The C4, however, is always a different story, mostly because it will have a chemical signature specific enough to track." Matthews removed a cigarette from his pocket and lit it up—that also was against policy. "So that's what we're going to work with. Anything else for me, Steven?"

"No, sir, not at this time."

"All right then." Matthews picked up a file and looked at a piece of paper with a picture of Hanson, "Now, this guy Hanson is the only one we know who can recognize our bomber. So I need him watched. I don't need to deal with a bomber and a loose asset."

"Yes, sir, I got him under control." Matthews signaled to the technician, who ended the video feed.

INQUIRY

2037 hours, July 11, Girishk
Helmand Province, Afghanistan

Jakub had been standing on a wooden stool in his kitchen for nearly an hour, all the while his efforts at replacing the light above the counter being frustrated; he had gone through at least three lightbulbs. He had both hands working with the socket, one holding the connecting kit and the other frantically turning a screw rapidly into its rest. Finally, it caught itself in place, and he was able to finally let go, as the rigging kit was now held in by three separate grips. He reached down and grabbed the last screw from his hand and began to twist it into place; as he did this, he grabbed a screw driver and began to tighten the others in an alternating fashion. It was during this time of focus that he failed to notice someone had come in and taken a seat behind him, then Jakub smelled the smoke.

Trying to seem calm, he acted as though he were reaching for a clamp when he was actually placing his other hand onto a small revolver in his right pocket, but he abruptly stopped when he heard the voice.

"Hello, Jakub." The steely chill that accompanied the voice could never be mistaken for anyone else.

"Zahid," he said, still not turning round. "A pleasant surprise to have you hear so late. Is there anything I can help you with?"

"Yes." Jakub heard a crunching sound as the man behind him put out what was left of a cigarette. "First you can take your right hand away from that gun and then you can come and sit with me for a moment." Jakub sighed and slowly took his hand away, allowing his loose shirt to drape over it once again. He turned to face him but never looked directly in his eyes; there was always something about Zahid's eyes that made him decide against staring at them.

"What do you need, friend?" The word barely made it out of his mouth before he clamped it shut again.

"Am I a friend? Is that how you see me, Jakub?" Zahid put one of his feet onto a chair and rested his hands across his knee.

"Yes. Now what do you need?" He became a little more firm in his inquiry.

"Cut to the chase? Fine." He took his foot back down, sat slightly inclined toward Jakub, and didn't move again. "The pieces that you gave to Behnam's men earlier today, do you remember what you told them about the power supply?"

"Yes, I told them it was different. But when I tried to explain, they cut me off, told me they could handle it, and then left without another word. I figured you had sent them."

"Well, I didn't. Tell me, have I ever sent someone else to pick up a package from you?"

"No." Jakub rubbed his head. "No, you didn't."

"Exactly, I always pick up, and you should never give my equipment to anyone but me. Clear?"

"Yes, but…"

"But what?"

"Well, you mentioned the power supply, is something wrong with the device?"

"It never detonated, Jakub. The Americans have the bomb." Zahid had seen Jakub's reaction to bad news before, always starting with an attempt at staying calm and rolling into a rant. It was like clockwork, and as Jakub's pacing quickened, he could see that he was just about to go over.

"What have you done, Zahid!?" He turned, fear mounted full-force in his eyes. Zahid held back a proud smile. "They will find me, now, they have too much to go on, don't you see?"

"No," Zahid said calmly. "They won't find you."

"How would you know? I've watched others get taken down in my business with less than what they already have. I cannot be tried for terrorism!"

"Jakub, sit down!" Zahid ordered, still seated in the same rigid form. "You might think that they know things, that they are unstoppable once they get a trail, but you are wrong. They will not be as interested as you might think with a single bomb maker. They probably won't even be looking for you." The lies flowed almost easier than the truth, and Jakub seemed to be buying it. Zahid knew that it would only be a matter of a few days before the Americans would contact Jakub, but he needed him calm, he needed him willing, and he needed him to keep a steady flow of materials to him.

"No." He finally smiled, enjoying his control over the angry man "They will not find you."

"And what if they do, Zahid, what if they track me here and come for me?"

"You are in Afghanistan, friend, and it took them a decade to find their greatest enemy in places smaller than this."

"But they did find him, and they killed him and dumped him into the ocean."

"Yes, but you didn't kill over three thousand people on their turf. They won't look that hard for you."

Jakub clasped his hands on the top of his head, closed his eyes, and slowly sighed out his fear. *Maybe he's right,* Jakub thought. He turned and sat back in his seat.

"So then you think we'll be okay? Me and my wife?" He gestured into the side room where another light was on.

"Yes, I do." Zahid stood and looked outside, the sun just beginning to set and thus casting a warm embrace onto his skin. "Now, I need two more sets, do you have them?"

"I have three." He went into the next room and returned a few moments later. "Take them all."

"I can only pay for two right now, Jakub."

"Don't worry about it, just take it, and pay me the rest the next time you come in."

"Jakub, I will take two, and that is all, when I come back, I need four total. Then our business will be complete and I will allow you to run where ever you wish."

"Why won't you just take it, Zahid?" Zahid smiled again as he stood, placing the two plastic bags Jakub handed him into his duffel as he looked back at him.

"Because you might feel like because I have extra, you'll have time to leave without saying good-bye." He turned and opened the door, not even looking back as he mentioned the money he had left in Jakub's "secret" safe.

SECTION TWO

BLAZE

NEXT STEPS

0245 hours, July 14, Residence in Sangin
Helmand Province, Afghanistan

After what seemed like only moments, Zahid awoke to realize he had been asleep for the last few hours. He sat up, sweat glistening off of his skin, which he could see as a small drop rolled itself along the top of his cheek until it came to a stop and disappeared, vaporized by the heat in the poorly ventilated back room. A blacked-out window sat cracked slightly open, allowing a long stream of wavering blue light to cast vague shadows against the wall behind the small cot on which he had been resting. It was this room where he had spent the last few days, preparing himself for his self-appointed task. In fact, he checked his watch again; he had only ten minutes before his self-assumed watchman, would walk in and tell him that his men were waiting in the next room so that he could inform them fully.

Zahid stood and stretched his arms into the air, his triceps bulging as they extended till they ached with the strain of pulling as hard as they were; they were relieved when he let his arms collapse atop his head, all the while his mind pouring over what he was doing and why. In the darkness, he could see a crowd of people, arranged as silhouettes behind what looked like a dark fog. He couldn't hear them, but as he watched, they seemed to move, or maybe it was the fog—no…smoke—starting to move away. He started to see shapes, hundreds of people all slowly moving toward him but doing so soundlessly. In their hands he could see rifles; in others he saw books, and then he saw their clothes; it was all camouflage. They started to move around him, and he started to feel heat, though no one was near enough to touch him. The heat grew, and slowly light began to penetrate the smoke so that he could see their faces and their bodies, but there was something different, something covered them in patches, and there seemed to be a trail of it running all around him, he looked closer: blood. Behind them, he started to see light, which then turned into a wall of fire. He gasped, tried to turn away, but before he could, there was a flash. The world around him fell away into the light as it focused in at one point, nothing more than a picture in his memory of a woman holding a little boy's hand. His mind gripped itself onto the picture, holding onto it as his anchor as he moved. He could see a boy sitting in a car, the sun pouring down its power all around him, save for a wavering shadow created by a pillar of smoke. He could hear screams, he could smell burning wood and scorched flesh in the air that seeped in through the cracked windows, yet all the while, he never looked up, never ventured to see what was happening to his family on the other side of his small protection. He heard gunshots, each one shaking his concentration, rattling his nerves, his breathing quickening with each resounding shock. The screams stopped, along with his breathing, and he remembered the little boy peeking through the window just enough to see the women who held his hand crawling from a burning home, a man standing behind her doing nothing but watching; he remembered his face. He held a gun in his hand. He remembered the look on her face, a final gift of comfort to the scared boy in the car. He remembered closing his eyes, slipping back down into the small cavern where he had rested his feet. Then another shot, another breath, and a face seared into his memory, the face of a white man, the one who killed his family.

Zahid opened his eyes, sweat now pouring off him and his heart beating like the drums of war. He took out a flashlight and walked over to his pack, only just barely visible in the darkness where he unzipped and removed a small leather pouch. He opened it, took out a folded piece of paper, and placed on his desk, where he turned on the small light that sat upon it. As he unfolded the page, he saw a small insignia at its bottom corner: "Iranian Intelligence." His eyes jerked to the middle of the page where a single picture stood alone above a small bit of writing, the face that still was burned into his mind. He remembered taking the page from the Iranians before he left, and then he remembered the look on his uncle's face when he told him he was returning to his home. The man who saved the boy from death, who brought him away and lied to all to make it seem as though he were his own son, felt betrayed by this angry boy's emotions; he never understood, but that was how it had to be, until he could find the man. He remembered a simple plea from his uncle, the last time he saw Zahid, when he asked him to survive and come home; Zahid never gave him an answer. It had been years since he'd been there, years since he had done what many would call desertion. Most who would know him still reside there, and him going back would give them a chance to remember, and he would most likely pay the price for their memories.

A knock on the door brought him back into consciousness, his time was up, and so with a renewed sense of purpose, he put on a shirt and walked into the next room.

"How long do you want us to wait, Amir?" Behnam was bowing in front of the Amir, his eyes locked onto the floor.

"I am not sure, our Brother Zahid stated that he would return over an hour ago. Have any of the guards seen signs of him?" He looked to one of the men standing near the wall.

"No, Amir," a man answered but then turned to leave. "I will inform you when they arrive," he remarked as he walked outside.

The Amir stood, his chair sliding backward as his legs straightened, and walked over to a pantry where he removed and opened a plastic bottle of water. When he turned around, he heard the sound of a gunshot, though it was far too quiet to be anything near. His eyes glided over the windows, all the while men were bustling around outside, most of them unsure as to where the sound came from or if anyone had been hit. Then a man who had been standing just behind a plywood covering jolted backward and fell to the ground, the wood jerking with the impact of a soundless killer; another shot was heard. The Amir barely had the word "sniper" out of his mouth before the glass shattered in front of him, and a hard push in his shoulder forced him back against the pantry, pain shooting down his arm as he collided with the furniture and slid to the ground; the bottle fell and spilt, mud curdling in its puddle at his feet. His eyes watered with the pain, blurring his vision, but he was still able to make out the arrival of a grenade as it landed inside the window, accompanied by several separate automatic weapons plowing large holes through the stone, spraying large chunks of earth and dust as they entered. He covered his face with his hand, but just barely, and so a light far brighter than he had ever seen sent him into a white blindness, followed by several different shades of blue and green that alternated with the ringing in his ears. He barely even noticed several pairs of hands grab him firmly by the arms and set him in a chair, all the while pain from his shoulder reaching out and paralyzing his body. After a few moments, however, his sight returned, followed a little later by his hearing. He looked around to see several men with rifles standing in the room around him; none of them were his men.

Another gunshot rang out in the room, grabbing his attention to the door on the far side of the small room. A man in a black coat and face covering walked through the opening, a Makarov pistol in his hand. It took the Amir a moment, but after a long look at the man's eyes, he could see who it was.

"Zahid, what the hell are you doing?!" He stood to try and assert himself as if in charge; Zahid let him know with a simple shove back into the chair that he was not.

"Where is the other site, Abraham?" Zahid put his hands on his knees and eyed the old man.

"How do you know my name? I never told you th—"

"There's a lot I learned about you, Abraham. Now, where is the rest of the Brotherhood?"

"Why do you want to know, Zahid? So you can kill them off too?" He clutched his shoulder, blood spilling in between his fingers; he winced with the contact.

"No, I need them to do God's work." Zahid reached over and rested his hand on the Amir's shoulder, pulling his mask down with the other. "Now tell me where they are."

"First you tell me why you are betraying us. Is it that you have found a love for the Outsider?!" Rage poured from the old man like fire; however, his fit was short-lived, as Zahid began to push hard into the bullet wound, the pain forcing the old man to scream and tip his chair backward; Zahid landed, straddling the old man's chest with his thumb still pressed deep into the wound.

"I have no love for the Outsider! But you were going to send me to Iraq, through Iran!" He removed his hand from the Amir's shoulder and stood. "I cannot go back there, you know more than anyone that to return would mean my death." He glanced at his men, all of whom had come back to Afghanistan to avenge what he had lost. "And I cannot leave. If I do, I may never get the chance I need."

"The chance for what?! What must you stay here for when you could fight the Infidel, the Outsider, anywhere?" The Amir looked up at him, now seeing for the first time raw emotion in the eyes of the young man he had believed to be a simple killer. "What have you lost here, Zahid?" The change in his voice, the strange understanding of the question, and the nearly compassionate look in his eyes all gripped Zahid, to which he replied in anger.

He looked down to see an old man, one who could see his pain; Zahid didn't like that. He pointed the pistol at his head and pulled the trigger; the old man's body shuttered with the impact.

"Zahid, we needed the location from him?" Zahid never acknowledged his partner but just stood breathing heavily as he gazed at the dead body. He did need to know. Then he heard moaning, barely audible but loud enough for him to tell it came from the other side of the window. He walked and stepped over the low set window pane; below him a man laid with several holes in his chest oozing deep, red blood. Zahid sat him up, one to allow the blood to drain away from his lungs to give him some extra time, and two so that he could use that time to tell Zahid where the others were. When presented with the question, he simply told him it was back in Kajaki Ulya, at a small warehouse called Al Bnayuh. With that, Zahid picked the man up and carried him into the house, his men following suit with the other three bodies outside of the house, and set them on top of the table. Then Furan, who casually dragged two large containers full of kerosene, began dousing the house and the bodies. When he finished, he placed a small black box in between the two gas cans and left them in the center of the room; the rest of them filed out and walked across the street, in between the houses to a second street, where they had parked several vehicles along the side.

As their vehicle roared to life, Zahid opened his jeep's passenger door and pulled out a small handheld beeper, and then he turned and waited. He closed his eyes for a moment, the times he had spent working for the Brotherhood squeezed together in his mind, each face and conversation a blur of time spent in servitude to a cause that was not his own; it would be different tomorrow. He raised his hand, opened his eyes, and pressed the trigger down. Inside the building, a spark lurched out from the box, starting a chain reaction of bright yellow fire that danced its way over the bodies and the wooden floors. After a moment, once the flames had grown to touch the air above the cans, the fire erupted in a cloud of hot, red fire mixed with black smoke. The flames expanded, engulfing the inside of the house and forcing itself outside like a geyser.

Zahid opened his eyes, the heat hitting him like a wave of relief, telling him that he had rid himself of another pain in his life. In his mind, the hoard of dead passed by, but instead of pity, he felt a sense of accomplishment; he had brought them there, and he had done it with fire. He turned away from the flames, the light turning what little night vision he had into pitch blackness till he started his car and turned on the headlights. In front of him, the red taillights glided away; behind was nothing but darkness. It was, as strange as it sounded to him, as if they were calling him to where his next step would be taken, and in a sense, they were.

OBSESSION

**0318 hours, July 14, Camp Bastion
Helmand Province, Afghanistan**

The door slid silently open, only pulling a slight draft into the under ventilated computer room. The lights were almost completely dimmed, save for a deep blue light that washed the room in an eerie paleness. The walls were dark, refracting little of the light onto the floor, which resembled something of an abyss. Thus, as a man stepped in, quietly working his way through the poorly lit maze of desks, he failed to notice movement behind him. The man moved as a cat after an insect, sleeking slowly in an attempt to go unnoticed, until he reached the room just past a line of computers. Carefully, he opened the door and walked in, shutting it behind him. With no windows, he removed his jacket and laid it against the bottom of the door and then turned on the lights, safe to move about unimpeded by darkness and unseen by unplanned observers. He turned and on a desk that cloned the rest in terms of color sat a computer with a screen a little larger than those in the previous room. Behind it were several rows of large, steel shelves, hundreds of boxes full of hard copies of most of the files CID had in their computer, save for personnel and current-case files. The man approached it longingly, no longer feeling as though he had to sneak as his feet pounded across the hard tile floor and turned the screen on. The monitor buzzed energetically as it lighted, causing his eyes to water a little while showing a quick pop-up that stated the security system had been updated. He closed it and clicked on a tab that had been left readily available at the bottom of the screen. The window displayed several folders with a text bar beneath each, requiring a password to be opened that was specific to each folder. He scrolled down the page until he came to the bottom. He dragged his pointer over, searching the names until he came to the *S* section and found her name; he clicked on the file, typed in a single-word password, and immediately, "Salviana, Cpl. Celia" appeared at the top of the screen followed by her picture.

He was about to print the photo when he heard a sound outside of the room, a nearly inaudible, high-pitched whine like that of an engine or motor that had been overworked. Hurriedly he turned off the monitor and drifted over to the door. The whine continued, and like the curious cat he was, Chris Thompson opened the door. As he did, he realized he had left the light on in the room behind him, so he frantically turned it off. He peered through the crack he had made in the door and into the darkness, searching for the source of the noise; he saw nothing, but the whining was still there. He opened the door further, searching carefully with his overacting senses that made him feel like a good sprint was just what he needed. He heard the whining louder to his left, and though it didn't sound as though it were moving in any direction, it seemed to be changing pitch, getting higher with each step nearer. He noticed it seemed to be coming from one of the data towers, which resembled a large stereo with several ports for computers and hardware. He could see that there was a static red light on the tower, indicating an issue with one of the components inside; it made an eerie contrast with the perpetually blue lights of the adjacent towers. He knelt down in front, following the sound to the cooling unit just above the floor, behind a small slide-up door. As he lifted it, he could feel the heat pour out of the small compartment, the smell of burnt electronics wafting around him gripped his attention, enough that he missed a shadow that moved ever so slightly toward the room Chris had just exited. Quietly he cracked the door open and disappeared into the darkness beyond. And as Chris worked to find the source of the heat, the smell of burning plastic nearly making him sick, he didn't see Hanson close the door or hear him place the jacket back under the door.

Hanson turned on his heels and removed a slim, black penlight from inside his shirt, the light shining off the glossy white walls shocked his eyes for a moment, but he quickly accommodated. In front of him, the light glared off of the dormant computer monitor, standing out against the almost invisible backdrop of file shelves. Quietly he moved past the computer and through the middle row of files, the shelves casting scraggly shadows onto the tile ceiling. He looked at the box covers, each with a different name and number that had to make sense to someone, just not to him. After about a minute of opening boxes and seeing only files from 2010, he saw that they were at least kept by date—something he did understand. He took a step back and looked at the top of the shelf and found a piece of tape attached to the center of each column of boxes that gave the name of the month and then the year; behind him was 2009, so he figured the other side would have 2012. On the other side, the shelf was only around half full, and so he went to the very end; the top read "July 2012." He looked the boxes over, most able to fit two months' worth of files inside, except for two: March and July. He opened July and instantly was surprised to find it nearly full so early in the month. When he looked through the dates, however, there was only one that actually was a case file, the rest all had to do with manufacturing companies and shipping manifests; the date July 2 wasn't even listed. Defeated, he backed away from the shelf and racked his brain as to why they weren't keeping a file of the attack. Suddenly the door jerked part of the way open, startling Hanson and causing him to drop the flashlight from his mouth. It was stopped by the jacket, however, creating an obstacle just big enough to keep Chris from coming through.

This delay allowed Hanson to reacquire the light and switch it off before Chris was able to open it again.

Chris, now flustered by the ordeal with the fan in the cooling unit being cracked, which caused the tower to overheat, the door jamming because he left his jacket too close to the bottom, and the fact that he no longer felt like he had enough time to do what he wanted, approached the computer, completely ignoring the lights. He reached the computer, turned the monitor back on, and printed off her picture, nearly tearing the page as he pulled it from the printer under the desk. He then clicked his way out of the program, then he returned to the computer and was about to initiate the shutdown when lights from a vehicle outside shown through the glass door and into the room, startling him so that he simply pushed the off button on the monitor as before and left the room. The light dimmed as the vehicle passed, allowing him to sneak by unseen by the outside world, and with that, he disappeared into the maze of the barracks.

In the room, Hanson's heart was beating faster than it had ever beaten before, with exception to his first bomb disarming when he arrived in Afghanistan. He sat with his back against the small end of the steel frame of the shelf, breathing to regain his composure. He looked up at the wall of files as if they were a cliff, un-climbable and mocking in its simplicity. He sat wondering how he would find what he needed and remembered that Agent Windburg would tell him only what he wanted him to know; the chief would know even less. He then heard a whirring sound, low and nearly inaudible, coming from the front of the room. He clicked his flashlight back on and walked over to the white desk in front of the door where he noticed a faint light coming from the computer. He clicked on the monitor, the rest of the room going pitch-black as it flared to life inside the small room. Intrigued, he closed the door that the clumsy Chris had left open, and he sat down in the chair. On the screen, there were several icons arranged it what seemed to him to be a random order, each with their own small subtitle. He searched optimistically for an icon that might give him the current case files, careful to read each word, but to no avail. He moved the mouse to find the pointer on screen, then went to the bottom left corner and clicked on the small icon, another list of files appeared on screen; it was there, in the center of the list, labeled, conveniently, "CASE FILES: JULY." Hanson opened it and was instantly assaulted with pictures of the attack. He could see an aerial view of the area where it all took place, two large blackened areas of smoke and sand spaced fifty meters apart, bodies still resting in a radius around the epicenter of the blast zones. Hanson scrolled down the page, each photo of an injured soldier and piece of armor that had been blown from its respective vehicle or helmet and thrown as if by a windstorm into the ground seeming unreal. He closed his eyes, trying to push back the anger that welled inside of him, trying to concentrate. He opened his eyes, and he was in the middle of the desert, with the sand and smoke and fire converging around him, that drifting curtain that has claimed so many now thirsty for his blood, for one more body, just one more KIA, Killed In Action written on his description on some officer's desk. He could see the wind as it pulled up sand and smoke from the ground around him, uncovering the bodies of soldiers whose names and faces he didn't know, but they were there. Then, with a fit of pure fury from his heart, he roared out, screaming as a lion in a cage, searching for his freedom. Then he opened his eyes, and he was again in the dark room with the computer, his eyes blurred by tears that formed from his clenching his eyes so tightly. He looked over the page again, avoiding the pictures as best he could till he realized there was nothing new to learn from it. He pressed return and was about to exit out and leave when he saw another file with a date even newer than the attacks, and when he opened it up, a small smile appeared on his face; his friends in the agency had done pretty quick work. Someone was gathering tools and supplies from a weapons company in the Czech Republic, and it was all headed to Sirak.

Hanson walked briskly back to the hospital, his mind now swimming with renewed thoughts of revenge, and his senses tingling as if they were on fire; he was close. The course in his mind had now been adjusted, and his anger was serving as his sights. He had never felt more focused, more driven, and less prepared for any other undertaking in his life; it was as though he were holding Pandora's box, and he had no idea how to deal with it. But now he felt like he was going hunting, his momentum gaining as if he were already chasing his prey. Yet he was reserved in his standings, assured in his convictions, and no matter what happened next, he would reach the end of this road.

CROSSING

**1025 hours, July 14, Camp Bastion
Helmand Province, Afghanistan**

Agent Steven Windburg flipped through the file, ultimately unimpressed with the man who all the evidence pointed to as being behind the bombings. The man's photo actually seemed promising, as he had the face of a hardened survivor; however, his record of low-level arms dealing and assault charges just made him seem more like someone who only tried to look tough and therefore made Agent Windburg think that he wasn't the bomber, but he definitely knew him. The scowl on the man's face was almost comical in its anger; Steven was looking forward to flipping him because chances were good that with moderate pressure the guy would snap like the preverbal twig.

"Well, what do you want to do, sir?" A man in a black uniform sat in front of him, his eyes shrouded by the bill of his hat.

"In my opinion, this is not actually our bomber, his record is too messy, and he just doesn't have the background to be capable." He tossed the file onto his desk.

"We could buzz him, get him to flip, or we make him think he won't survive the night."

"True, but then he might go to his 'friend' for protection, the friend may get spooked, kill him to cover his tracks, and we lose him." He sat straighter and adjusted his tie to make it loose. "No, I think we'll let him think he's taking the rap for whatever we say this bomber has done, then he might think about flipping to our side for a deal—a whole lot easier than bringing him back from the dead."

"All right, so do you want to go in, scare tactics full, or just yourself?"

"Yeah, I think the single would be more motivational for him, or at least make him feel more comfortable. But I want you ready, violent people will jump to violence." He looked at the file, reading again over what the guy did for a living. "I think we'll make a meeting with Jakub Sorvi."

Leena Sorvi had been married to Jakub for nearly twelve years, and she had never been more confused about a person in her life. She picked up a long pair of socks from the foot of her bed and placed them into one of her wicker baskets in a corner of the room; they were his, and still they reeked of stress and dirt. He had been, at a time when she had first met him, the kind of man who never was afraid and was always pushing to fight someone. But he changed; he became not only angrier, but also more scared after being there for so long, trapped doing another's work. And to her, she figured it had to do with the men he was working with, or over the last few days, more like men he worked *for*. Any time when people came who wanted his other merchandize he acted rough around her, as if he had to prove he was still strong; but he wasn't, and she knew it.

She poured some water from a pitcher into a bowl and washed her hands, a bar of soap she made herself sliding back and forth between her hands. She thought about asking him if they could just leave, get out of Helmand, out of Afghanistan, or maybe even the Middle East itself, maybe live somewhere that these people couldn't find him. She wondered what he would say, if he would even listen to her; she assumed no and so decided it was best not to ask. It was while she was still washing in the room when she heard him come through the front door, and when she didn't hear anyone else with him, she felt truly happy. Maybe, if she could make him happy again, he might listen to her. So she went to her mirror and took down her shawl, her face still surprisingly pretty for being hidden away for most of the day. She walked to the door and peaked through; he was sitting at the table writing out a receipt for someone and was pretty focused; although she knew that she could make him a little less focused. She nearly opened the door when a voice came from the hallway behind him, and she closed the door mostly but still had enough time to see Jakub stand, that familiar anger in his eyes and his gun pointed at whoever had just entered the house; she returned her shawl over her face.

"Whoa, Jakub, don't be too hasty with that trigger." Agent Windburg would have turned himself sideways, but at this distance, that guy wouldn't miss, and so he'd just get more of his organs shot up if this guy didn't feel like talking.

"Who are you, and what do you want?" Jakub still had the silver revolver pointed at the man's chest.

"Just put the gun down for a second so we can—"

"Who!?" Jakub clicked back the hammer.

"Okay! My name is Agent Steven Windburg. I work for the CIA, and we have reason to believe you have connections with some very bad people."

"We?" Jakub asked, and before he could react, a heavy hand struck the back of his head while a second hand grabbed his gun arm and pulled him into the table, slamming his head into the hardwood surface. The gun was yanked from his hand as he was flipped over and literally tossed into the chair in front of him, and as he turned to see who had disarmed him, he felt a cold blade touch his neck. He followed the arm up to a man with a mask covering his head, and Agent Windburg now sitting on top of the table, his chest toward the opposite wall and the revolver in his hands.

"Let's start over, Jakub. You can remove the knife." The man in black pulled the blade away and stood back. Jakub sat up and rubbed his neck, glad to feel only a scratch instead of a deep gash. "We have found out something out about you, Jakub, and have reason to believe that not only do you have connections with terrorists, but that you are the bomb maker responsible for several attacks on US troops." Zahid's face flashed into Jakub's mind, he shook his head in near disbelief, and he stayed silent.

"The bomb materials we tracked all point to you, and seeing as that's all we have to go on, you're the perfect fit."

"If you really believed that you would have come with more men," Jakub remarked, still keeping his eyes lowered.

"What are you saying, Jakub, that I have the wrong guy?"

"I'm not saying anything."

"Good, then you'll come with us without trouble, and then you will be sent back to the States, where we can prosecute you for terrorism, and well, I'm sure you know the rest." He nodded to the man in black, who walked behind Jakub and stood him up, cuffing his hands together as he stood.

"Now, are you sure that you have nothing to say, Jakub, or is the death penalty too good an opportunity to pass up? I can never tell with want-to-be martyrs." Jakub wanted to say something, wanted to yell out that he hadn't killed those men, but he stayed quiet just a little longer until he looked back and saw his wife through the door that had been cracked open and realized that he wasn't getting out of this with silence.

"Wait!" he yelled. "Just give me a minute, and I'll tell you who is actually responsible, but I want something in return!"

"I'm listening, Jakub." The man in black sat him back in the chair.

"I want full immunity from any accusations, and sanctuary in the US with whoever I bring with me after I am done. Is that clear?"

"Of course. Now tell me about the bomber." Triumph was brimming in Steven's eyes.

Leena's ear was pressed to the edge of the door between two of the hinges, trying as best she could to calm her breath so that she could hear, but even then, they were speaking too low. She turned and looked through the crack, her husband facing a man in a gray suit, who seemed to be doing all the talking with his hands. She couldn't see the other one, but she knew he was there. Frustrated, she watched her husband's face, watching his eyes shift between the man in front of him and the other who must have been in the hallway. After a while, though, it changed. He had a face she had never seen before; the face of someone trapped and have already given up. She heard chairs scoot over the floor as Jakub and the man in the suit stood, still they were talking low until the man in the suit stuck out his hand and said, "Have a good day, sir. Keep in touch, Jakub." A shadow passed in front of the door as the other man walked past and followed the man out of the door; though she couldn't see, she knew it was safe when Jakub closed the door, and the dead bolt slid into place.

She opened her door; he was again seated at the table. However, he had his eyes covered by his hands, and his revolver was lying on a pile of papers in front of him. She walked over and grabbed the gun from the table and set it in a drawer behind her then turned back and rested her hands on his shoulders.

"Jakub?" she asked. "Jakub, what did they want?" He stayed silent but rose swiftly; her hands falling off his shoulders as he walked past her and grabbed his revolver, returning it to his pocket. "Jakub, please tell me what happened," she pleaded. His large blue eyes locked onto hers, his jaw muscles flexed, and he looked away; he didn't want to tell her.

"Jakub, I know you don't want to hear me right now, but I need you to listen." She walked over in front of him and looked at him again. "We can leave, Jakub, you don't have to help those men or the other man who you used to work with. We can just go and disappear."

"But, Leena, I cannot just walk away. I have to—"

"No!" she begged him. "No, you don't, I will be with you, and we can have a different life somewhere else. Please, Jakub, they want too much from you now."

"If I leave, then Zahid will hunt for us, he will—" He realized he had used his name, and fear once again covered his face. He grabbed her shoulders and yelled, "I can't talk about this, Leena, there is no way that we can do that, don't you see!" His eyes were now wet with emotion, tears ran down her face. "I can't put you in danger, and I can't tell you anything else, to keep you safe."

"Jakub, as long as you are with these men, then we will never be safe." She tried to turn away, but he held her fast, his grip firm but still gentle.

"I won't let them hurt you, and we will be safe soon. I will take us to America, and we will be safe. You hear me? We will be safe." She held back more tears, and he held her close again, but still, in the back of his mind, he knew that the most danger was still to come. For him, he would have to cross the most ruthless and cunning man he had ever known, and he hoped to God he would make it.

RECRUIT

1640 hours, July 14, Al Bnayuh Warehouse
Kajaki Ulya, Afghanistan

Al Bnayuh warehouse was nearly in the center of the small metropolis, towering over the markets that stretched along the already cramped inner streets of Kajaki Ulya. It was nearly three stories tall, its edge wrapped by the rough plaster that covered the framework designs were etched into the wall came up to form a Victorian-style bust. The building was actually rather well-built and would have been better-looking if it weren't for the immense number of advertisements for shops and sales that had been written in large red or yellow letters and slapped over a majority of the wall that faced the street. However, these ads were unable to clutter over all of the design, as large arches allowed the wall to sink in beneath them and open into either windows, near the front of the building or large lift gates near the back for deliveries. It was within one of these arches that a young man sat, holding a small yellow radio, waiting to signal inside if any vehicles came up to the door and gave the word, to which he would radio to a man inside, who would open the gate and allow the vehicle to drive through. Thus, the young man became rather excited whenever any vehicle larger than the small coupe cars that were so popular came driving near. At least, he was excited near the beginning of his long shift, but as the hours dragged on he became rather lethargic. He was thus unprepared when a large white van pulled around the corner and drove up in front of the gate; the driver waited impatiently for the boy to get closer before he leaned out of the window and spoke a one word password. Frantically, the young man fumbled with the radio till he was able to turn it on and he spoke into the microphone. A few moments later, the door started to open, the van drove inside, and the boy sighed with slight relief and went on with watching the roads.

Inside the van pulled around a wide corner, lined on both sides by large towers of shelves, packed fully with wooden crates and boxes, this setup continued the expanse of the warehouse till it ended abruptly at a large open space, catwalks running back and forth over the area for three separate levels. The only light came from long lights that stretched along the sides of the open space and a few hanging industrial lights along the inside road. It was at the end of the small road that the van parked itself next to a pile of open crates, several men arranged randomly on the catwalks, and on the ground, all stood watching. The van's engine quieted, and it seemed that no one would move until a man walked from a large steel table and stood in front of the van, his hand very lightly resting atop the hilt of his pistol, covered up by his brown jacket. It was when he jerked his head slightly up that the door of the van opened, and Zahid stepped out, followed by three other men, one from the passenger door and two from the back. They all stood watching as Zahid walked over to the man in the jacket, a serious look on his face, but it soon died away as the man in the jacket met him halfway and smiled, shaking Zahid's hand with both of his and greeting him with a blessing from Allah.

"And to you, Nadeen? How is the fight from this side?"

"Oh, Allah has seen fit for us to have killed twelve Outsiders over the last few months, we have also taken a few men prisoner and have even found a way to place one of our own into their ranks." His hands dropped away, and he raised his arms. "It is a great time for the Brotherhood of Cleansing Fire!" he shouted, the men behind him all joined his celebration but Zahid's men stayed quiet; Nadeen noticed.

"I do not recognize these faces, are they new to our cause?" He watched them judgingly.

"They are of the cause, Brother." Zahid patted him on the shoulder and had him turn and walk to the table; Nadeen's men watched Zahid, and Zahid's men watched them. Tension was nearly tangible when newcomers showed up. "Now I have some very bad news for you, but try to understand that we will have faith, and we will still fight on."

"What happened, Zahid? What has changed?"

"The Amir—" he cut himself short and lowered his voice, wary that such news of a dead leader would cause some substantial waves with the men. "The Amir and several of his men have been killed."

"What!" Nadeen whispered, taking a step back as he looked at Zahid in disbelief.

"Last night, me and my men came near to the house and heard gunshots as we approached, but when we got there, the house was already in flames, and lights in the distance were moving very fast to the south."

"In the name of Allah, what…no, who is responsible?"

"From what my men tell me, the tracks belong Outsider vehicles. Americans, Nadeen."

"How did they know about them?" Nadeen turned toward the table and rested his hands on its cold surface; Zahid turned with him.

"Did you hear of the school bombing that never happened? The authorities said it had to do with the police finding and stopping it." Zahid smirked. "They aren't smart enough for that. What happened was that the bomb never went off. The explosive was no good, and the Americans came in and took it."

"How do you know it was the Americans?"

"I had one of my men watching in the town after I found out that the bomb didn't do its work."

"So they used what they found and tracked it. But what about our contacts, did they just make them talk, are they still around?"

"It was just one man, he was taken, and he told them all about the Amir. What's more, he told them of our meeting, to which me and my men were only a few minutes late when we arrived. But that was enough, everyone else had already arrived, and they all were killed."

"Then we are all that is left?"

"Yes."

Nadeen walked away from the table and rested his chin in his hand. Zahid watched, waiting to see if the seeds would take. Nadeen turned back around, looked at Zahid as if he were looking at the savior, and shouted, "Brothers, the Amir has graced us with his presence!" He held his hand out toward Zahid. The men shouted their excitement at finally meeting their legendary leader, Zahid's men shouted in their approval, and Zahid bowed slightly, a smile creeping lightly over his face; the seeds were planted.

OUR MAN JAKUB

**0115 hours, July 15, Denver,
Colorado, USA**

Matthews yawned as he slouched in the now very warm chair he had brought in from his office into the conference room; he still waited for Steven's call that had been due over an hour and a half ago. In his hand, a cigarette, nearly down to a small stub, was still smoking lightly. On the floor, several coffee cups were arranged in a star pattern, one of them with old cigarette butts swimming in a small puddle of now-cold coffee. He laid his head back, pushing somberly against the headrest that was nearly parallel with the floor from the weight of his head. His hands folded over his stomach, his eyes were starting to close, and he had just reached the point where he no longer felt the need for a blanket when a loud beep came from the speakers, followed by static, the video screen only just clearing up by the time Matthews opened his eyes, sat up, and looked on. Agent Steven Windburg walked into the screen and adjusted the camera, still panting from what Matthews assumed was a long run.

"Sorry I'm late, sir, just had to finish up a meeting with the senior agent over at CID. He was telling me how he still needed a—"

"Honestly, Steven, I don't care what he wants." He sat up and rested his elbows on his knees. "Information is what he wants, and he can only have so much. Are we clear?"

"Yes, sir," Steven answered, a little less excitement in his voice. "Sir, early this morning I had another talk with our man Jakub." Matthews stayed silent. Trying to get his boss interested, he took out file and began flipping through the pages as he explained, "Sir, he gave us our bomber and a location on where he might be. From what I have written here, it's a small house in Sirak where the bomber's name…Zahid al Khatri is working with a militant group independent of the major players."

"Jakub told you all of this?"

"Yes, sir."

"And what did he ask for in return?"

"Sanctuary…in the States with his wife, who is with him, and a new identity. Apparently this guy he's crossing is quite the boogeyman."

"Well, let's keep this 'boogeyman' under the bed until we can get a better handle on him. Does Jakub have a picture?"

"He says he tried to get one for security, but the guy never shows up when he's prepared, and even then, he isn't dumb enough to let Jakub point a lens in his direction. As of right now, he could be trying to play you and could himself be the bomber."

"Well, we wouldn't want to bring a bomber back to the states now would we?" He stood up, kicking over his empty coffee cups as he went to leave the room. "Steven, keep him under close watch until we get our bomber."

"Yes, sir."

"What was the man's name again?"

"Zahid al Khatri, sir, the rest of the information on him will be on your desk when you get in tomorrow morning."

"Steven, it already is tomorrow morning for me. I'm going to sleep in the loft, and when I get up at 0630, I want it exactly as you said it."

"Yes, sir." Then the feed went dead.

REUNIONS

1025 hours, July 15, Camp Bastion
Helmand Province, Afghanistan

The weather was strange that afternoon, the sky seemingly far too dark to belong to such a desert. A dust storm the size of a regular squaw line was rolling along the eastern edge of the camp, casting a long, nearly gray shadow over the generally scorched area where the base resided; it was like a cloud, but no water to be felt if it were to pass over. The winds blew with and across the path of the sand giant, and so whereas most days helicopters were landing more frequently there than any other base in their area, the weather was causing just enough ruckus to keep the troops' movement limited to the distances of their Humvees. Thus, as would be expected, air traffic was light, but the vehicles moving in and out of the camp were at some of their highest numbers, and so most people were far too busy to notice much difference in their generally busy days. In fact, most of those in charge were too busy even to notice a man standing out in front of a building what appeared to be the most strange thing that could be imagined for a worker; he was simply waiting. Hanson was waiting for Agent Windburg, in fact, whom he had asked to meet over an hour ago to ask about what he and his men had found, but he still waited, and Steven was nowhere to be seen. Hanson took a deep breath, all the while looking around at the strangely dark shade that covered everything around him, but his mind lay on things other than the weather; he still held the paper clip from the office in his pocket, twisting it back and forth between his thumb and forefinger as he wondered why someone would use such a strange adaptation for a bomb. The bent piece of metal in his hand caught on the inside of his pocket with each twist he made, eventually lodging itself in a small loop that had formed from the constant shifting from the small shard of metal. *A strange tool indeed*, Hanson thought to himself, but he didn't wish to complain, at least he knew what to look for. He gazed at it a while longer after taking it from his pocket, only taking his eyes away from it when the door to the CIA office on base opened and Agent Windburg stood at the door.

"Corporal Hanson"—he offered a handshake—"I hope you're enjoying the shade, we don't get much of it out here." His smile was warm and genuine; Hanson forced himself to return the kindness. "What can I do for you?"

"Sir, I was wondering what you found out."

"Found out about what, Corporal?"

"The bombings, sir."

"What about the bombings, Corporal? I hardly have time to give you a summary."

"Sir, I just—" the wind picked up immensely for a moment, sand ripping from the ground and raking across his face. The wind nearly drowning out his low voice. "Sir!" he yelled. "I want to know about the bomber, I want to know if we have him."

"Why do you want to know, Corporal?"

"Because I lost a friend to that bastard, and I don't feel like me knowing would hurt the cause or anything, sir."

"Corporal, your job"—the door behind them opened and a couple men walked past, pulling their clothing up over their mouths and faces. Steven caught the door and motioned Hanson inside. He closed the door and turned back to Hanson. "Corporal, you have done well, already given us more than we hoped. But your job doesn't make you privy to that information, at least not yet."

"Can you at least tell me if you know who he is?" Hanson was nearly pleading. Steven sighed, glancing around the room as he considered either walking away or giving the young patriot what he wants. "All right, we do know." He finally gave in. "We are working on getting a location, but we still may need to get more evidence if we're really gonna get this done."

"Okay."

"You cannot talk about this, Corporal. Not with anyone, you understand?"

"Yes, sir, thank you."

"Don't mention it." Steven put his hands in his pockets and shook his head. "Not anyone, remember that."

"Yes, sir." Hanson shook his hand again, pulled over his collar, and walked back out into the wind, leaving Steven to return to his office in silence.

As he left, Hanson felt small, insignificant in the role that he played. He was proud to be able to help, but he felt as though he were simply a tool in the hands of those who don't trust him, or anyone for that matter. He knew that he wasn't part of their circle of trust, but what was strange to him was that they acted as though they knew he craved revenge, as if he were the dog on the chain, only let go of when they needed him to sniff something out; it pissed him off. One thing was for sure: he needed to know more about the bomber, he needed to find him, he needed to kill him. It was that simple in Hanson's mind, but it wasn't as simple to do. Before he could get back at this man, he at least needed to know who to look for. He thought about breaking into CID again, but chances were that the CIA had already relieved them of their files about the bomber, and he had already run into their brick wall. He was at a loss.

The wind picked up even more as the sand storm began to cast its weighty shadow over onto the camp. The world around seemed almost surreal behind the shroud of moving sand, thus he didn't even notice someone approaching behind him. He opened the door to his barracks when he felt a hand on his shoulder; he immediately spun into the room, knocking the hand off his shoulder; however, as he turned, he was immediately tackled over and into the ground. He felt as though he were pushing against a piece of metal. Then his assailant started to laugh, a low chuckle that became more and more familiar as the man rolled off Hanson and onto the floor next to him. Hanson immediately felt foolish with his fear when he realized it was Daniil who had spooked him.

"I should have known it was you, Danny, only you and my older brother would ever pummel me then laugh about it."

"Hey, bud!" Daniil was barely able to speak through his laughter. "Don't be too hard on him, I've met your brother, he's a really nice guy."

"Whatever! You're both too strong to be shorter than me." Hanson was now laughing nearly as hard as his gasping friend. "What are you doin' here, Danny?"

"Oh, well, I thought you would have figured that out already. I still have to finish you off." He quickly jabbed Hanson in the ribs. "Now I'm done."

"All right," Hanson grunted as he stood himself back up, his ribs still throbbing from the well-placed strike "get up." He reached out his hand and helped Daniil off of the floor. As they stood, Daniil pulled a chair from a large desk they were standing next to and offered it to his friend, Hanson said no, and Daniil sat instead. "So what were you doing up with the CIA, still singing for and dancing, or are they making you part of the club?"

"Well, they don't seem to want to tell me much, but I have been able to do some work, I just don't think they're comfortable with me knowing much more than I find for them." Hanson leaned against the wall behind him and sighed, still disappointed.

"Well, it's not like they're the nicest guys to get to know, you yourself remember just how rude they were to me before I kicked the instructor's—" The door opened and a man walked in with a stack of mail, which he set beneath the bed nearest the door and then left again. "Well, you see my point. They'll warm up to you after a while, you just have to make sure you don't warm up to them too much, or they'll have you singing and dancing all over again, except then you won't be paid for it. You'll feel obligated."

"Sounds like your talkin' from experience, they make you teach them how to wrestle or something?"

"Nah." He smirked. "It's just what I know." He was quiet for a moment, staring off at the far wall like there was something important written on it and he just couldn't read it. He turned back to Hanson. "Anyways, we're not here to talk about them. How have you been?"

"I'm fine, Danny, just fine." Hanson looked at his friend for a moment; the guy seemed like he actually cared. It was good to have people; all Hanson was missing was one of the females, one in particular. That's when he remembered Celia. He needed to talk to her. "Hey, Danny, I still have to go over what information about the explosives they did give me, it's not much, but it could take a good part of the evening so I'm gonna get to it."

"You sure? We still have to fight a little, don't we?"

"No, maybe next time, bud, I have to keep this whole thing up for Billy at least. But I'll see you later all right?"

"All right, you don't have to tell me. I get it, I'm not wanted." A fake sniffle and teary eyes made him actually look sad, but he couldn't hold it for long. "All right, I'll go find some other people to mess with."

"Adios." Hanson saluted him with his two first fingers and Daniil backed out the door, replacing a pair of heavy-set field glasses to cover his eyes from the storm. That's when Hanson started back for his trunk to retrieve his doctor act and start hiding again. He was going to pay Celia a visit, and it made him happy that it wasn't just for information.

—◦◦◦—

Celia grabbed a blank piece of computer paper from underneath her desk, scratching notes onto it frantically as she reached for a file with her other hand. On the computer screen in front of her, several files were open at once, each a piece of the case that pertained to this new bomber who surfaced not more than a day ago. At the bottom of the screen, a small loading bar was slowly reaching the end of its boundaries, signaling the removal and deletion of the files from the CID server, after that the only ones with info on bomber would be the CIA. Celia never liked the CIA, not because they didn't do good work, but because they never liked to share; they were so childish. As she wrote, she lost track of the timer, and when she looked back to see how much she had left, the pencil in her hand slipped out, rolling nearly off her desk until she caught it with the tip of her finger and pulled it back over to the page; she was only able to finish the sentence she was on from the screen before the files crashed and were gone. She stood, trying to see if what she had would make any sense, be any help, but so far, it was more random facts than anything; she tossed the page back onto the desk and sighed with disappointment, knowing that she was still in the dark. She grabbed the files off her desk, dropping them into a small plastic crate, and then she backed through the door into the computer lab. People moved about through the room as if they were all alone, some seemingly too busy to even say "excuse me" when they nudged one another going from the data towers to their desks; this was especially true for one data tower on the other side of the room, where someone apparently had "kicked in the cooler unit" as the technician put it. When asked as to whether or not anything else had happened to it, he gave her an impatient glare and returned to his fixing; apparently he wasn't into sharing information either.

Eventually she reached the filing room, opened the door, and kicked down the door stop. However it failed and closed behind her; no matter, she'd be gone soon anyway. She took the crate of files to the far right wall and started to load them into the box that represented July's cases. Each one she put in seemed to be more and more irrelevant with each moment, petty theft or loss of equipment seeming unimportant in comparison with the bomber case. This guy, from what she had been able to learn, was an absolute ghost—not even a picture or history besides what the forensics and field guys had given her. What's more is that he was almost too good at setting his traps, as if he knew exactly what our guys would do and when to strike when they think they're safe. It was strange, though, that he was only scary because he existed. The troops knew nothing of him, only that there's a fight, and that they will have to keep fighting it. But this man scared her, made her feel unsafe—a faceless enemy. But she guessed that that's what fighting the insurgents is really like anyways so she put it behind her, closed up her box, and started out toward her desk to think about how she could still help put this guy away. Then she remembered the computer tower in the other room, the one that crashed. It had been taken offline before the CIA could have drained it, and so maybe... She dropped the plastic container in the room and exited, especially interested in when that tower would be fixed.

Hanson opened up the door to the CID building in surprise. It opened without a sound, and no one seemed to notice the presence of a doctor in the lobby. A couple of MPs were talking at the end of the room, so Hanson thought about asking them why the door was open, but they had habits of asking questions in return, so he decided against it. He walked through the room and out to where Celia usually sat. He looked to her empty desk with a disappointed glance; however, he didn't look long when he noticed another man come out from the computer room that he recognized. It took him a moment, but he eventually got his name.

"Chris!" he called out to him, and the scrawny man turned with a shocked expression on his face. "Chris, do you remember me?"

"No." His answer came bluntly, and Hanson, still trying to be nice to the recluse, tried to explain.

"Hey, come on, I met you a week ago, here with Celia."

"*Special Agent* Salviana," he corrected Hanson.

"Yes, the special agent, do you remember me?" Chris had a blank look on his face. "Rick." He tried to remind the man of his name, relieved himself that he still remembered it "From the hospital?"

"Oh yes, Dr. Rick, why are you here?" the man's blatantly annoyed demeanor was starting to eat at Hanson, but he continued to let it slide. Never make waves with cops or MPs nearby.

"Uh, right, I'm here to see Celi—" He caught himself. "Special Agent Salviana. Is she around?"

"Why? Get done watching CSI and just had to see if it was real?" With Chris's sarcasm, Hanson's patience was quickly dwindling.

"No, I just wanted to talk to her about some things. Is that all right with you?"

"Not really, non-CID personnel aren't usually permitted in here."

"Look," his voice was lowered as his patience had run out, "I'm asking because I have some important things to ask her about a case. I have a friend who lost a partner in one of the attacks, and he really wants a checkup. Now where can I find her?"

"Sorry, Doc, I just can't help you." With that, Chris grabbed a file from Celia's desk and walked back into the computer room, leaving Hanson to fight it out with his inner soldier on whether or not to strangle the walking rule book.

Celia grabbed a flash drive from the files' storage room and checked to see if the tower was still under maintenance; both the yellow tape and the technician were gone, so she assumed the best and started toward it. In the back of her mind, she realized she was basically stealing from the CIA, but to her it was already her information, they just wanted it to be theirs; problem was, so did she. As she neared the tower, she heard a phone ring at a desk on the other side of a short wall of desks. She couldn't see who picked it up, but she knew it was the chief agent. She caught him saying that it was ready, and that whoever was on the other side of the phone should send someone over to pick it up; this time she assumed the worst and quickly made her way to the tower and plugged her device into the USB hub. She guided the cursor onto the explore button and opened it; the files were still there. A small group of agents walked past, laughing and completely oblivious to her save for a small "hello." She smiled back, and they continued joking with one another as she copied the files onto her flash drive. It took only a few moments, and she then removed the drive, closed the computer, and walked away, checking behind her and around as she went; she had remained unnoticed. As she exited the room, she was proud of herself, but she was still trying to seem inconspicuous, and thus was too preoccupied to notice someone on the other side of the door to her desk, until she opened it and sent the man standing behind the door, tripping into the desk and onto the floor.

The bump was unexpected. Hanson was already off balance from trying to look incognito as he glanced over the files on her desk. He was leaning just enough so that the door hit him in the head which forced to trip him over and off of his feat for the second time that day. Above him, a brightly lit office light blinded him for but a moment, until the light was blocked by someone standing over him. It was when he realized who it was, that the word *déjà vu* popped into his mind. But then, his head started to hurt.

"Oh my God! Rick, are you okay?" She knelt down next to him and tried to move his hand from massaging his head; he allowed her and tried to keep from groaning again.

"Yeah, yeah, I'm fine. I'm all right." He stopped moving for a second and looked up at her as she looked at the top of his head, when she looked at him he started to laugh. "You seem to like knocking me over, Special Agent. Did I do something to make you mad?" She giggled and retorted with.

"Well, you haven't called or written, so I had to do something to get your attention." He laughed again; he lowered his head and immediately felt pain again from the bruise that was forming. She started to rub it gently as he grabbed her desk to sit himself up. It was then the MPs walked over and asked if they could help.

"Oh no, guys, don't worry, we're fine."

"So she says. She didn't get hit with the door." The MPs snickered and migrated back over to their post where they had been standing for a while. Celia smiled and told him he was just being a baby.

"Baby or not, you need to watch where you decide to shoulder rush things, you might just hit someone."

"Or maybe you shouldn't spend so much time near doors."

"I'm a doctor, Celia, I can't be wrong." He stood and leaned against her desk. "Well, at least I hope not." She smiled and rolled her eyes, taking the flash drive in her hand and placing it into the laptop USB port, all the while Hanson covertly watching what was to come up on the screen. It was when the computer recognized the drive, and she realized that she still hadn't exited from the explorer section of the last computer, and the CIA would be there soon to pick it up. She told Hanson to wait a moment as she needed to go check on something.

"Ma'am, yes, ma'am," Hanson said jokingly as he saluted her, she only barely acknowledged him. As the door closed, however, Hanson took his chance. He opened the flash drive's icon, and instantly, a page appeared, but only one file was present. Quickly he accessed it, and immediately a picture appeared of a Middle Eastern man, seemingly unaware that his picture was being taken, walking toward a house. To the right, Hanson looked for a name, something to identify him with, but he couldn't see it. He scrolled down, still searching until suddenly, below the picture the last paragraph had one name in its midst. He checked the file one last time; it was him. "Zahid al Khatri" was in red letters, surrounded by suspected attacks and dealings with another man in the black market. The picture was taken at an angle, still a little hazy as it had yet to even be cleaned up by the techs in forensics, but he could see his eyes. Dark, lifeless, reminding him of a shark just before a kill, only taking the time to look before it struck like lighting. The man was a predator, and Hanson could see that; from the description that followed, he seemed even worse. He was entranced almost, reading everything about him that was listed—suspected to be from Iran, dangerous, unstable. The list went on, but Hanson read without fear. Instead, he saw himself as a hunter and this man his prey; a wolf does not fear a rabbit. He then heard Celia's voice behind him, on the other side of the door, and quickly, he clicked, trying to exit, but he wasn't sure he had. Time's up. He stayed in front of her screen, this time just far enough away to avoid getting hit by the door. She entered and found him playing with a couple of paper clips that were left on her desk. He turned around.

"Hey, good to see you. What took you so long?"

"Oh, I didn't take long." She adjusted her uniform, straightening the crease in her arm when she noticed Hanson was staring; he noticed she saw him and looked away. "C'mon, I'm hungry, we need to catch up, and now I'm on break."

"Yes, ma'am," he said again.

"And don't call me ma'am."

Daniil Brish watched them as they left the building. He remained unnoticed in the heavy shroud of the sand. It wasn't interesting to him that Hanson was talking to a girl; Daniil had already been over to the British side for a little chat with a tank technician who had surprisingly cute bangs for always wearing a hat. Instead, he was wondering why Hanson was dressed like a doctor; it was something he was more than interested in finding out.

REVEALED

1530 hours, July 15, Camp Bastion
Helmand Province, Afghanistan

Celia burst into the hospital, the anger almost like smoke pouring out of her ears. She stormed down the main hall; soldiers who passed by seemed to want to get out of her way. Only one tried to hit on her, but she held up her hand—not a good time. She came up to the nurses' desk; the woman who was sitting there barely even noticed her until she slapped her hands onto the counter.

"Excuse me, do you have a 'Dr. Rick' on staff?"

"Yes, ma'am, just went down to surgery, he'll be out in around an hour. Would you like me to take a message?"

"Is it urgent?"

"Is what 'urgent'?"

"The surgery, is it urgent?"

"Well, it's just a little bit of reconstruction, so not really—hey! Where are you going?"

"To see Dr. Rick." Celia moved down the hall, following the signs that read "Surgery" and made it all the way to the door before a couple of MPs came up behind her and asked what she was doing. "Agent Salviana, Army CID, I have a couple questions for Dr. Rick."

"Well, ma'am, you're going to have to wait until he comes out of there, no one is allowed back except staff and patients." Suddenly the OR doors opened behind them and a tall, bald doctor in scrubs walked out and tried to pass. Celia was just about to ask where she could find Dr. Rick when one of the MPs waved him down.

"Excuse me sir, this women from Army CID wants to speak with you."

"Wait, you're Dr. Rick?" She was stunned—but not entirely.

"Yes, although I do prefer my last name when I'm getting yelled at, sounds too much like I'm in trouble when you use my first name like that." He laughed a little, the MPs laughing with him. Celia cupped one of her hands to her eyes and rested the other on the hip, shaking her head as she looked back at the group of men.

"Sir, do you know if there was a patient here by the name of Corporal Damian Hanson? He was a bomb technician who got hurt in a blast a few weeks ago."

"Well, ma'am, I have a lot of patients, and I barely even get to know many of their names for time's sake, so I'm afraid I can't help you."

"All right," she sighed, still obviously fuming "thank you for your time." She turned to leave.

"Well, wait a minute. If he was a burn victim, he probably spent time over in the east wing, you should try the clerk's desk there." He pointed down a hall, and she thanked him. A few moments later, she had made it to the desk.

"Excuse me," she asked, a short nurse with pudgy cheeks and black hair turned toward her and smiled. "Hi, I was wondering if I could see to Corporal Damian Hanson, I believe he was here being treated for burns."

"Well, I'm sorry, but he's no longer in the hospital, we released him a good while ago."

"Do you know where I can find him?" her face reddened, her eyes evermore impatient.

Hanson grabbed his doctor's uniform and was about ready to head out and see Celia when he started to change his mind. He was starting to feel bad, starting to feel a lot like Billy's stepdad who kept lying until he lied himself right into prison. He wanted to tell Celia who he really was; he wanted to get that cleared up the first time he met but he just couldn't. Every time he was going to tell her, at dinner, at lunch, on brake, the list went on, and each time he wanted to say something, but then he'd think of Billy and the hundreds of people already dead and hurt from that bomber Zahid that he couldn't close himself to finding him—not yet. But he'd done it, he knew enough about him, and he was going to tell her; but he would have to break it slow. Knowing her, she might go into interrogator mode and put him in the stockade, but he had to try. So he picked up his clothing, set everything ready, and was just about to leave when the door opened, nearly hitting him, but he had stepped back. Agent Salviana slammed it behind her.

"Hey." He was shocked to see her. He tried to play off his shock "Um, you almost hit me again." He joked, but she didn't seem amused.

"Oh, I'll try harder next time."

"Are you all right?"

"No, why the hell would I be all right, Rick?" she paused for a second. "I mean *Damian*." She gave him a knowing, pissed-off look, and guilt covered his face. "Why did you lie to me?"

"Celia, I had to, I couldn't let anyone know what I was doing."

"What? You didn't want to get caught fraternizing with a female? Had to protect your honor?"

"No, Celia, it's not like that. I like you, I wanted to spend time with you, but—"

"But what, Corporal?" Her tone had turned derogatory.

"Celia, do you remember when I asked you questions about the explosion a couple weeks ago?"

"Yes, but what does that—"

"Just listen!"

She immediately quieted down. As she watched him, she could feel the pain as he pleaded with her. "I told you, I was asking for a patient, but that wasn't true. I was asking for myself." He sat down on the bed, clutching his hat in clenched fists. "I was in that attack, Celia. I was one of the technicians that tried to stop the bomb from going off. My partner and best friend from back home, Billy, was the other. He didn't survive that attack."

"I still don't understand. What were you looking for?"

"I had to know what you knew, what the CID and the CIA knew. I had to figure out who killed my best friend. I had to know, and I only knew one way to find out."

"So…" her eyes watered a little; she was torn between pity for him and anger. "So you used me?"

"No, well"—he shifted in his seat—"well, yes, but not entirely. It wasn't fake, Celia, I really do like you, but I lost my best friend. I'm sorry."

"Today, after I came back from being with you, I found my files on the computer still open, I thought I did it, but was that you?"

"Yes." He lowered his eyes, his knuckles white. "Celia, where did this come from? Who told you about me?"

"Why is that important, Damian? You already have everything you *really* wanted. Why do you need that?"

"Please, just tell me. You'll never have to see me again if you don't want to, but I need to know who else knew."

"Or what?" She looked up at him, wiping the glossy wetness from under her eyes.

"Or I may never get to pay back that bomber for what he did to my friend, what he did to Billy's family, and what he did everyone else."

"Don't forget about yourself, Damian, you wouldn't want to forget about that." She looked away for a moment; he could tell she was thinking. Finally she turned back and said, "He said his name was Brish. That's all I know about him."

"Thank you, Celia."

"You know what, Hanson, don't thank me. If anything, I'm one person who you shouldn't thank." It took everything in her not to scream at him, yell some more, tell him to go to hell, but she was done. "You were right, Corporal, I won't be seeing you again." With that, she turned around and left, didn't turn back, and didn't listen for his calls.

Hanson sat in his bed, emotions running through his chest like a stampede, his mind ached, and his hands were shaking from the tightness of the clench he had on his hat. He looked over to his right and saw the green turban lying to his right. He remembered her saying she liked it, that she liked the color and how it made her feel happy. He grabbed it and tore it in half, tossing the remnants into his trunk and slamming the lid.

Daniil stood under the rotors of the Black Hawk as they rotated faster and faster, kicking up plumes of smoke around him. He looked on, out toward where Hanson's barracks were and watched as the girl stormed away. A few minutes later, Hanson emerged but then went back inside, kicking sand as he went. Daniil chuckled a little. It had been a long few months of work in the camp, watching and waiting and playing the soldier game to get something important out of his presence. This was just a part of the plan; he hoped he could explain it to Hanson someday, but for now, it wasn't time.

"Sir!" someone called from behind him in the chopper. "We have to get going, sir, you're wanted in Kandahar in twenty minutes."

"All right, let's move." He jumped in the chopper, and it lifted off the ground smoothly. He closed his eyes and tried to ignore the sound.

IT WAS NIGHT

1918 hours, July 15, Al Bnayuh Warehouse
Sirak, Afghanistan

Hassan watched as Zahid spoke, amazed at how the man's mind seemed to churn with cunning preparations as if he were made for the plans that he was laying in motion. Every question, every retort or doubt, was met with shining black eyes and an answer that defeated the pestering of fear from each man who questioned him. They knew that what he proposed would be something unheard of and would insight a battle more fierce than most of them felt prepared to wage, but they trusted their Amir and believed ever more in his words. Yet even with all the questions, the men had yet to ask the right one; they had yet to question—

"What about airpower?" Hassan's ears perked up when a man sitting on a large wooden crate behind him finally asked what he was thinking; all turned to Zahid for his response.

"We have none," Zahid joked, some of the men snickering at his humorous answer.

"I mean, how do we deal with it, Amir?"

"Ah, now I understand." A ghoulish smile appeared on Zahid's face as he prepared his answer. "As I said, we will begin the assault with a strike at their collection team when it leaves to get supplies. We disable them so that they need armored extraction from the base itself. When that occurs, there is a good chance that they will send out at least two of their Apache helicopters.

It is when those come that you will be using the devices in that crate you happen to be sitting on." The man looked down to read the crate but was unable to do so before Zahid continued. "Once that happens, we will need those things out of the sky before we reveal the mortar teams that surround the base itself. If we don't, those helicopters will change assignments and we will lose the mortars." The men nodded in agreement. "When we start the barrage, there will be a second armored response, ground vehicles, yes, but their air support will be delayed until another base can assist them."

"But didn't you say that they had helicopters on base?" another man from the crowd questioned.

"Yes, but only a couple will actually be able to leave before they realize that we will be close enough to hit them as they are taking off. Then they won't take the risk, and they will rely on their ground strength."

"Once that happens," the man standing next to Zahid interjected, "we will utilize our killer rounds and force them to send more toward us."

"It will be then"—Zahid regained command of the conversation and pointed to the western edge of the small compound—"that we send our tuck from behind. The target will be identified once inside for sure, but we are hoping to strike at their hospital. We need to avoid destroying their transport helicopters as best as we can."

"Amir," Hassan called out from his seat, "how long is this supposed to last?" Zahid eyed him for a moment and then smirked as he replied, "When our truck reaches the hospital and the eastern end of the compound, you will know it. It is then that you will pull out. Clear?"

"Yes, Amir." Hassan looked around once more; no one seemed willing to question him again.

"All right." Zahid turned and looked over the small crowd. "You know the rest, now get ready. We go tonight."

—⦅∞⦆—

Sound carried as if the earth were in a perpetual winter; each motion and step making a crisp crunch against the surface of the cooled sand. Light was only visible from its origin, and as the power of the lights faded, the rest of the world was lit by a dull moon, casting its miniscule brightness as a wave over the dunes, and the wind followed suit. The cool air whipped through the expanse of the darkness, only to meet the rigid walls of the hangers that were arranged mechanically over the expanse of Forward Operating Base Edinburgh.

Known formally as an FOB, the relatively small camp in the Afghan desert is home to several hundred men who have resided there for a tour, others even more. It was a place where camaraderie was the backbone, the structure—in essence what kept the secluded place alive. This was engrained in the minds of the Marines on base, especially for Corporal Mitchell Ramsey, who was making his way back from the hospital after giving blood, saving the life of a wounded soldier brought in only minutes ago on a rugged Black Hawk. Several other choppers in fact were due in to the camp over the next few hours, but strangely, two attack choppers took off frantically nearly ten minutes ago.

Ramsey walked at a subdued pace, although it was a relatively quick motion for someone who had just given blood, but he still felt as though he were moving far slower than his long legs usually carried him. Exhausted, he clumsily brought his hand to his face, rubbing off a small layer of sweat that had accumulated while he was waiting to be released from the hospital, but he apparently hadn't waited long enough, for as he brought his hands to his face, his consciousness began fading, and he nearly lost his balance, saving himself from a rough contact with the ground by grasping a large pole that held a triplet of high-powered floodlights. After a moment of rest, he inadvertently struck a match and lit a cigarette, not realizing that it would put him to sleep as his mind was already lacking oxygen. It was, in fact, about to complete its unintended purpose when it was flicked out of his mouth. Enraged, Ramsey turned to begin scolding when he was struck again, but this time, by the presence of a staff sergeant symbol on the outstretched arm that now firmly grasped his shoulder. He looked directly into his officers eyes, straightened his back, and attempted to give some semblance of an attention pose while holding on to his consciousness. The sergeant dropped his hand.

"Corporal, where were you for the last hour and a half?"

"Uh…" he tried to remember where he was, already having trouble knowing where he stood at that moment. "I was giving blood."

"You say that like it's a question." The sergeant smirked.

"I was giving blood, sir. Just on my way back to barracks."

"So if you just gave blood"—the sergeant walked over to the smoldering butt on the ground—"and you are already 'out of it,' then why would you think it a good idea to smoke?" The young soldier grinned, knowing full well that the sergeant didn't like smoking anyways, and that he was enjoying every second of protecting yet another set of lungs.

"Well, sir, I just needed to calm down after all the stuff I saw in the ER," Ramsey mused. Bantering like this with the sergeant was usually reserved for the more advanced soldiers, but the sergeant had taken a liking to his humor, although most of the time his jests were all but laughed at by the strong-jawed man.

"Good excuse, but not good enough. You're up first tomorrow morning and get the others out of bed too. We have first escort with EOD tomorrow, and that'll take all day." Waking the others up was another responsibility usually reserved for the higher ranks, but Ramsey guessed the good standing also meant more standing and less lying down. The sergeant stepped back, Ramsey saluted, and the sergeant returned the motion; both men parted ways.

As he walked away, Ramsey noticed a small light to the west, peaking in and out if the small hills as it moved southbound on the road that ran almost parallel to FOB Eddie. As it ran, he could make out that it had headlights and was rapidly approaching; although he couldn't tell the type of vehicle besides the fact that it wasn't military. But before he could point it out to his staff sergeant, who was still within earshot, Ramsey heard a sound that was so sinister and unexpected that he barely understood what that distant boom he heard was, until his fears were confirmed as the sound of the air unzipping above ripped its way through his haze. He looked up just enough to miss the impact of a mortar shell a few dozen yards in front of him—directly onto the tent full of Marines he had been walking toward.

Outside the Base, a few moments before the mortar attack, a voice cried over the sound of gunfire. "Sergeant!" a soldier screamed from behind a burning barrel. Gunshots rang out in the distance, followed by shots far louder being returned to the enemy on the adjacent hill. The man called out again, searching carefully around for his CO, but still, no answer. He stood halfway up to from behind his bright barricade, only to be forced back to the ground by several bullets smacking into the earth around his feet. He covered his head with his free arm while holding his rifle in his right. "Sergeant, where are you?" A voice started to answer from the other side of a vehicle, but it was cut short by the arrival of a rocket propelled grenade that screamed overhead until it detonated on the side of a large forklift. He called once more, glancing over the darkened drop zone until his eyes locked on a man crawling away from the now-burning forklift; even from where he was crouching, the young private could see a blood trail behind the poor man. The private gripped his gun tightly, rapidly exhaling as he prepared for his sprint to the soldier, but someone ran to him first and picked up from the ground, trying desperately to offer support to the now single-legged soldier. Then a sound from above alerted the private to what was coming, but when it contacted, its power ripped through his consciousness and sent a storm of debris flying in several directions; the forklift had been mortared, and those two soldiers were gone. The private stumbled backward from the crater, shocked by what he had just seen, and oblivious to the world around him. Only barely was he able to notice someone grab him and force him back to a bunker made behind supplies that were air dropped. When he looked to see who had grabbed him, relief flowed through him when he saw it was his lieutenant who had come to get him, several other men were also gathered around the man, a couple wounded, but most seemed to be unharmed. The lieutenant started to shout orders to them above the sound of mortar rounds hitting near their position. The private looked over the dry landscape, amazed that only a little while earlier it had been a place to receive help, several large airdrops full of food and supplies were all left for them, but they were some of the only cover the men could find. As he was speaking that, a new sound appeared, a steady beating that resounded above the noise of the battle, followed almost immediately by two Apache war helicopters. As soon as the men saw them, they began to cheer, feeling safe as their men of steel fought from the skies above them; they jeered even louder as the mini-gun began to spray suppressive fire onto the hill from where the mortars were being fired from.

The men started to disperse as the lieutenant ordered, spreading out in several directions as they moved toward the hill, all the while shells were falling from above like a fiery rain, light from the small fires around the battlefield reflecting off of their hard, bronze siding. It seemed to the men, especially for the private, that these birds of prey were unstoppable; he was absolutely invigorated. But it had lasted for only a short time that had been too good to be true for the lieutenant, and his fears were confirmed when he called for the men to hold as one of the choppers took a direct hit from a shoulder-fired AA missile. The men scrambled as the steel beast rocked backward from the impact, smoke sputtering out from its engine as it began its swift descent. It seemed like it was only a matter of seconds after it crashed into the ground that the other took a hit, quickly spinning out of control as it plummeted to the earth until it stopped abruptly atop a bunker and the lights went out for the private.

⟞⟋⟍⟍⟍⟍⟞

It hit with what seemed to be the force of a thousand hammers striking the earth, as if thrown down from the sky by Zeus. The ground shook beneath his feet for only a brief moment, just long enough for him to lose his balance and fall to the earth, scraping his hands across the gravel as he protected his head from smashing onto the rigid stones. Landing, he could hear the angry buzzing of the shrapnel and plastic fly overhead, but the sound soon faded. Wearily he looked back to the tent, only to see the deep blurs of smoke and steel that obscured his view, but he could still see the people. One man had run out blindly, cupping his ears in his hands and screaming out in pain, pleading for whatever devilish noise had taken control to subside. He collapsed against a crate a ways in front of Ramsey, his voice now mixed with the sound of people yelling as soldiers rushed by Ramsey to attend to the man and whoever else they could find. But the screams were too much for Ramsey; he couldn't handle the sounds of their suffering, knowing he should be helping, so he did. Gathering his strength, he rose from the ground, the muscles in his arms quivering as he forced them to work on depleted amounts of oxygen. He wiped his eyes, smearing some of the dust across his face as he removed the tears from his eyes that had formed from the wave of small particles that hit him only a few seconds before. Another man hobbled out of the now-cratered structure, dragging what seemed to be clothing and a bewildered look, as if he had no clue as to where he was. Ramsey made his way over to him, stepping over a couple pieces of steel and a backpack. He reached the poor soldier, now able to see a long stream of blood flowed from his head, and guided him away to a larger building just a little ways away from the barracks and sat him down. A siren now blaring from the speakers positioned just beneath the lights pierced its way through the destruction, offering a strange security. He turned to see if he could get anything for the man to put on the large gash atop his head, and he remembered the backpack. When he reached it, however, he realized that rather than a back pack, he had stumbled over to the body of his friend, curled in a strange position as if he had been rolled up and tossed along the ground. He bent down and listened for breathing, feeling the neck for a pulse at the same time—nothing. Horrified, he retracted himself from the body and returned to the man who he had left sitting against the wall. However, he found him slumped over to the side and lifeless.

He sat down next to him, unable to move. He couldn't take what was going on around him. The rhythmic cracking of rifle fire from a distance, only interrupted by the horrible crunching of metal and earth as another shell announced its arrival wouldn't allow him to concentrate. The screams coming from around him, and the screeching of angry, frightened soldiers as they attempted to keep a handle on the fight over the radio just made it worse. After a little while, he just turned the radio off. He sat there for what felt as though an eternity had passed. He watched nearly out of body as a chopper pilot tried to get an Apache off the ground, but was thrown back down as a missile flew over the short wall and detonated inside the cockpit; the chopper hit without a sound. Clouds of dust and earth carried their ways past him, obscuring almost everything from view. And besides the deep rumbles of the artillery and the moan of a hurting soldier, he felt as though he were alone. He looked down at the dying man next to him, feeling as though he were the lucky one. The person was allowed to just skip all the pain and suffering that raged around him and just fall asleep, to wake up in a place far better than this. It wasn't envy, but it wasn't pity either, and Ramsey had no idea what to call it. It was after a long time it seemed that the world began to clear, and he remembered that there were others out there that would need help, so he gathered his strength and began to stand.

All of a sudden, as he stood back up from among the rubble, he saw that the same vehicle that had been moving through the night had just came through the western entrance, stopped, and dropped what looked to be a man out of the back. The SUV skidded forward at an immense pace, headed past Corporal Ramsey and disappeared behind the building. Ramsey feared that the vehicle was part of the attack, se he turned on his radio and began to shout what he'd seen, all the while running toward the man he saw released from the trunk of the black SUV. As he neared, he could see that the man was wearing a US Marine uniform and seemed to be tied at the feet, laying on his side and facing away from Ramsey. He reached the downed soldier, looking for any signs of blood as he slid onto his knees beside the unconscious man. It was then, as if the whole world had turned its head upon the small place in the desert, an immense light filled the night, followed instantly by a sound of thunder so great that the world shook with its presence. Shocked, Ramsey turned away from the man and gazed at the hospital, where he had been resting just a few minutes earlier had just been obliterated by some unknown monster of fire. Before he could see the rest, however, a sudden, sharp jerk pulled him down to the ground and onto his back. Startled, he tried to fight the hands off, turning his head until he could face his attacker and stared directly into the darkest pair of eyes he'd ever seen. It was a dark face that had been cleanly shaven, the downward angle of a large knife looming over his head. They looked for just a moment, Ramsey now realizing what was soon to transpire. It was then, with that silent farewell, the blade dropped from its perch, and the darkness quickly followed.

NIGHT STRIKES TWICE

0815 hours, July 16, Forward Operating Base Edinburgh
Helmand Province, Afghanistan

Lt. James Marlow looked over the field as if it were the place where death itself had landed, every hole and crater acting as the tracks along the trail of its path. He walked down the hill, now standing atop the place where only a few hours earlier his enemy had rained fire down upon him and his men. He felt the heat from behind him, the sun casting it's light upon his shoulders, but the field itself was still shrouded in the shadows of the early morning, the hill acting as the wall that kept the rest of the world from seeing the atrocities laid out before his eyes. He felt heat; it came from within.

"Sergeant Havash!" immediately a man at the bottom of the hill turned, faced the lieutenant, and called out a "yes, sir" in the strongest voice he could muster. "How many?"

"The count has reached twelve, sir." A man then walked over to the sergeant and gestured to a severely damaged forklift. The sergeant staggered his step slightly as he tried to hold in his emotions. "Make that fourteen, sir." He looked away for a moment, taking in the scene around him until he could take no more, then he turned back to the lieutenant. "Sir, what happened last night?"

"We fought a battle, Sergeant. It was in a warzone, and from what I can see, we prevailed."

"Sir, how did we prevail?" another man was walking up from a pile of debris near the bottom of the hill. "How could we have prevailed when what's left of the men looks like this?" He pointed with his fist at the morbid plain; dog tags dangled from his hand.

"Were you with me last night, Corporal?"

"Yes, sir." The muscles in the man's cheeks pulsated, rage purely apparent in the young man's eyes.

"And you are still breathing. Behind me is what is left of the enemy we faced out here last night, and they are not breathing, Corporal. It is because of you and me, and the men who stand around you that I call this a victory." The lieutenant sighed. "And it is because of our dead that we are able to say so." He stared at the corporal with a serious piercing in his eyes. "We will call their triumphs what they are."

"Yes, sir." The Corporal finished his walk and handed the lieutenant the tags; the first one was the private's.

As the chopper flew over the base, Hanson could see the wreckage in its entirety. Below him, hundreds of men, most of whom were medics or corpsman trying desperately to salvage life from the savagery that had taken place the night before. Even at that height, Hanson could feel a twinge in his heart, knowing full well what those men were feeling and wishing to God he could help. But he was a soldier, and only him doing his job could offer any solace to these men, not his words, or any man's for that matter. The chopper landed, and he and his men unloaded from its lowered backdropped ramp, several soldiers, CIA, and CID technicians and himself, all there for one purpose. Hanson hoped he wasn't wasting their time. Hanson looked around at the buildings, the smoke, and the men, all having received several years' worth of ware on them in just a matter of hours; in his mind, he could almost hear the explosions that no doubt rang throughout the night. Hanson felt like he had seen enough, but knew he had to see more, so he urged that they work quickly.

"Corporal Hanson?" A man walked briskly toward him. As he neared, Hanson noticed the bars on his shoulders.

"Yes, Lieutenant?" He saluted him, his fingers lightly brushing against his helmet that rested low over his eyes.

"Good to meet you. I'm Lt. James Marlow, and I'm in charge here at FOB Edinburgh."

"Likewise and understood, sir. Where to?" The rest of Hanson's team finally came up from behind, followed by a black-vested Agent Windburg.

"Follow me, gentlemen." The lieutenant turned and led the group through a field of tents, broken buildings, and craters; however, no path could avoid the debris that was strewn all over the area. Several other soldiers were still cleaning up the heavier pieces of building and equipment when they were ordered to clear the area for Hanson's group, and a couple men tagged along to see why these people were even there if not to help the wounded or reconstruction. Even Hanson was still in the dark as to what they were doing until he rounded a small building to find what was left of a medical holding facility; a large blast radius was obvious as even some of the telephone poles had been laid out pointing away from where the bomb had gone off. The medical building hadn't been completely destroyed, as two of the four walls still stood, and a small portion of the ceiling was intact but sloping down toward the blast zone. Yet a majority of the building was either collected in a pile of rubble at the base of the building or outside the walls adding to the chaos of the rest of FOB Edinburgh. At the base of the debris, the remnants of a vehicle rested, much of the undercarriage still intact but were blackened from both the ash and the heat of the blast. Hanson noticed this first.

"A car bomb, Lieutenant?" Hanson asked.

"Yes, from what my men told me, it made it through the gates when the mortar barrage started on the other side of the base. Most of our men were moving in on the mortar teams when they came through and blew out the med center. From what my men could see, the guys who drove this knew exactly where they were going."

"There were multiple suicide bombers?" Agent Windburg asked as he looked around.

"Yes, one of our guys near the gate said that he saw two people in the vehicle when it entered the premises."

"Why would they need two bombers, Lieutenant?" the chief asked.

"I'm not sure, sir, I just know what I'm tellin' you. Why does it matter?"

"It matters because there is a chance that one of those men didn't die in the explosion, and that means there could be another bomb," Agent Windburg remarked. He then motioned for Hanson to walk with him for a moment; they spoke low as they moved away from the group. "All right, there's a good chance that another device is placed, and since this place is a lot bigger than the school where you went bomb hunting last time, you're gonna need help finding it."

"Well, I already know where it will be, sir."

"And how's that."

"Our guy wants casualties, he'll hit one of the hangars because that's where the people are, either the makeshift med center in hangar 1 or the motor pool in hangar 2."

"That's very good, Hanson. Here's what I know." He stopped walking and turned toward Hanson. "I have good information that tells me you're looking for det-cord."

"Det-cord? How do you know that, sir?" Hanson was now very intrigued.

"We have sources that know this kind of thing, Hanson, now what should we expect with det-cord?" Hanson stared coldly. Windburg was keeping Hanson in the dark but still wanted him to roll over, and it wasn't like he had a choice.

"Det-cord is used for bringing something down, demolishing, and such. When it comes to a building, you can do a lot more damage by bringing it down than just blowing a hole in it. Only thing is, it takes time."

"All right then. Take whoever you need, find it, and keep down. We don't need other people knowing about this."

"Sir, I think we should get people away from there first, get them out of harm's way." Images of the dead flashed into his mind; he didn't want to add to the collection.

"Hanson, if there is a bomb, and we start pushing people out, whoever set it could still be around and could trigger it."

"Then what do you suggest, sir?"

"I think you should only use a couple people to look for this thing, the rest should act like they're analyzing what's left of the med center."

"Act like?"

"Look, chances are, we won't get much from that blast sight besides some chemical traces. No DNA. No prints. Nothing. Now if we keep this guy feeling safe, maybe we find him and have a whole lot more than we would have." He shifted his eyes to make sure he wouldn't be heard. "Besides, this attack is our guy, we know that."

"More from you're mysterious source, Windburg?"

"I don't need any more questions from you and have no desire to explain. You have enough information to do your job." He stepped toward Hanson, both men staring each other down. "So do it."

"Yes, sir." Hanson didn't wait for anything else, but started back to the rest of the group, most of whom were already unpacking forensic equipment.

"I need five men to come with me." No one moved at first, most still too interested in finding the key evidence than listening to orders, so Hanson played to their liking "We're going hunting for another bomb." Seven men stepped forward, and Hanson took the first five with him toward the hangars, assigning two men to each, including himself.

⌁◈◈◈⌁

Soldiers moved about relentlessly in the small building, making contact with superiors via radio or accessing and filling out data sheets to catalogue the happenings of the previous night. The door opened and closed constantly, and a steady flow of traffic kept most people waiting, jammed together in an uneven line until they were given a brief window to actually get inside. On the really bad days, however, most would just wait at a couple of tables and chairs outside of the office (although the chairs were really moderately sized boxes and cases). Many people would come and just sit for a moment, resting themselves to blow off steam or catch up on what was going on in the world by asking people on their way out. Thus, one from Hanson's group, who was notorious for his procrastination, had made his way to the area and plopped himself atop one of the crates near the back, just obscure enough of a place to avoid being seen by the rest of his team. It was here that someone began speaking to him about the attack and asking him as to what he was doing there.

"Well"—he noticed the "Corporal" symbol on the man's uniform and felt relieved that he didn't have to follow his intro with a 'sir'—"I'm not really supposed to talk about that; hush-hush sort of thing."

"Oh yes, I understand, sir." He also enjoyed being called sir. "It's just that I noticed you all were working around the medical center, and I was wondering if you guys were looking for something."

"Like I said, Corporal, I'm not allowed to talk about it." He then leaned in to the man and said, "but we haven't found nothin' to speak of anyways."

"Okay—yes, sir, I mean. Sorry, sir."

"Don't worry about it, I have to get back before they start bitchin'. Enjoy your wait, Corporal. It looks like this line'll take a while." And with that, the man stood and walked back to his group, still smiling at his opportunity to use his rank.

The corporal sat back in his "chair," his head against the wall as he watched the man walk back to the bomb site. Then he noticed another group heading away from the site, he watched them move slowly but in a straight line, directly for the hangars. This didn't worry him at first, but when they split themselves up, he knew that they were looking for something, and he knew he had to find out. He stood to walk over when another man came up to him, also above his rank, and told him to go with him and help move supplies into a truck; they started walking the other direction.

The hangars were massive compared to the small rooms Hanson searched through at the school. It looked, to an untrained eye, that every shadow, every closed space, could offer a hiding place for a device. Hanson knew who this was; however, he knew he was too smart to place it somewhere it would do little more than create heat. Thus, as Hanson looked about the hangar, he knew that the only places this thing could be were the support beams that lined both the ceiling and the walls, all seeming to give their strength to the central beam that ran the length of the hangar; below it a catwalk ran parallel.

"Teams one and two, this is Corporal Hanson, I want you to start on the catwalks, and if he can bring down the ceiling, he won't need much more." He waited for acknowledgement from the radio; 'yes sir's" followed, and Hanson moved into the hangar on the far left and in turn walked directly into a sea of wounded soldiers covering the floors. To the right of the entrance, a single ladder ran straight up to a platform, from which two separate sets of stair cases began; one along the wall and another straight up to the catwalk. When Hanson and his partner reached the platform, he sent his partner along the wall, and he moved up to the catwalk. When he reached the top, he saw that much of the walk had been obscured by the lighting, now he was able to see that it ran in several directions, with much of the walkway still blocked by supplies and equipment. He knew he wouldn't have much time, so he decided to stick to the central walkway, carefully adjusting barrels and boxes as he made his way through to the center platform. He could see three other walkways branching off of the platform, even more debris collected in its center. He had just reached it when his radio came alive.

"Sir, this is team one, we have nothing up here, sir." He was referring to the hangar full of vehicles.

"Aren't there debris up there, or stored equipment maybe?"

"No, sir, there's nothing."

"All right, then try looking over the larger vehicles, maybe there is something there."

"Yes, sir." The radio went quiet again. Hanson picked himself up over a box as his partner came from the walkway to his right and informed him it was clean.

"With all this stuff up here, I wouldn't just assume that we're clear." Hanson eyed the long beam, only just then able to see that electrical wiring ran along its top; a possibility grew in his mind. "Corporal, let's try on top of the beam. Tell the others to do the same." Hanson then stood himself atop the railing, giving him just enough height to look over the beam's lip and into the space between the I-beam bottom lip and the ceiling itself. He took his penlight from the front pocket of his uniform and shone it into the dark space; he was immediately rewarded with a first-person view of a system of detonating cords that ran along the sides of the I-beam. As he looked, he could see every few meters another detonator was attached, remote detonated receivers paired with each; he was gonna need a lot more men.

"Teams one and two." They responded a few moments later. "On the I-beam along the top, can you see any det-cord?" A few moments passed until both replied, that there was none. "Then you all need to get up here right now, because we found our bomb, and it's primed to bring the whole roof down on the med center." Seconds later, the men were already in the building and scrambling their way to Hanson's position. When they reached the platform, Hanson started to explain, "Each detonator can set off most of the explosive system, the far ends being the only parts that wouldn't detonate if only one receiver was disarmed, but that's still enough to bring the roof down. As most of you know, bombs like these are notorious for being tricky, and with this, the trick we have to pull off is simultaneous disarming. Now pay attention." Hanson turned back up to the detonator above his head and adjusted himself so the others could see. "Right here is the receiver." He pointed to a long metal casing, a small antennae pointing at an angle away from the rigging. "And this is the power supply." A second box, no bigger than a cell phone had a single wire connecting it to the receiver. As Hanson explained, his mind began to focus on something else attached to the bomb, something he forgot about but now remembered perfectly and realized exactly what it could mean. *The paperclip*, he thought. It was the bomber's trademark, and he only just now realized why. "Windburg," he whispered into the radio, "looks like your source was right, this is our guy." He turned back to his men. "Now look here, this wire connecting the receiver to the power supply is actually a paper clip, which is bad because that means it's a live wire with no insulation."

"So what does that mean?" One of the men asked, apprehension apparent in his wavering voice.

"What this means is that if we're not careful, we could short this thing out before we disarm it, then *boom*."

"Then what do we do, sir?" a younger member of the group asked.

"I need you all to get ready to pull the clip from the receiver, but we need to do it at the same time, or they go off. And if you touch the paperclip to the I-beam's surface or just connect the two with pliers, then you will short it out, and chances are, it blows." The men were completely silent, all perfectly aware that they were facing death. Hanson, understanding their fear, attempted to lighten the mood. "Although I'll understand if curiosity gets the better of you." They all laughed for a moment;

they were ready. "Gentlemen, here we go." With that, the men made their way to the receivers. Hanson thought about how he was accustomed to disarming explosives like this, compared to the usual MO of simply blowing the bombs with smaller bombs. That was the way it's done on the roads—that was the safe way, but he couldn't do safe, not in a hospital like the one he was standing over. So he needed to do it old-fashioned, and his men would follow suit with the pliers and risk of having their world explode right in front of them. At least he wasn't alone.

Windburg walked around to the other side of the old med center, out of site from the rest of his men and immediately began to vomit, his back reeling with each strain as his body tried to cleanse itself from what he had just seen. He rubbed his face, barely able to control the shaking in his hand and his mind flashed the images of when they removed the rubble from the floor. There were bodies, faces, people who were barely recognizable as being human from the blast that had ended them so violently. Blood was like jelly, making the dust and dirt into a pasty mud that covered what was left of the walls. He had even seen an arm that seemed to be attached only by a strap of clothing that used to be, from what he could tell, a patient's gown. He tried to push the images out, trying to focus on the surroundings that seemed far more peaceful at first, but he received no relief as body bags now lined the perimeter of a field in front of him, it was the faces of war, the darkness and sickening repetitive nature of the combat the made no distinction between soldier and survivor. He wished to give them peace, he wished to push the images from his mind, but both were out of his grasp; he would just have to push through. He took several deep, long breaths, holding them slightly as he calmed himself and prepared to return to his work. He turned to leave when a voice from behind him asked him about what had happened, and he turned to acknowledge.

"What?"

"I'm wondering what happened here, sir. Were we hit by a missile or something?"

"No, Corporal." He struggled to recall, faces still flashing into his mind. "No, it was an IED. They were able to drive it in during a mortar attack." He looked up at the corporal, something oddly familiar about him made him think he knew him, but he decided he didn't. "We're just cleaning up after the bastards now."

"Sir, I noticed some of your men heading to the hangars. Is there more wreckage on that side?"

"Um…" Windburg searched for a reply but could find none, so he simply agreed. "Yes, they're just cleaning up too."

"Well, it's pretty messy over there, I'm guessing, do you think I could go help them?"

"I think they have it under control. You should stay here." He turned to leave when the man grabbed his shoulder.

"Sir, there were no mortars that hit over there, and from what I heard, the hangars are the only things that weren't. Is there something else they have to do?"

"Listen, Corporal…"—he searched for a name patch— "Ramsey, I'm not going to talk about this with you. If you are so interested in helping then come with me, and I can find you work to do around the corner."

"Sir, are they looking for another bomb?"

"Woah, no one said anything about a bomb. You need to stop asking questions or I'll…" the corporal then turned walked quickly away, ignoring the agent's threats. Windburg, too angry to pursue, shook his head and started back but was again stopped by a voice, but this time it came from his radio. Hanson had disarmed the bomb. He immediately ran to the med center.

The corporal watched as the men began to bring out pieces of the bomb, each man smiling with accomplishment. Even though most of it was covered, the corporal could still see a strand of det-cord hanging out of a bag, which to most people looks simply like a large white wire. But he knew what it was, and he knew the way it had been set up that it had to be taken apart by someone who knew exactly what they were doing. He was about to walk up to the group, ask a question or two when the last man of the group walked out, speaking happily with the man whom the corporal had been speaking with before. *There you are*, he thought, thinking that the man being congratulated had to be the one who disarmed it. He looked carefully at the man's uniform, searching for a name, but he couldn't see it from the angle he was looking from. So instead he watched his face, he memorized it, and then walked away. He needed to get out of view, get a call out that the bomb had failed, but he couldn't do it there. He knew that if he made a call right then, they'd find him; this man he'd seen, the man he'd talked to, they were looking for him, and Zahid knew why.

SECOND HAND

2350 hours, July 16, Denver, Colorado, USA

The CIA in Denver had been relatively calm for the last few months, having very little in terms of serious business since the manhunt for Bin Laden had finally hit its climax, and it ended abruptly after his death, putting nearly the whole building into a state of assumed dormancy. Most nights, in fact, it would have been odd to see more than three or four lights on within the entire building, as most work could be done and finished during an eight-hour work day. Yet for the men and women working there, the night was anything but quiet.

"Sir, casualty reports are still counting but they're saying overall at least fifty dead, two hundred–plus wounded."

"I don't care about the stats right now, tell me what the situation is with security in that area."

"Sir, minimal chatter was recorded on Taliban frequencies or regular insurgent channels, it's like these guys didn't even exist." A young girl yelled from her desk. She was about to say more, but a man behind her spoke up.

"They exist, son, you can tell because of all the craters up on the map. Ghosts didn't make those, mortars did."

"Gentlemen," agent Matthews spoke again, "I said I need to know about security. What has happened and what are the risks as of now."

"Sir, just received reports that a large bomb system was disarmed in the medical center. But for safety, they are moving the wounded to higher-class facilities. As of now, no enemy sightings or chatter besides others praising the attack."

"What are they worried about? No one is getting in there now that security's beefed up."

"Agent Roberts," the chief analyst on the floor spoke harshly toward the man, "the bomb system was placed after the attack. That means that there is a chance that more explosives could be there—just too many unknowns to leave hundreds of people at risk at a bombed out FOB!"

"That'll do, Charley!" Matthews snapped. He had grown tired of all the speculation and incessant shouting. He simply wanted the facts, and so far, it seemed that he wouldn't be getting them any time soon from his floor. "Victor," he called out over the noise. A moment later, a small, smug-looking man with long black hair stood up from his computer to acknowledge his boss. "I need to talk with my contact on sight. Get up to the vid room and set it up for me."

"On my way," the man said, already jogging toward the nearest set of stairs near his desk.

Matthews then turned to the elevator behind him, holding the door open briefly for another agent to clamber himself through the opening with a pile of loose papers in his hands, already losing a few as the door closed itself. He stayed on board to retrieve them when Matthews exited onto the second floor, walked only a few steps to the video conference room, and opened it up. The man with black hair had already opened up the link and was making the call. A few moments later, after a small session of static and white noise, Agent Windburg appeared on screen.

"Steven, my watchtower is a madhouse right now, and I'm not getting squat for a sit rep from these desk jockeys. Tell me what's goin' on."

"Sir, we think that our bomber is a part of a new insurgency network, one far stronger than our man Jakub had let on before. As you can see, these guys don't just have the resources, but are also the planning to hit us hard."

"Sure, I get that. But what about this second bomb you all found in the med center, what did you get from it?"

"We're still running the information through, but we think that the bomber, the same one from the attacks and the one who built this bomb, is possibly still on base." Agent Windburg's face slowly started to change, as if he were remembering something he only just then understood. Agent Matthews wanted to know why he did that.

"There's something you want to tell me, Steven?"

"Uh…no…it's probably nothing."

"You know I don't like 'probably's, Steven."

"No, I know, sir, it's unrelated."

"Fine. Anything you thinking about that is related?"

"Sir, Jakub has done his part, and we think our bomber is still hanging around his last job. Not sure why as Jakub gave us just enough to find it."

"Well, he's not done yet."

"What do you mean?"

"I mean, we still don't have our bomber, and he is the only one that this man would recognize and possibly go after. We use him as bait since you seem to know where this 'Zahid' is still hiding." He smirked and eyed Agent Windburg. "You don't like it?" It was more of a statement than a question.

"No, sir, its fine. I just thought we were done with him, that's all."

"One thing you need to learn is that if you can still use an asset, then you are not done with him. Make it work, Steven."

"Yes, sir, I guess we still need to learn what else Zahid has to be able to defend against it."

"No, you need to find out *where* Zahid is so that you can kill him and save the money for something more useful than defense."

"And save the lives of our men, sir."

"Yes." Matthews smiled. "And the men."

"I'll keep you posted on anything else that we find."

"And make it quick. I can't handle all this second-hand screaming from the floor."

"Yes, sir." Then, for the first time, Windburg ended the feed. *This is starting to get out of hand,* he thought to himself, only barely noticing the black-haired man walk out of the room. However, he did notice the door close slower than usual and guessed someone else was in the room.

"Can I help you?" He turned to find a particularly edgy secretary standing near the door.

"Yes, sir, um…" She resituated herself and pointed to the door. "Um, you're wanted in… you're wanted in the main conference room. The director and his associates want to speak with you about the Edinburgh attack." He walked over to her, both angry that he had to go talk to people who wouldn't understand what he was saying, and infatuated with the way her auburn hair fell perfectly over her ear and shoulder. He walked over to her and touched her shoulder.

"Now that wasn't so hard, was it?" She smiled and shied away. He smiled as he turned, but then sighed as he reached the room. He would have far preferred staying with the secretary.

ROCKS AND HARD PLACES

1018 hours, July 17, Girishk
Helmand Province, Afghanistan

Jakub looked out from his roof with a feeling of desire overpowering his thoughts, capturing his mind as he waited for the outside world to decide what to do with him. That's how he felt, really, as though whatever happened next had nothing to do with his desires or his decisions—that his future rested on someone else's shoulders. He hated that feeling. He wanted control, but the world wouldn't give it to him anymore. He remembered reading an article in an old newspaper when he was younger, about being trapped by decisions—being stuck between a "rock and a hard place" as the writer put it. He remembered how free that article made him feel, because he was the master of his own fate with no lack of options. He was allowed to be anything he desired simply because the world wasn't about to step across him; he stood in charge of those around him, and no one could tell him how or what he could do. But that was how he felt before he met Zahid, before that rock showed up and slowly roped him tighter into his plans until one day, he found that not everything was under his control now, not everything he had before was still his; a part of his life now belonged to Zahid. He hated that feeling too.

He heard a car honking below, loud and long enough to shock him out of his daydream, and the goats out of the road; the goat herder was still jeering at the car even after it had moved on.

For a moment, as that black car had passed, Jakub thought it might be the other side of the world coming to knock on his door, the CIA reaching out through one of their most famous ways of getting people to feel indebted to them. This character he had met only a few days before now had quite a handle on him. Somehow, someway Jakub could barely understand, Agent Windburg and his men had found out almost everything about him, and they knew not only what he was doing but who he was doing it with. Now, all because he made a profit from one guy, someone else was there to make their own profit from him, but they would have to use him like bait. He felt like bait, too, as if he were simply hanging out so one animal could snatch another. *A rock and a hard place,* he repeated in his mind, he hated that feeling most of all.

Leena closed her eyes and waited for him to move again, waiting for the stairs to creek or the boards on the roof to whine, to just make some noise to let her know he was still there. He was always quiet now, no real conversing with anyone besides the occasional purchaser looking to buy something from him—especially with her. When he ate, he ate quickly and went back upstairs so that he wouldn't feel obligated to talk to her about what was going on inside his head. In truth, she already knew what was in his head, already understood what was eating at him, that wasn't what she wanted, wasn't what she was looking for. She wanted to talk to him about it, to be informed by the man that she had stood by and trusted for years, but he was afraid. Yes, the CIA, she had figured out from his small rants he would give after drinking a little too much, but even then he was angrier at them than afraid. It was this *other* man who he had only named once; this Zahid person seemed to be the only one who was keeping her husband's mouth closed, hands tied, and holding him down as if he were simply a pawn in this man's game. A small piece in the puzzle that created a picture that she couldn't see, but she didn't want to either. She only wanted her husband to understand that he was strong, to know that she would stay with him, and fight with him if she had too. She didn't care about who these other men were; she knew they were just taking up his strength and stifling him but that was all, and she knew she could beat that if he would just let her in.

Footsteps above her caused her to open her eyes; she could feel herself hoping he would just open the door and come down the stairs or even call for her to come to his side. She wished to be near him so badly, everything inside her telling her that he needed her, though she knew she had little to offer. But he was alone, and she wished she could make him feel as he had done for her those years before. She was a young woman without a home, living off from people who used her, made her steal, and made her feel alone. But he helped her. He was the one who, even though he at first seemed just like the others he saved her, protected her; made her feel like she wasn't alone or afraid. But now he was sitting by himself, asking for nothing and slowly letting the time around him slip by just as she had done, when she still prayed that her time on the earth would come to an end. She knew what she had to do, she knew that to help him; the only thing she could do was to act as he had done and ignore the protests and simply protect. So she rose from where she had been sitting, apprehension taking the form of a lump in her throat as she climbed the stairs, opened the door, and found him standing with his arms resting against the roof, his head drooped as he stared blankly at the ground below him. He reminded her exactly of her when she was still alone, and so she decided she would ask him the same question he had asked her.

"Who can I beat up for you?" He didn't move for a moment, still and calm as if he had heard nothing from her, but he only lasted a few moments until she heard him laugh just a little, a small jerking in his shoulders and a long, choppy sigh as he tried to stifle his laugh. She smiled, satisfied with the fact that she might just get him to talk.

"Uh…everyone would be nice," he answered sarcastically. She giggled and walked over to the edge of their loft next to him, all the while still looking up at his eyes. He smiled at her, his eyes still as caring as they had been when he first came to her.

"Is there anything I can do, Jakub?" His smile started to fade; he didn't want to talk of his problems. She noticed. "You don't have to worry about me, Jakub, I fended for myself before you, and so I can handle whatever you feel that I can't."

"I already told you, Leena."

"Yes, you told me that you can't tell me anything. I can't accept that, Jakub, not after all the other things I've seen."

"No."

"Jakub, you told me you would get us out of here. Out to America, right?"

"Yes, and I will."

"Then if you know what's going to happen, why can't I know why it's happening?"

"Because telling you could have both of us killed! You want me to have that to worry about too, Leena!" His shouts stunned her; she wasn't expecting it, but she knew exactly how to deal with it. She smacked him across the face.

"You have no right to keep this from me, Jakub! I have watched as you fought for everything else as if the world couldn't touch you, and now you let men step in front of you and change your mind for you." He stayed silent, covering his eyes with the palm of his hand. "You know that I love you, and I know you are scared, but if you will just trust me it will be easier for you. I promise, Jakub, I can handle it."

"Leena, get back." His voice was cold, and he began to stand straight, the muscles in his back shifting underneath his shirt as he moved her away from the edge of the loft.

"Jakub, you can't just shoo me away like this, I want to know what—"

"Leena!" He turned, his steely blue eyes hard and forceful as he toned his voice down and whispered. "Get back and sit down."

"Okay, I'm sitting." She noticed he was watching something below, something moving toward the house. "What is it?" she asked. "Who's there?"

—∞—

Jakub held his hand against the door, waiting patiently for the knock to come. His other hand rested loosely on the revolver in his pocket, the cold steel giving a small comfort to him as he waited for whoever was coming from the road to touch the door and announce who he was. What happened after that would depend on whatever Jakub decided: either the door or the trigger. Then the knock came, a loud, heavy knock that seemed almost urgent. "Can I help you?" Jakub called through the door.

"I am here from our mutual friend, Mister Sorvi." Jakub removed his revolver and pointed it toward the door, prepared to fire.

"Would you like to tell me who that friend would be?" Silence followed for a few moments until he heard more steps come to the door, and a more familiar voice called through.

"Jakub, this is Agent Windburg, you're gonna need to put that gun away and let me in."

"How do you know I have a gun?" A familiar chill touched the back of Jakub's neck, a circular hole that would most certainly be attached to a gun.

"I told him." Jakub instantly remembered the voice; the man in black was who it belonged to. "Now open the door." Jakub slowly unlocked and opened the door, stepping back widely to the right. He set his gun on the ledge near the door.

"When will there be some trust between us Jakub, hmm?"

"Around the same time you stop sending your dog through my back door. You talk about trust when even you don't have any." Jakub was still scowling at the men as two more came through the door, dragging a large case inside and setting it underneath the table. Jakub sat and offered the men seating as well, all but the dark-clothed man, who opted to stand near the window. "Why are you here, Agent Windburg?"

"Because it's time, Jakub. We know what our man looks like, we know what he's going to use, and we're pretty sure as to where he is. You've done your job, and we feel pretty safe in letting you through to the other side of the hole you've dug for yourself."

"And apparently someone else as well." The man behind him nodded toward the door at the end of the kitchen. Jakub froze in his seat; he had wanted to make sure it was safe before he brought her out.

"Tell her it's all right, Jakub, we'll not let anything happen to either of you."

"Leena." Jakub waited for a moment, looking around at each of the men to see if anything seemed to be off; he had no choice in the end. He called her out.

"Ma'am," he greeted her, standing up and offering the chair as he did. She only eyed him a little then walked directly over to her husband and stood next to him. She grabbed his hand beneath their line of sight, and he gratefully held her. Agent Windburg just smiled.

"We've been waiting for a while, you know." Leena broke the silence. "You know we're in danger and yet you took your time, even though we had given you everything days ago." The words were cold to the tongue and, she assumed, stinging to this agent's ears.

"Listen, ma'am. I can understand your frustration. Apparently you and your husband have talked enough to scare you, but I can assure you that you shouldn't be scared."

"I will be assured when both I and my husband are sitting in one of your American planes." Her eyes never left his.

"Jakub." He looked over to the now far less tense man. "You should have let her negotiate, she probably could have got you a job at the CIA," he joked, although for him it was more an attempt to regain supremacy in the conversation, but for Jakub, it just made him angry. It felt good to just be angry again.

"I am tired of waiting, Windburg, I want to leave. Now!" One of the new men jumped at the shout and reached for his pistol but was waved off by Windburg as he himself stood and handed Jakub a large folder. Jakub opened it, finding several pictures and documents, all with information about him, or at least who they decided he would be once he made it into the States. But there was a problem that became immediately apparent. "Where are the rest?"

"The rest of what, Jakub?"

"The other papers, the one's for my wife, where are they?"

"Jakub, you never showed me her, gave me a picture, nothing. She's not in the deal, Jakub."

"You son of a bitch!"

He arose ferociously, pure fury pouring off of him. "You told me that all this would be for both of us!?"

"Jakub," his voice was still eerily calm, "as far as I see, you never gave me enough information to help her, and so now, you need to do just a little bit more if we're gonna make this deal count. Am I making sense?"

"Yes." Jakub started to sit, feeling like he was still trapped, again held between the two parts of the world. His fear returned, and Leena noticed.

"Listen, you take my husband and let him go, I don't need to go yet. I will be safe here."

"No!" Jakub shouted.

"Jakub, they can't keep controlling you like this, or it will never end. I say no, we've done enough!" She turned her fiery gaze toward Agent Windburg, who averted his eyes and stood, walking toward the door.

"No, Leena, I will not leave you here."

"Jakub, she will be protected, that I can promise you. By the time you're done with just a small amount of information, she'll be on her way to you."

"Forgive me if your promises don't assure me," Jakub snapped back. He stood to go with Windburg, still holding her hand as he pulled her along. Unwillingly she went. As they did, Agent Windburg nodded to the box under the table, and the two agents pulled it out and began to remove tools, along with gasoline and several other tools. Before Jakub could see what else, however, the man in black closed the door and herded the couple toward an armored Humvee at the end of the short road. It was when he finally sat down inside that Jakub realized, finally, that he had made his choice, that the world never really controlled him, just limited his options. He had removed the rock and now was climbing that last hard place. "What else do you need me to do?" he demanded from the agent, who only just then had made his way passed him and into the rear of the passenger seat.

"Jakub, good things come to those who wait."

"Apparently not," he remarked. Agent Windburg just smiled.

"You will be informed at the base."

"What base?"

"Forward Operating Base Edinburgh, Jakub. That's your last stop till America."

BATE

1800 hours, July 17, Forward Operating Base Edinburgh Helmand Province, Afghanistan

Calm, quiet, unmoving, and soundless. The desert sat in a haze of blistering heat, stagnate winds, and shimmering sand from the now-uninterrupted light of the sun. The hills around the camp that were once ominous in their darkness became intimidating in their size during the day. It seemed as if, like the stories about most deserts, that the only thing residing here was death itself. A wasteland of only ash and sand, at least until the uniform nature of the desert abruptly ended at the base of the now bustling grounds of FOB Edinburgh. It was around and over this area alone that the silence was interrupted by the eyes-in-the-sky, with both reconnaissance fighters and fast-moving Apaches constantly scanning the hills and valleys for a threat. For those who would see this, it provided a sense of safety, a sense of control over the land where death roams. For a soldier, those sounds were the gentle hum of strength or the roar of power to out muscle any enemy. Yet to others, those who would fight against it, those sounds were of a different world entirely—one that would over power any foe that met with it on flat ground. For those who could not fight it, the sound meant fear. For those who would, the sound simply meant that the ground was no longer flat, and the advantage would go to whoever struck first. It was inside the base one such member was stationed, listening carefully to the sounds and watching the sky with the same mind as a hunter after dangerous game. He sat in the small room knowingly behind his enemy's believed defenses, careful to let no one see him in true form. Now alone, in a small tent where most that come have already moved on. It was a place of solitude, and now, a post for him to make his call, and so Zahid removed his radio, still on a frequency too encrypted to be broken, and used too little to become a trace.

"Saben," he spoke into the radio and waited patiently for the response. A few moments later, it came in as an echo of his phrase.

"What do you know, Amir?" Hassan, his friend and former squad member, used the name sarcastically, as neither he nor Zahid believed in the cause that the name came with, but it gave useful assets to him so he used it.

"It would seem that, despite our careful work, we have a broken link."

"One of the men?"

"No." Zahid gave a small sigh, disappointed but still unsurprised. "It would be my armor bearer. He has opted to fall on his sword and take me with him."

"What has he told them?"

"Enough for them to know I'm here and what to look for. One of their agents went directly to where it was, as if he knew exactly where to look."

"What about the rest of this does he know?" Hassan's voice was now very tense, noticeable even over the grainy noise of the radio.

"Nothing, his involvement ended with the last shipment."

"Then the threat has passed."

"Don't assume, Hassan. I need to make sure he knows nothing more, and then I need to remind him of why he shouldn't have been speaking." Zahid moved up from against the wall and toward the entrance of the tent, slowly letting his eyes adjust to the light.

"What do you need me to do?"

"You know where he lives, yes?" Hassan said he did.

"Then you will…" Zahid's eyes finally adjusted, and as if he were meant to, he caught a glimpse of someone on the other side of the camp, someone he recognized and immediately knew who it was. "Hassan?"

"Yes?"

"I need you to go to the house, bring the other two, and see who is there. Report to me as soon as you can."

"Yes, sir, may I know what we're looking for?"

"Well, you can be sure that Jakub won't be there."

"Why?"

"Because I am watching him right now."

Jakub sat at the long picnic table as a child who knows he shouldn't be in his parent's room, too many things flying through his head about how he could get caught. Everywhere he looked were Marines, notorious for being the ones who would bring a hell of a lot of pain to an enemy they found, and there he was sitting inside their turf like a bee in a hornet's nest. He felt like praying but then remembered he helped a terrorist and started feeling even less welcome. It was in this attitude that he had been walking for the last hour with Windburg and was still jumpy when Windburg finally came up from behind him and offered him food. His fearful reaction was almost comical for those who watched him, but for him it was just another chance at getting found out.

"No, thank you," he spoke in a low voice, no real expression of gratitude present in his voice.

"Suit yourself." Windburg sat down across from his informant, calmly picking away at a plate full of what appeared to be food. However it smelled rather different.

"What am I doing here? You told me I would be working, and now you have me just sitting here."

"You need to be patient, Jakub. Why must I keep explaining this to you?"

"Because I won't be satisfied till my wife is here with me. So I'll ask again, what am I doing here?"

"Are you really not hungry? There's plenty of these Meal, Ready to Eat left." Windburg evaded the question, so Jakub evaded the answer. "Come on, we'll talk while we walk." He stood, leaving much of the meal left on his plate. The two walked passed a long line of soldiers, all waiting for their share of the meals and all still very agitated by the cleanup they have been forced to do. Jakub could smell the fight in those men, each was trained and ready to fight an enemy; they just needed a target. Thus Jakub felt a lot more secure once he got away from the group; he didn't fell like becoming their target. "Basically, Jakub," Agent Windburg broke the silence, "you are here because I can't find him, and I think you might be able to help with that."

"What do you mean? I already told you what I know about him."

"I'm not convinced. I mean, don't you find it convenient that he disappears, any trace we have on him gone as soon as you finally spill what you say was 'all you know'?"

"Hey, I told you what I know, I left nothing out, and you want to blame me because you guys can't find him." The two stopped in the middle of a large gravel field; it felt to Jakub that he was surrounded—out of place and vulnerable. Something was wrong.

"Jakub, what else can you tell me of Zahid? What are you hiding?" His voice was growing angrier.

"I have nothing to tell!"

"Bullshit! What are you hiding, Jakub?!" Jakub started to realize what was happening.

"You don't want to hold up your end of the deal. You don't want to help me."

"Jakub I can't help you unless you tell me!" People were starting to look, more and more watchers and wonderers paying closer attention.

"Why am I here? You know I can't get you anything more, so why do you demand I give what I don't have?" he spoke softly, trying to bring the tone of the conversation back to a calm level. It was then he saw the young agent's face; he could see something near shame for just a moment, but it quickly reverted back to anger, and he grabbed Jakub by the arm.

"All right, seeing how you don't feel like helping you are going to spend your time in the stockade until you're more agreeable." With that, two MPs approached and took Jakub away. Within only a few moments, he was being walked back through a building and into a cell, cursing at Windburg and the guards as he went. Once they were alone, Windburg ordered Jakub to be quiet, his face now as guilty as it had looked before. "Listen, the reason you are here is because I have reason to believe that Zahid is in this base." The news shocked Jakub into submission, total fear of him, but not enough to keep him from protesting.

"You brought me right to him you bastard." A sinking pit was forming in his stomach.

"I'm sorry, but that is exactly why I brought you here. We need him to show himself."

"So you want him to come after me."

"You should have just told us about your wife the first time, then this wouldn't—"

"He will kill me, Windburg. If he knows I'm here it doesn't matter what you do. I won't survive the night."

"Not if we catch him first."

"You have no idea who you're dealing with." His voice was chillingly low. "Someone who has taken on a base such as this, and decimated soldiers and still remains untouched and you believe he will fall in just one night?"

"We have to take that chance."

"He is not normal. He has a fight unlike anyone I've ever met. He will not fail in this—especially because the CIA is involved."

"What do you mean?"

"You'll find out."

—◦◦◦—

"Saben." A voice came through the radio, far more crisp sounding in the evening hours now that there was less traffic. Zahid acknowledged. "Amir, we are at the house, there seems to be at least two men inside the house and a woman. His wife, from what I can see."

"Well then, get control of her, kill the men guarding her, and inform me when you have her." Zahid looked out toward the stockade, watching as a lone guard paced back and forth at the entrance. "I think we may have one more use of our old friend." He clicked the radio off.

WHITE NOISES

2216 hours, July 17, Forward Operating Base Edinburgh Helmand Province, Afghanistan

Hanson sat motionless in his barracks, the hours already having slipped by with him still on his back, thinking incessantly about what he could do, how he could keep searching for Zahid. He knew he might be on base, but he also knew he might have already left and Hanson could just be waiting for nothing. He wondered aloud, or at least it felt aloud, of whether he was close, whether the dark-eyed thing that plagued his dreams had finally slowed its run or was out of his reach again. He closed his eyes, the face of the one he was after, the picture that seemed so normal for any other person was instead the mug shot of a real-life monster. The picture was strange, as he remembered it, as the person in it was looking past him, unaware of the fact that a picture was being taken but still he had an aura around him. His jawline seemed to be set in stone, yet his arms rested as though he could flow himself through the picture in his mind; his persona commanded fear, yet Hanson felt something more. As he sat up from the bed, he looked around him, feeling completely alone inside the dark barracks. He didn't want to be alone; he wished he could go back to the camp, go to the place where he knew he would find a girl he still had feelings for. He hated the fact that he lied to her, using her to learn the face he wished he could forget; he hated himself for that.

Hanson remembered this feeling of loneliness, as if his whole skill set was useless and he couldn't do anything about it;

it reminded him of being in the hospital. He remembered the one soldier he didn't know, the one that had a heart attack while rooming next to him. He remembered the other men, who he didn't know, some dying and most hurting, all wishing they were somewhere else just like him and all needing someone to talk to, or at least someone to care. So Hanson decided to head out from the barracks, grabbing his uniform jacket and wrapping it around his shoulders on his way out of the door. He knew the med center, a place far less comfortable than the hospital he had stayed at, was only just on the other side of the line of buildings in front of him, so slowly he made his way around by the road, eventually coming up just a little short so that he could still see the stars without the bright lights of the hangar drowning them out. As he watched, he noticed the stars were immensely bright, as if they were glinting with pride that they were so peaceful while the world they smiled upon fell further into violence. But tonight it was calm, at least so he thought, until he made his way finally to the entrance of the med center and found the whole place bustling with something near chaos. Hundreds of people, all wearing white, moved as if they were in trenches, quickly shuffling their way by each other to tend to the next wounded soldier. The beds were white, the sheets were white, even the lower part of the walls was covered by white drapes the sectioned off patients that were more stable than the ones in the center of the room, where much of the white was mixed with a crimson that most people never see. The colors were striking, vivid enough to bring a memory of a bloody arm, a torn patch, staples in a wound and crimson in the sand all flashing through his mind's eye. He looked up to the rafters, trying to clear his vision of the vicious scene below, but instead found that as he looked up into the darkness he swore that he could see movement, all across the ceiling something flowing. First sand, then smoke, he couldn't tell for sure. As he watched, he realized what it meant, why he continued to see this shroud over death; it was what brought it. The sands and smoke had become to him like the harbinger of the dark, the bringer of something he couldn't pin down, but he knew existed. Trying to clear his mind, he looked to the ground, concrete smoothly carrying him toward the side of the room until he found his way through one of the side chambers, separated by the white curtains, where another soldier lay. The man wore a medical gown, but above that, a large patch of gauze wrapped from his neck up the side of his face, pools of red still pushing their way slowly through the bandages. Yet Hanson was calm, the man seemed calm, and both men had their scars. Hanson wished he could go back, wished he could've pushed Billy that much farther, and even died himself to save him. Hanson couldn't stand the feelings he had; he was already so fatigued from the constant roar of anger, and the incessant white noise of revenge, gripping his dreams and blurring his vision. Then he realized that had Billy been in his place, he would have to deal with the same pain; he wouldn't wish that on anyone. As he watched the poor man's breath slowly, he saw something that, strangely in his mind, felt peaceful; even though both men had seen some of the worst that war could throw at them. Hanson wanted to talk to him, ask him how he felt, what he was going to do, but then he realized that he had been through what this man had, and the soldier still had to wake up from the pain and realize that the same world he knew was gone. Hanson knew the killer he was hunting; this man was as any other soldier in that his enemy could be anywhere, he had nowhere to pin his anger, to direct his vengeance besides the next battle he faces, the next enemy he kills. Hanson had seen enough; he couldn't be in that place anymore, and so he forced himself back through the labyrinth of beds and medics until he made his way out into the night once again.

It was strange for him, as he looked up into the night sky, because it still hadn't changed. It wasn't strange because he expected it to, but rather because even with the things he'd seen, even with all the blood and all the wreckage that this fight had left the stars still were shining; the night only waits, only watches, but still won't change. He hated that most of all.

———◦◦◦———

Jakub sat in his cell, thinking about Czechoslovakia, about the last time he had gone fishing in a lake. He wasn't thinking about the peace he felt, or the happiness that he gained from catching the big fish. Instead, he was thinking about the worm, how it had no choice in the manner of its demise, but he simply had to wait in a cold, dark container for either the day to end or for fisherman to jab a hook through it and send into the murky depths of some unknown pool of water. It was only then, sitting in the cell that he'd ever really thought about the bate, never really felt bad for it or wanted to give it a better option, because sitting in that container waiting for something to happen just gave him one more reason to compare himself to the worm, and either the fisherman or the fish would be coming around soon.

A noise came from the end of the hall, a subtle, very muffled squirming in the rubble outside the stockade. He scooted off his cot and pressed his head against the bars, trying to see what was going on at the front. He heard the guard start to move toward the noise, but he said nothing, only shined his flashlight back and forth over the area which cast a dark shadow on the barred windows through Jakub's cell. The light had just died away when Jakub finally noticed something on the floor in front of him. It was white, only a piece of paper wrapped around something else. He reached out and picked it from the ground, his hands shaking at the ever-growing sense of a predator nearby; the object wrapped in paper was a knife. It was as he unwrapped it that he knew who had sent it, for it only read a few short sentences followed by an order at the bottom for him to destroy the note before he left the cell the next morning. He read the text, and immediately the coldest chill ran down his now burning back. The note was simple; its orders were clear and the consequences were chilling: "I Know What You Have Done" it read "Now Follow What I Say or Leena Dies."

WHERE ALLEGIANCE LIES

**0800 hours, July 18, Forward Operating Base Edinburgh
Helmand Province, Afghanistan**

Agent Windburg sat fuming in the passenger seat of the Humvee, driving clear across the base to the stockade wondering what he was going to do to Jakub. A few minutes ago, he received word that his guards who were watching Jakub's wife had been killed; the girl was taken. Originally he suspected the bomber or a band of the same organization the bomber works for, but that idea had passed when he realized that she was not dead and Jakub was safe in his custody. Jakub had some explaining to do.

The Humvee pulled up alongside the entrance of the stockade, kicking up gravel and clouds of dust as it skidded to a stop. The dust was still rolling beneath the vehicle when Windburg opened the door and marched through the entrance; Jakub was just sitting up from his bed when Windburg opened the door kicked Jakub in the chest, sending him hard into the concrete wall of his cell.

"What the hell happened to my men, Jakub?" He reached over and grabbed him by the collar, yanking him back to attention.

"What are you talking about?"

"Don't play dumb with me!" He clenched his fist and punched him in the jaw, Jakub kicked him away, but the guard drew and aimed his rifle at him. Agent Windburg stood straight again. "Who did you send, huh!? Did you tip off the bomber; you think he's worse than me on a bad day!?"

"Yes." The answer came with a voice of forced anger; Jakub's eyes showed pity instead.

"Well, you're mistaken. Now if you want anything beside a bullet to the head or a military tribunal, then you better start talking!"

"I'm saying nothing until…" he hesitated clearly not wanting to speak.

"What, what do you think I'll give you?"

"I need to get out of here. I'm not speaking until you get me out of here and on the road and on our way back to my home."

"I could just leave you here, leave the door open, and wait for your Zahid to come kill you. Is that an option?"

"Not if you want to catch the kill team that massacred your men." He stood and looked directly into Windburg's eyes. "Now get me out of here."

Jakub watched the mirror to see how far away the base was behind them, watching each small spec as it lifted and moved from his vision; he assumed they were helicopters. He eyed Windburg, who sat with his side pressed against the glass of the Humvee while staring out the window, his whole mind focused on what he would do next. He watched the guard in the passenger seat, watched how every few moments he would close his eyes in the warmth of the sun, resting from a knight that had had little for him. He looked back up into the mirror, the base shrinking ever smaller into the horizon behind them, the helicopters no longer visible from their distance. Then he looked at the driver, calm and fluid with the long turn, skin dark from the time he'd most likely spent in the sands of the desert. Something was strange about him, something familiar, but Jakub couldn't place it. Jakub tried to get a better look, but Agent Windburg spoke up.

"All right, Jakub, your out of the camp and safe, now what the hell happened?"

"There is a group of men, they work for Zahid, and they are very dedicated. From what I know, they were with him even before he came to Afghanistan, and they do his heavy lifting."

"Well, what about them, how did they know about you, huh?"

"You're the one who brought me to that base, trying to make me bait. Well, he outsmarted you."

"No, he outsmarted you," Windburg retorted, sitting up and turning toward Jakub. "It's not my wife he has, Jakub."

"He knows that, I'm all he needed."

"Well, it looks like you won't be very helpful way out here."

Jakub turned his head away angrily, getting one last look at the guard in the seat, who had had his eyes closed for over a minute. He looked into the rearview mirror, trying to see the driver's face but stopped at his eyes. They were black as night, cold and stern. The driver's hands flowed from the steering wheel to the shifter and then back to the wheel. Then he looked at Jakub, and he knew who the driver was. Time was up. Jakub leaped forward, removing the blade he had concealed the night before, and rammed it into the guard's neck, blood spattering onto the windshield and roof of the car while a torrent of crimson flowed down his neck. Agent Windburg went for his gun but was knocked off balance as the driver of the Humvee fish tailed, allowing Jakub to lurch backward and pin Windburg's arm against the door, striking him in the head several times with his elbow as he fought for control of the gun. The vehicle slowed rapidly, then the dead body of the guard smacking up against the hard dash as it did. Agent Windburg, trying desperately to keep Jakub from getting the gun found the handle with his free hand and burst open the door, causing him to fall out but allowing him to free his gun hand. From there, he could see everything that happened, his consciousness amplified by the adrenalin surging through his blood stream. He could see Jakub's face as he fell out atop of him; sweat glistening as the shadow of the Humvee passed over his face into the sunlight. He could feel the rigid resistance of the trigger as he prepared to fire the pistol in his hand, aiming closer and closer to Jakub's chest. It was as he contacted the ground with his back, the hot sand spreading beneath him like an opening grave that he finally overpowered the trigger, and a shot rang out.

Jakub barely felt the round hit his chest, only he knew it when he smashed into the ground and tried to push up; his arm was useless. He rolled over onto his back, clasping his right side with his left arm while pushing himself up against the Humvee. In front of him, Agent Windburg stood, the pistol in his right hand and the knife being dragged up from the ground in his left. They eyed each other for a moment, realizing immediately that the agent still stood. Jakub closed his eyes, darkness filling his mind until he rested on one image; his wife standing before him on the roof of their home. He could even hear her voice, smell her fragrance; he had failed her, and so he waited for the second shot. Then he heard a struggle, someone else was fighting before him. He opened his eyes and found the driver had forced Windburg to the ground, the pistol already pulled and thrown away. Jakub could only watch from behind as the driver rammed his leg down upon Windburg, holding him still as he wrenched the knife away. It was then that Jakub froze, watching in horror as the knife was raised high above the two, then fell like a guillotine; it took only a few moments for Windburg's legs to stop squirming. He looked up as the driver stood, removed his helmet, turned around, and found himself staring again into the cold eyes of Zahid. He looked at the man fearfully, silently praying for something in his mind until he wanted it enough to ask.

"I did what you said, will you spare my wife?" Jakub felt warm streams running down his face, and as the wind blew slightly, they cooled.

"You did what I asked, your wife is safe." Jakub sighed with relief, his heart lifted by the words. "But you will not be spared."

When Jakub heard this, it surprised him that he was still calm, still happy. He didn't care, as long as she was safe.

"Thank you." He barely had the words out before Zahid lifted the pistol from the ground, aimed it at Jakub, and fired once again. Darkness filled Jakub's mind again; the last he saw was the image of his wife. Then his mind went black.

—◦◦◦—

Zahid dropped the pistol, his gloves and the knife all glazed with blood. He looked around him; the three dead men all silent as if waiting for him to move. So he did. He reached back over to Agent Windburg's body, taking off his gloves to search through the pockets until he found a phone. He removed it from the pouch and unlocked the small touch screen. He found the message system and began searching for the name. It had been several years since he learned the name of the man who killed his family, several years since the little boy holding his mother's hand lost everything to someone who used them to steal. Now he was there, holding the cell phone that on its screen had his name as if it were just any other. He clicked on the name "Matthews" and typed a short message into the phone. It was something he'd seen in his dreams, written on the walls of his mind, a few words that he'd held for so long that they felt like fire in his fingers as he fixed them to the message. He stared at it before he sent, still shocked and invigorated at seeing them written on a piece of his enemy, and so he waited; he read it one last time for the world around him to hear.

"This is my fire, it burns for you." He pressed the send button and threw the phone into the sand. Carefully he removed the pistol again and aimed at his own arm and fired. He would radio back to the base, they would come to take him away, and he would soon be standing on the grounds of the Outsider's beloved Camp Bastion.

CALLED OUT

0305 hours, July 17, Denver, Colorado, USA

Agent Richard Matthews was sound asleep when he heard a very faint ringing. At first he took it as just a noise, something he would allow to just fade away into his subconscious and allow himself to rest all the more. But something else inside him stirred. Slowly he began to awake, gripping the walls of the deep slumber his mind had fallen into and chasing the ringing, edging closer and closer to consciousness. Another ring, another surge until finally he broke through his dreams and opened his eyes, the ringing now pungent sound in his ears; someone was calling him. Slowly he slid his legs out from under the blanket, his taut calves flexing as he pressed them into a warm pair of slippers. As he walked toward the large dresser, another ring shouted through the air, reminding him that it wasn't a call, but a message. He wondered who would be sending him a message so late, then he remembered that his subordinate Steven Windburg would already be up and working, and so a slight bit of anger came over him as he wished the man would just wait for some things, but it must have been important. He picked up his phone off the dresser and checked the screen; it was a message from his office. "Be ready at your door in five minutes." It read, "Meeting with directors." Something important had happened, and it seemed Agent Windburg had decided not to inform him.

Matthews sat in a large chair at a semi-circular desk in the main conference room, a printed copy of a message and pictures spread out before him; all taken less than twenty minutes ago. On the white sheet of paper in front of him, the message that had been sent from Agent Windburg's phone sat in bold print, a grainy picture of his body below it. The surrounding photos all were of far better quality, but they were of two other bodies from the Humvee crash, along with several from a torched building where the Jakub contact had been; three bodies including a woman were only partly pulled from the rubble. Four large computer screens were on the wall in front of him, aligned so that each was facing him to allow for the director and his advisors to all have a clear shot of Matthews. All were silent as Matthews poured over the things on the table, focusing intently on the message. It had been sent to him, but he had never received it; instead it was intercepted and blocked by the agency, shown directly to the director; now everyone sat watching what he would do. However, after more than five minutes of silence, the director grew impatient, and so he asked a question.

"What do you think this means, Richard?"

"Well I'm not sure, sir. It seems to have been sent to me."

"Yes, it does." Matthews tried to find a way to play it off, act like there was no reason for him to have gotten that message, but he knew it would be a thin excuse.

"Sir, the best I can gather is that it was someone who doesn't like the CIA, found out Agent Windburg was one of ours and decided to make a point. This doesn't have anything to do with me, gentlemen."

"I thought you read the message, Agent Matthews. I mean, that plus that picture of our boy there makes it look pretty personal, don't you think?" one of the advisors said, trying to back his director up.

"Listen, Windburg and I contacted each other all the time—"

"So you must know what he got himself in to?" It was a question, but it sounded like a statement.

"What I mean by that is that I was the last one on his phone, the perp just pressed redial."

"You sure seem a lot more interested in telling us what you didn't do than telling us what you know." The director resituated himself. "I don't have much time for more of this so I need you to tell me. What the hell was Agent Windburg wound up in?"

"Sir, in this picture here"—he held up the picture of Jakub—"this is the body of Jakub Sorvi. He was the supplier to the bomber we have been tracking throughout Helmand Province. The reason we're so interested is because he is a part of a brand new insurgency group grown right in the heart of enemy controlled zones. He and this group—"

"Is that the Fire Brotherhood or something like that?" The deputy director asked.

"No, it's been called, at least by what Jakub told us after Agent Windburg turned him into an asset, the Brotherhood of Cleansing Fire. As I was saying, before it and the bomber are responsible for the last eight of the worst attacks in Helmand, Afghanistan, and the rest of the world, including the FOB Edinburgh attack."

"Then it's safe to say they found out about your asset."

"Yes, sir, it seems so."

"Now, because this character seems relatively attached to you, it would seem that there are some things we should be looking into during your time in Afghanistan."

"Are you accusing me, sir?"

"I'm not accusing you of anything, but there is too much in that message to say that there isn't at least something we'll need to look into."

"Sir," one of the director's assistants spoke up, "I can get our people running the investigation by tonight."

"No, we're going to use CID, we'll give them the records and they can look 'em up." That news was not easily accepted, as the CID would love to find something and get their hands on information; that meant they'd be thorough. Matthews didn't like that.

From then on, the meeting was a blur; most of it spent with Agent Matthews in silence. He listened only halfway as they explained that everything was getting too out of hand, too much damage over too little time, and it needed to be fixed. He partly heard them complement him on his earlier work when he was still in Afghanistan, when he destabilized a group just like the Brotherhood that seemed to be dominating the area. Instead of really paying attention, however, his mind drifted back to the message on the table. As he searched through its words, he confessed to himself that it was sent to him, that the dead men in those pictures were all a part of the message that its writer was after him, and now he had done enough to bring him Agent Matthews in reach. He realized that whoever this was remembers something that only he knows of, a time when he grew rich; and in order to hide where he gained his wealth, he had to eliminate his assets. This bomber, this "Zahid," was after him, but now he was after Zahid.

"...so we will need you to go back to Afghanistan in order to clean this all up." The words seemed like they were just a little too late. He already knew where he was going, all that remained...

"When do I leave for Camp Bastion?"

SECTION THREE

INFERNO

ARRIVAL

1025 hours, July 20, Camp Bastion
Helmand Province, Afghanistan

"Celia, did you grab that file?" one of the analysts bellowed from his desk.

"Yes! It's on the desk behind you!" She smiled at his laziness, and he accepted it with a grin.

The entire building was buzzing with activity, everyone wanting to have a hand in an investigation as exciting as the one they'd been handed. For them, getting information from the CIA was great, but getting those files and using them to investigate a company agent was literally Christmas in July. It seemed like every person that she worked with was analyzing some string of data or another file to try and find something interesting. That was the strange part for Celia, the fact that they were more interested in just knowing what happened in a situation rather than figuring out why or who; they just wanted the information, but Celia wanted more.

"Hey, Chris, do you have that Kandahar file?" she called out, scanning the room to see if she could catch a glimpse of him. No reply. "Chris!?" she called out louder, still no answer. However some of the people began to clear an area near the far left wall, and she saw him sitting at a desk staring into a file with several other's stacked at his side. As she approached, he noticed and quickly turned the page he was on; Celia paid no attention.

"Hi," he sputtered, seeming very uncomfortable as he squirmed in his chair to stand.

"Hi, Chris." She noticed he wouldn't stop staring at her eyes. "You all right?"

"Oh…yeah, I'm fine." He looked around him for a moment, noticed the mess, and started to straighten up. "Um…did you need something?" he tried to sound busy.

"Yes, um, do you have the Kandahar file?" within three seconds, it was in her hand, the pile of folders neatly cut in half to give it to her. "Wow, thanks." She smiled, and he gleamed with pride; however, he looked away to try to avoid staring again. "Okay," she started, "I'll get back to it then."

"All right."

She turned and walked back to her desk, unaware that he was still watching her as she went. She sat down, obviously excited by some of the abnormalities she had already noticed in some of the other files and hoping to figure out what they meant. They weren't large; in fact, they were almost small enough to overlook, but still something was off in the accounting, other things were off in communications with contacts, abrupt disinterest by assets and increases in taxes despite no apparent increase in pay. Whoever this "Agent Matthews" was, he had spiked enough interest in the agency to get CID involved, and that meant scandal. Being a girl made "scandal" all the more interesting; being an investigator made it her job to be interested. From where she sat, she couldn't lose. Thus, she began to dig into the file, marking each abnormality she could find but focusing on the assets; there were just too many changes, she noticed, right before Agent Matthews left Afghanistan for his swivel chair in the States.

As her mind chewed through the file, she began to see the names of assets formed in Kandahar with more and more frequency. Each asset, which she found strange, seemed only to be used for small-time locations on ammo caches or the occasional red flag for a terrorist, but none were ever really dealt with. Frankly it was strange that ammo plots and low-level terrorists would mean much for the CIA. Cleanup wasn't their job; that belonged to the guys in camouflage. Then, without much warning, a steady contact would drop off the radar, no record of fighting or abduction; only a report that the contact had failed and contact had been severed. Now, this was relatively common in that type of work, she knew, but to have four or five all near the departure date was odd. So she started to study the contacts, and things were becoming interesting.

Hanson stood at attention with several other men, all standing around two flag-covered caskets just behind a C-17 Globemaster doing their "run-up" before takeoff. Most of the other men were there for the young soldier in the first casket, who had been one of the guards in the Humvee attack a couple days earlier. But Hanson stood with two strangers and the chief at his side—all with their eyes on the second casket, a CIA crest pin stuck into its side; the body of Agent Steven Windburg resting inside. Hanson barely noticed one of the flight crewmen slowly making his way toward them, trying to think of a way to tell them their time was up, the plane had to leave. Hanson did see him though, and so he gestured to the other men, the chief standing to his right following suit, and all moved around the caskets and in true military fashion for both began to carry them up into the plane. Most men began to file out then; the chief was one of the last to go, but Hanson stayed, and once he was alone, he stood at attention once more, and even though Windburg wasn't military, Hanson saluted the Agent in silence exited out the back. He watched the plane taxi away from him, slowly building speed as its powerful engines pulled ever harder on the atmosphere until it eventually climbed its way up from the runway, leaving its heavy roar behind it as the only lasting sound in the quiet of the desert. Hanson thought back to the med center, where they had taken

Agent Windburg after the crash. He was barely breathing and his mind was slipping, gurgling blood in the back of his throat as he tried to explain something, trying to make someone listen. He remembered the looks the doctors gave each other when they saw the wounds. He remembered some leaving so that they wouldn't have to watch. Yet of all that, he was still having trouble remembering what the dying agent whispered. He had gotten close after the doctor had given the green light for him to stay after they knew he couldn't be saved. But the blood was too much, it made it hard for anything to be heard, but Steven pushed himself to speak. It was his last try that made it through, but only in spurts. "Drive... drive..." he sputtered "drive". Hanson didn't understand, he tried to help, asking him questions, but eventually the coughing came, the words stopped, and soon the motion and the fighting died away as his eyes rolled back, then back to Hanson. He closed his eyes, and he was gone. Now Hanson was watching his plane fly back to a family Hanson had never met, but he wished he could have at least said something, and he wished he knew what he said. *Drive?* He repeated in his mind, he pushed himself to understand, but none of it made sense.

He checked his watch, reluctant but aware that he had to leave soon. *Ten forty-five already*, later than he thought. Camp Bastion was a good ways away from the air field he was at, and it was today he would be meeting the new man from the CIA; apparently a big name when it comes to the Afghan deserts.

In the desert, black was definitely a strange color to be wearing, simply because it grew so very hot in the desert sun, but it wasn't like he had a choice. Too many people around knew what he looked like, and if he was going to work with this new boss as he had worked with Agent Windburg, then the black clothing was a must. He didn't conform simply because he liked his job, always being the one who was rough with people and lying to others, but it gave him a chance to fight on his own terms, instead of flying out on a mission he knew very little about; although he had to say that his bosses were never really interested in sharing much with anyone when it came to information either. So he just waited, standing in the sun with several other men, all waiting for a brand new Black Hawk to touch down on one of the Camp Bastion landing zones. As he stood, he thought about whether or not it was his fault for not being with Agent Windburg, maybe he could have saved him from Jakub. No, he was sure he could have, but he was also sure that Windburg could have saved himself from someone like Jakub. That's what didn't add up, Jakub killing both a guard and Agent Windburg and severely wounding the driver, all by himself. He had read the records. Jakub was tough, but he was just a brute, with little skill when it came to fighting other than a brawling. Windburg was trained for close combat and was hard to surprise; he had a nose for things that weren't right, *So why didn't he stop it?* He racked the question in his mind over and over again, trying to make it understandable, but he didn't finish his train of thought as the helicopter finally showed up, kicking up huge plumes of dust and sand that had gathered over the tarmac. The door opened as the man in black neared, and a gray-haired man with surprising grip strength exited and shook his hand.

"Agent Matthews, good to see you made it."

"I'm not, could've been sitting with a bourbon back in the states about now." Both men smiled as the made their way away from the helicopter to a parked Humvee. As they got in, Agent Matthews asked a question. "What's your name, son?"

"I'm Agent Black, sir." Agent Matthews smiled, always intrigued when he met someone with deep cover in the field.

"Nice to meet you, although I got to say, your cover name isn't very original," he remarked as he looked at his clothes, another smile grew on his face.

"Where to, sir?" the driver asked.

"Where? Oh…um, the office, I still need to acclimate here, and I figure there'd be some good reading up in Windburg's old office."

"God rest his soul," the driver spoke again.

"Yes, God rest it." The engine started up, and within a minute, they'd reached the office building; he was in the office in two.

"Anything else you need, sir?" Agent Black asked.

"No, not unless you have a bottle of Jack sneakin' around here."

"No, sir," he replied.

"All right, shut the door on your way out."

Agent Black wasn't particularly sure how he felt about having this new man hanging around the man's office that hadn't been touched since before he died. It was like an intrusion, but it wasn't for him to judge or to speak up about. He did have other things to think about, however, and standing outside wondering what the new boss would change was a waste of time, so off he went.

TROJAN

1427 hours, July 20, Chinook In-route to Camp Bastion Helmand Province, Afghanistan

Zahid knew that the ride over would be tough, mostly because of the sedatives they were giving him so that the bumps wouldn't cause him too much discomfort. He never really minded discomfort and never had a problem with sedatives, as long as he wasn't using them. He never liked losing the feeling of control, never liked being in a state of mind where he couldn't tell what was going on. But to him, not many who had been shot would refuse a pain killer, so he sucked it in just like all the others; now he was reaping the benefits because instead of pain with each toss and turn, he had a slow, nauseous perception of everything; his stomach felt like it was doing loops as he sat in the harness, watching everyone on board as carefully as his subdued mind would allow. Two men in front of him, both standing while holding on to the rails that ran along the inside wall of the helicopter, seemed to be very interested in a piece of metal jutting from one of their rifles, one actually bickering with the other as to why the damage wasn't his fault. To his right, there was a long double row of cots, with less injured soldiers harnessed in same as Zahid, though he had more without a cot in front of him. The man across from him was out completely, smirking quietly or giggling as his head rocked back and forth nearly more often than the helicopter actually rocked itself.

A larger jolt rocked the small aircraft, causing a few to cry out in shock as they worried about hurting themselves more. Zahid actually knocked the back of his head up against the top of his chair, but he didn't utter a sound, only used his arm that was still free of any bandages to replace his helmet so he could rest his head back on the seat without the impact. It helped very little with relieving the jarring, but he didn't feel as much and that was enough. As he watched, he began to hear loud voices coming from the cockpit, and as he looked, he noticed that the two who had been bickering over the rifle were now keenly paying attention to their head phones, the one facing Zahid is who he watched closely; his face said it all: dangerous airspace ahead. As he watched, his mind began tossing strange thoughts through his imagination. First was a what-if; what if he were to die on that helicopter, how strange it would be to be killed by his allies and to die with his enemies; he would be thought of as a soldier by both sides. He liked that idea; in his weak state, he found it poetic in its dark irony: death but in the wrong order under the wrong name.

He snapped back into consciousness when he heard several men screaming, and the sound of tearing metal as large caliber bullets rocked the bottom of the aircraft. All of a sudden, seemingly out of the blue, a new feeling came over him, something he never thought would be in his mind, but he knew it was there: peace. As he thought of his own demise, he realized he wasn't one to care; he realized that he didn't fear death and wasn't too interested in stopping its approach. In a sense, he felt relieved for just a moment, and he welcomed the feeling. But his memory did not allow it long. Soon, as if prompted from inside, the picture of the woman and the boy, he and his mother, tore itself into his mind, as light through a boarded window. It reminded him of why he still breathed. Peace left him then, and it seemed as if the warriors that were attacking the helicopter agreed with his remembrance and decided to let him go, to allow him to finish what he had started. So there he sat, waiting patiently for the chopper to make its approach, to land, and to allow him in.

He looked up, resting his head against the chair while following the fuel lines that ran the length of the chopper. As he looked, he realized that this metal beast he was in was simply a vehicle, nothing more, but still trusted by so many to bring only help. Either relief for wounded to a hospital or relief to men fighting on the battlefield. Yet again, very poetically, it was bringing him across, the one who had bested one of their own bases, and they themselves were flying him back so they could fix him and bring him back to fighting health. He remembered learning of a story, from his uncle, about the great deception of the Trojan horse. Zahid assumed that, in a sense, this vehicle had become an involuntary Trojan, and he, the secret, it kept. In his mind, he started to run the story, a Trojan horse bringing his vengeance to bear like an infection; though he didn't like to think of himself as something as vile as an infection. No, a soldier, a warrior more so, one who would go into the heart of his own enemy and bring it down, to bleed him out.

The helicopter started to slow, the bumps becoming less frequent but slightly more violent. He turned to the window at his left, just before the cockpit, its view still was dominated by golden sands and a steady stream of light flowing over the chopper, though it didn't hurt his eyes much to gaze out into the desert many feet below. The whole of the desert changed then, shifting from waves to walls, from sand to concrete and tarmac; they were now hovering over the inner walls of the massive Camp Bastion. Its sheer size surprised him, made him realize just how deep of a grasp the outsiders had on the land. It seemed like their vehicles and buildings stretched for more than mile, and as if to make it seem all the more daunting, large tanks and attack helicopters seemed to be lined in battle array at the edge, as if to warn him of what he had just stepped into. But still, he remembered the picture, and still he remembered the story. For him, this helicopter had become his Trojan horse and this base his own city to conquer. Yet as he knew even before seeing it; there would be no destroying it—only distraction, diversion to the most violent degree. He wasn't going to release their grip, rather he would simply tighten his own around the neck of his enemy; he was there to kill their Agent Richard Matthews.

TRACKS

2300 hours, July 20, Camp Bastion
Helmand Province, Afghanistan

Keeping his eyes closed for so long had actually begun to make him tired, especially with some of the sedatives from the flight still drifting through his mind every few minutes. Still he kept them closed, pretending to sleep at least long enough for the nurses to assume they could leave him be. So in a forced darkness he waited, breathing slow and calm to keep his heart rate low until the time came. Then he heard a noise in the room, a shuffling of feet followed small tugs on the tubes and needles attached to his arm. He opened his eyes to find a doctor standing over him, lightly pulling the tape and needles slowly off and out of his arm. When Zahid's eyes opened, the doctor looked at him for a moment, smiled, and finished pulling of some of the connections and disabling the machine. It was as he was helping Zahid sit up that a nurse walked into the room and was strangely surprised to see the doctor.

"Oh, I thought there was something wrong with the machine."

"No, ma'am, just moving our boy here to a barracks, he's stable enough now."

"Um, I didn't know...well," she stumbled over her words.

"Ma'am, I don't have very much time, so if you could hurry."

"Yes." She pushed a small lock of her hair back from her forehead. "It's just that I'm head nurse over here, and I didn't get any message about a barracks move."

"Oh, I understand. Sometimes the papers just get lost is all."

"Sure, but I do need to check with Dr. Hammond before you move him out. Could you hold a moment?"

"Oh, sure, just hand me that arm sling behind you would you?"

"Yeah." As she turned, the doctor let Zahid sit up on his own strength and walked over to the nurse with her back to him. He reached his arm around her neck and clenched around her throat so that she couldn't scream. He then removed a syringe from his pocket and injected its contents into her neck; she slumped to the floor a few seconds later, and he pushed her into a side door with a few supplies, blocking the door with a bed. He turned back to Zahid and nodded to a black bag at his feet as he closed the door to the room.

"Hassan, how was your flight over?" Zahid asked mockingly, knowing that the flight that he and another doctor took on a Black Hawk was far more rough than his.

"It was fine. It's good to see you again." The two then began to remove articles of clothing, all of which was common wear by most of the cleaning staff around the American side of the base. They had just set in their boots when someone knocked on the door.

"Caroline? Carry, you in there?" As she asked, Hassan replaced his white lab coat and opened the door, Zahid simply acted as though he were cleaning up the tape on the desk next to him, tossing the strips into a trash bin at the foot of the bed.

"I'm sorry, you missed her by about five minutes. I think she said she had to go talk to Dr. Hammond, if you want to check with him." The chubby little nurse sighed and nodded then walked back to the nurse's station.

"Zahid, we need to leave."

He removed his doctor's coat, and Zahid picked up the bag from the floor, stuffing his hospital gown and the coat in and zipped it up as they left the room. Hassan looked back to the nurse's station behind him as they went; still the woman was clicking on a computer. Zahid watched in front, still no one even visible let alone watching as the two made their way through the halls, eventually reaching the doors and exiting out into the cool night. Hassan brushed his longer hair back behind him, removing a cigarette from his pocket and offering Zahid one; he shook his head.

"What's the time?"

"It's 11:08, we're making good time." He lit the butt in his mouth, sucking lightly on the filter.

"All right, we have another nine hours to find the itinerary. We need to know when he arrived." Bright lights passed over them, making them pause as the Humvee roared down through a gate to another part of the camp.

"It's strange, isn't it? Us being here, their greatest attackers and defenders passing us by as if we were one of them."

"It's far stranger when you're driving one." Zahid noticed a building just to the right of the road, looking off at an angle to face east. "Here," he said, and the two turned and entered the building. Guards were scarce, one near the front and another standing near the doors that lead to a set of offices. Zahid assumed he would find the office there, but he wasn't sure.

"Excuse me," he asked the guard, who immediately turned, his face stern but passive. "We were told to come here to work the main office earlier, but we missed Agent Matthews, do you think you could point it out for us?" It was a direct approach, he knew, but he was relying on the trust between soldiers, and it paid off; the guard simply pointed to the hall behind him and said, "Third door to the left, just after the fountain." Zahid nodded in thanks and Hassan followed him to the room, still watching behind just in case; no one came. As they entered, the first thing they saw was a large desk, all was in perfect order, save for one small pile of papers left on the desk. Zahid went for the desk while Hassan went out into the hall and found a vacuum in a closet; he had it plugged in and turned on by the time Zahid had sifted through the papers until he found the itinerary. Several items had been crossed out, others circled and a date at the top with a large check next to it, already used. He flipped it over and scanned the date; it was for tomorrow. He took out a piece of notepaper and placed it on the desk, lightly writing in the times between seven and nine, circling the one in the middle. Once this was done, he started to place things back the way he had found them, careful to place the itinerary back in the pile with the marked side facing up. The vacuum went off, and as he looked, he noticed Hassan was speaking with the guard again, this time with the guard less laid back. He turned round just in time to see Zahid walking out with a rag in his hands, the piece of paper folded and placed deep in his pocket and out of sight.

"Is there a problem, sir?" he asked politely.

"You said you only had the office, why is he vacuuming in the hall?"

"Just routine, we do the outside and then move in. I was just about to bring him in when you came over."

"Gentlemen, I don't think I've seen you before." The guard's face was rigid, his eyes locked on the two men. "Did you say you were here earlier?"

"Yes, sir." Zahid watched carefully through his peripherals as Hassan let the bottom hilt of a knife in his sleeve start to slip down into his hand behind his back.

"Well, I need to check and verify that, it's probably nothing, but we've had a couple thefts this week, and I can't risk more." He stepped to the side and gestured to a room filled with chairs and asked them to go inside to wait.

"All right," Zahid said but then dropped his rag just to the other side of the guard's feet, so that he turned and watched him pick it up. He was coming back up from the ground when Hassan grabbed the guard in a very similar fashion to the nurse; however, he took the blade and slid its point into his throat, pulling him into the room and laying him under a pile of chairs, a pool of blood forming around the feet of the stacks of chairs. They locked the door and moved on, leaving the blade in a garbage bin and covered it with the rag.

"Did you find it?" Hassan asked, turning up the sleeves of his shirt to hide the small patches of blood.

"Eight, he leaves at eight, and we need to strike just before that. Where did you put the radio?"

"It's in the barracks they gave me, but there are others sleeping inside, you'll have to be quiet."

He acknowledged in silence as he walked away, stuffing his blood-stained shirt into the black bag, removing a hat and putting it on. He disappeared around the corner the same time Hanson reached the tent, which Hassan said had the radio. He found it lying on a cot near the door just behind a small box. Zahid took both and left the barracks, walked for what seemed to be a quarter of a mile till he found a small parking lot, several vehicles parked, and the lighting extremely dim. He stuffed the box just beneath a pole at the center of the lot and turned on the radio. He fumbled with the switch for a moment till it snapped into the right frequency, and he waited. After a minute of making sure he was alone, he whispered into the radio, "Saben," and a moment later Nadeen answered back.

"Amir, you are truly inside?"

"Yes, where are you currently?"

"Praise Allah," Nadeen exhaled. "We are waiting nearly six miles from you, we'll be moving closer as you said all night till we're in sight, then we wait for you."

"Yes, but you will need to be here before seven, preferably before the sun rises."

"Why the change?" his voice sounded concerned.

"Because we have a rare opportunity, Nadeen. A general sleeps within these walls, and you will be the ones to bring him down."

215

Zahid listened as Nadeen transferred the message to his men, and he could hear their cheers fill the night air. He checked his surroundings again.

"This is truly good, Amir, you have brought us the enemy, and we shall take his head."

"I hope so. Your attack shall truly bring great opportunity." He turned the radio off when more cheers erupted.

EYES IN THE SKY

0715 hours, July 21, Reaper Drone Control Room
Location Unknown

"Sir"—the pilot motioned for his sergeant—"could you come have a look at this."

The sergeant made his way past the crowded control booths to the pilot, balancing his coffee as he moved. When he reached him, he placed his hand on the top of the computer and asked, "What's up?" sipping on his coffee as he listened.

"Um, right here, along this hill line here." He pointed to an indentation on the screen. Along his finger, a long line of white heat signatures, most covered lightly but still plainly visible through the heat-sensing lenses on the massive Reaper drone that circled above.

"Zoom in," the sergeant said.

"Sir, these heat signatures stretch for nearly a quarter mile. Have there been reports of enemy movement in the area?"

"Son, for you that doesn't really matter," the sergeant said, his eyes still locked on the screen. "But from what I've heard, there's none."

"What do we do?"

"Report it, you keep this pattern above locked and alert me to any movements. Richards!?" he called out.

"Sir?" Richards responded as he quickly laid down a racy magazine that he believed no one knew about.

"Put this on the main screen for me, and get Captain Marrow down here, he needs to see this."

Nadeen reached down into his bag and removed a monocular from a side pocket, the light of the sun just barely over the horizon casting everything in a dull grayscale. He peered through the scope, scanning the space just over the wall for any movement while careful to keep checking higher, in case a helicopter were to sneak past.

"Nadeen, have you heard from the Amir?"

"No, not since earlier. Why?"

"Well, when do we go? The longer we lay out here in the open, the greater the chance—"

"Don't talk at me about chances. It is Allah's will that we fight today, and with our Amir already inside, all we have to do is wait. Our time will come, Ahmed, just be patient." He smiled at the young man, and he nodded in submission. Nadeen looked around again with his scope, thinking he might have heard something coming from behind them, but the sky seemed empty. As he looked, he saw only that he was alone and waiting in the open; he said a silent prayer for secrecy.

"What is it, Mitch? I still have half the reports from yesterday to go through."

"Sir, I think we may have some insurgent activity."

"Big news?" the sarcasm stung. "Where is it happening? I'll try to humor you here."

"Well, sir, it's only about a half mile out from Camp Bastion. They don't usually come anywhere near there."

"Hugh…" he paused, watching the screen. The line of prone bodies all lined up toward the camp looked ominous. "All right, see if you can get a good picture of any weaponry or something, we can't go poppin' off rockets just yet. I'll go get on the line with intelligence, maybe they'll have an explanation."

"Yes, sir. Jackson!" the pilot acknowledged. "I need you to get confirmation on any weapons or other unfriendly things."

"I'll try, sir."

"Don't try, Jackson, we didn't let you play with that multimillion-dollar RC plane for 'trying.' Get to work. And two of you go help him if you aren't already flying a bird." He gestured to some of the other pilots, one of whom immediately jumped up, another followed a few moments later. "Let's see if we can't catch us some vermin, gentleman."

Agent Matthews grabbed his vest off the back of his chair and wrapped it around his chest, tightening the straps as he kicked the chair back under his desk. He was placing his custom Colt 1911 .45–caliber pistol when he heard a knock at the door. He called for the man to come in, carefully folding the snap around the stained wooden handle of his pistol as the door opened and Agent Black walked in, followed by Corporal Damian Hanson.

"You look tired, Corporal," he remarked then nodded to Agent Black who, now wearing a black mask, moved out of the room, shutting the door behind him.

"Ah, yes, sir, not much sleeping over the last couple weeks."

"I see. Tell me, you looking for something?"

"Excuse me, sir?"

"Oh, well I mean what are you looking for, working for me and the agency. Something special, I presume."

"No, sir," Hanson lied. "Just after the enemy in any way I can. Saving lives while I'm at it is just a plus."

The graying agent smiled, glistening from a layer of sweat forming above his brow. Apparently he liked the answer.

"Well, Corporal Hanson, I must say you have done well. Now tell me, what was the major difference between you and any other bomb tech out there?"

"It's because I know what belongs to the bad guy, especially the one me and Agent Windburg were hunting before he passed on."

"But what is the difference, hmm, what makes his stuff any worse than the next bomber?"

"Well, first and foremost, he has excellent timing and placement, when he hits, usually it's crippling as you saw with FOB Edie." More bodies flashed through Hanson's mind, they were starting to pile up. "The other thing is that he uses a paper clip. I'd never forget that, always a paperclip."

"Why a paperclip?"

"Could be for anti-theft, lack of funding for wires or because he likes paper clips. Frankly, sir, I don't give a damn." Hanson had already grown tired of the explanations. "I only remember it because I can track him with it."

He eyed Hanson, and Hanson felt as though he was wearing his secret on his face. He didn't like this agent much either, something in his eyes made him start thinking of an untrustworthy dog, but he was the new boss so he sucked it up. "Well, Corporal, I'm afraid we have little more time to talk, we have a flight out to a US consulate in Kabul. Long trip to go, but when they call for help, you get to get a move on."

"Sir, what's at the consulate?" Hanson had no real desire to go that far, he knew the bomber wouldn't be anywhere near there.

"Well, I received a ping on our bomber, seeing as how we put out some info on him last week. It seems he was working out at some newspaper in Kabul under an alias. Since you've done such good work, I thought you should be the first to get to see what he did when he wasn't blowing up bases and convoys. Besides, we have done enough with you when it comes to finding this guy, we know what he looks like and we know where we're lookin'. We'll find him soon, so I think this is my way of—"

"Firing me," Hanson finished, partly joking and the rest pure distain. He really didn't like this guy.

"Yes, however you want to put it. I'm being polite because of the work, other than that I just don't give a damn. Now let's get a move on. I want to be back tonight."

⸙

Zahid wrapped his turban around his face as he prepared to move in to the office. It would only be a few more minutes till his men would attack, and the base would be on full alert. Hassan came up from behind him and handed him a pistol, both men placing the black nine millimeters into their pants and covering them with their shirts. They were still resting behind the large row of Humvees, and the sun only just then breaking over the walls and spilling over into the parking lot. They watched the building, having already given the signal to attack and thus all they needed to do was wait for the fireworks to kick off. Zahid checked his watch, it was nearly eight in the morning and the door to the CIA building still hadn't moved since the night before.

"Are you ready, Hassan?" A smile slowly began to creep over Zahid's face, but it was hidden by his turban.

"Yes, Zahid, I am." He cocked his pistol, looked past Zahid, and nodded to the door. Zahid turned, and his heart nearly stopped. There, just walking out of the door was Agent Matthews, walking as if the only thing he had to do was relax. He could barely control his rage, but he did manage to hold himself back; he needed the base to go into alert before he went. Just a little while longer. Soon, very soon, as he judged how slowly he and the man next to him walked, he would be standing over the body of his enemy. The smile returned to his face.

⸙

"Sir!" a single analyst called out.

"What?"

"We've received confirmation from upstairs. We have permission to go weapons-hot in two minutes!"

221

"Good, why did they just give it?"

"Because they can see the guns, sir, from the feed. They think these might be the FOB Edie attackers."

"Well then, all weapons?"

"All weapons, Captain. Hellfire's clear."

"Good. Jackson, you ready to play?"

"Already in strike approach, sir."

"All right." the Captain sat down in his chair as if he were about to watch a movie. "Give 'em hellfire." The room went quiet.

FULL CIRCLE

0740 hours, July 21, Outside Camp Bastion
Helmand Province, Afghanistan

Nadeen and his men moved low over the dunes, dodging behind a stone or slipping back into the sand whenever movement appeared over the wall until they could get close. To his right, a man with two rocket launchers on his back took one from his shoulder and aimed up at the top of the wall. Although he couldn't see them, he knew that two mortar teams to his right and three to his left all were gauging the cannons to the distance. Behind, several men with light machine guns watched the gates and prepared to lay down fire as soon as anything made its way through the gates out toward them. Nadeen raised his hand; his men came to a stop and waited for it to drop. Before he did, however, he noticed a small glint in the sky, just to the right of the rising sun. At first he thought it was a plane, a helicopter maybe that was making its way to the camp. It was only seconds before it hit, however, that he noticed the trail and realized it was a missile.

—⟩⟨⟨⟨—

"First Hellfire is a direct hit, multiple targets down." Everyone in the room watched the screen, somehow mesmerized by sheer size of the white cloud that formed after the missile hit. Several bodies nearby seemed as if they were hit by a truck, picked up, and thrown by the blast and laid spread eagle in the sand, their white signatures partially obscured by the heavy smoke.

"Sir, enemies returning fire." Some of the white spots on the ground had moved away from where the missile hit and had collected behind small hills; small flashes of heat were shown, but they seemed to be spraying fire in several different directions. They didn't know what had hit them.

"Send another one then clean up with the gun."

"Yes, sir."

Zahid heard the explosion from where he was sitting as if they were only a few feet away. He turned to see where it came from and saw out to the east a plume of dark smoke rising. Hassan had just turned around when the sirens on base lit up the morning silence; both Agent Matthews and Hanson immediately stopped to hear any announcement.

"Zahid, what's going on?"

"I"—he hesitated for a moment—"I don't know." Over the loudspeakers, an announcer shouted for different groups or officers to report to different places. Already hundreds of soldiers were running, filling the area, only pausing for a Humvee that roared around a corner. Then the announcer stopped shouting, some strange voice in the background through the speakers and then he returned to the microphone, "Enemy activity outside, east and about a quarter mile out! Reaper in the air, Hellfire's mobile, all teams hold for direct." Zahid heard the word "Reaper" and immediately knew his window had opened. He could still see the smoke trail from the missile, but the drone was still invisible to him. He raised his head above the car to check on Matthews; he was already moving quickly toward a helicopter a few hundred feet away. He was getting up to leave when a voice came from behind him, the sound of a round locking into its chamber followed after.

Nadeen's head felt as though it had been hit with a club, and as he removed his hands from his forehead, he noticed blood had covered his fingers and was already flowing over his brow. He rolled over onto his belly, trying to bring his knees up under him, but as he dragged his legs, he immediately felt fire shoot up from his thigh and into his side, and so he collapsed back to the ground. He looked down; his lower leg had been snapped in half and his thigh had a long gash of red flesh from his knee all the way up to his hip.

He looked for what had snapped it; a few feet away another man lay, missile launcher in hand with a spot off blood plastered across its side; he realized that was what hit him. Carefully he used his other leg to lift himself up from the ground and balanced as carefully as he could, a dull throbbing still rising and falling from his right side. He called out for someone, anyone who could hear him and heard moans in response from the other side of the hill. He hobbled over, nearly falling as the sand tried to give way under his foot. However, through the smoke and dust that circled around him, he eventually found a couple men who had pulled themselves across the sand and to an indentation in the earth, laying themselves against it.

He had almost reached it when a rapid patting sound erupted, short geysers of sand leaping upward in two parallel lines that lead their way quickly to the men in front of him; shocked, he fell back, watching as the large caliber rounds smacked into the group of men. He closed his eyes when he hit the ground, wincing as he heard the sickening resonance of metal tearing flesh, as if the bullets were hitting a pool of water; the only other sound was the screams of the men.

When he opened his eyes again, the smoke had started to clear more, and a large, strangely shaped plane whooshed by overhead. He looked back down to his men then turned away when he saw the spectacle of death, crimson pools with rings of red mud had formed underneath the bodies. He could barely stand it. As he lay, the only light came from above, a blue sky through a hole in the thick, dark smoke that had risen above him. His head started becoming lighter, his vision blurring in and out as he could feel a chill filling his body as the blood flowed from his leg. He looked around him, trying to see if anyone else was around, if any had survived, but he could see nothing through the burning fog, only the sound of more bullets striking the ground somewhere out of his vision was what he heard. He heard no scream, but he knew that the silence was death; he stopped looking. Slowly a shiver came over him as he lay in the sand, the only warmth was just underneath the top layer of sand, so he dug his hand under to absorb some. His vision finally went out; only his hearing remained, letting him listen to the finality of the cool breeze that moved the sand and smoke around him. Then silence.

Zahid watched as the drone exited, the drape of smoke that begun to move higher into the sky. He watched as it flew over the camp and heard cheers from the men around him by the soldiers who watched its confident exit from the battlefield. Behind him someone was talking to Hassan and him, but Zahid could barely hear him, instead he was watching as the target he was after, the man from the CIA climbed into a helicopter and strapped himself in. Everything in him told him to pull his gun and shoot but he didn't; he didn't want to kill him yet. He wanted it to last.

He finally heard the voice behind him, someone shouting at them and Hassan returned the shouts. He turned around and found two guards behind them, both had their hands on their side arms and one had his hand out pointing. Zahid started to listen.

"... and keep your hands up!"

"Why? What do you want!?" Hassan bellowed.

"Turn around!" the soldier screamed. "Keep your hands up." he drew his pistol and Hassan drew his as well. "Put the gun down!" Zahid looked back and saw the helicopter start to take off, everything in him screamed for him to chase, but too late; he was going. He drew his pistol and pointed at the guards as well.

Now the guards, he and Hassan were locked in a standoff. Zahid looked past the guards and saw the nurse Hassan had drugged standing with a couple other soldiers, pointing out at Hassan and him. The window had closed. All of a sudden, Hassan started to speak in Arabic.

"Zahid, there is no way we both can run."

"I know," Zahid spoke with his voice reserved. Failure started to rise in his mind as a possibility.

"But I can hold them."

"Hey!" the guard yelled. "What are you saying?!"

"No, Hassan, he is gone."

"But he will return." He gripped his pistol. "You can still take him. He will return and you can hide until then."

"There will be no place to hide here!"

"Then you go after him."

"Put the guns down or I will shoot!" the guard yelled again.

"What? You want me to chase him with a car? I'll never catch up."

"Then take the chopper, we can hold them for you." He pulled back the hammer.

"We?" Zahid asked. His question was answered when Hassan lowered his pistol and pointed at the guard. Immediately a loud zip ran past Zahid and a bullet struck the guard, who sank as his legs gave out beneath him. Several more rounds went off, the second guard collapsed as they did, and Zahid looked around again. His men, the team he'd brought from Iran, his closest brothers were all around him and were firing, pinning down men as they tried to get close.

"Go!" Hassan screamed "Take their helicopter!" Zahid listened. He picked himself up over the Humvee and sprinted down the gravel road toward a parked Apache, the sounds of his men's machine guns urging him on. He threw open the door and immediately started the machine up, all the while trying to see how his men fought. Up in the building, two of them were firing from the offices, and Hassan was backing into the building as they laid down cover for him. To the left of the building, Zahid could see several American soldiers making their way toward the building, all the while firing up at the offices. Then Zahid stopped as he saw in front of him what looked like to be thirty men moving toward the building. They passed, and he started up the chopper, the large rotors gaining speed as he did. He expected to be shot, but they never looked at him, all still too preoccupied with the machine gun fire from the building. He looked back down at the controls, instantly memories of his training in Iran flowed into his mind, every control of American equipment having been drilled into his head. He knew how to fly it, now he needed to get it off the ground. The propellers whirred, the cockpit started to shake, and slowly the machine lifted itself up from the tarmac. He looked back once more to his men; it seemed as though hundreds of Americans and British soldiers had coalesced at the doors, protected from the fire by the overhang. None of them noticed him, or at least notice he wasn't one of theirs; all they knew was they had a chopper taking off. He looked up to the office and watched for a moment as his men fired down, bullets striking the ground and men pulling each other back underneath the building. Then they breached the doors.

He turned away then and started off in the same direction the other helicopter had gone. He removed the piece of paper that he had written the itinerary on and grazed the information quickly. It surprised him that he hadn't noticed before, he should have seen it. There, underneath the eight o'clock time was the name Kabul followed by the name *Daily Afghan* NP. They were headed for the paper, but they were going to miss their appointment.

UNKNOWN

0815 hours, July 21, In Route to Kabul
Helmand Province, Afghanistan

Hanson's headphones were not working at the moment, but he knew something was wrong. To his right, Matthews was shouting at the pilots through the microphone and they were shouting back at him some answer that he apparently didn't like. He took them off, noticed the battery was pulled partly out, and had just got it fixed when he jumped in.

"What's going on?" Hanson asked.

"Remember the missile that hit outside the camp?" Matthews said, already he was on his cell phone preparing a message.

"Yeah."

"Well, whoever they hit wasn't dead. Now we got a whole number of gunman inside the office building keeping everyone pinned down."

"Sir"—Hanson was still thinking about the bomb at the hangar—"Agent Windburg said that he thought that someone was impersonating a soldier. Back at FOB Edie."

"And why does that matter, Corporal?" the man didn't even look up at him.

"The bomb there was done on the inside; I think this might be him." Matthews stopped typing and looked up at him; though he was wearing sunglasses, it was apparent that he was worried.

"Captain," Matthews spoke through the microphone.

The pilot responded, "Turn us around, we're going back to the camp." A delayed "yes, sir" followed, and the large chopper made a heavy left turn back around.

———◈◈◈———

Zahid looked down at his compass on the instruments dash. It said he was still bearing northeast, and that's exactly where he needed to go. He checked the GPS map, still nearly two hours out, but he would most likely catch them before they reached Kabul, as his chopper was faster and lighter. He looked out the window, trying to see their metal reflection, but the sun was just rising to his right, making it too bright to see that far ahead. He looked to the copilot seat, trying to find a helmet or pair of sunglasses, but the helmet was down below the seat, and he had to stretch to reach for it. Still evading him, he removed his pistol and pulled the top of the helmet slowly toward him until he could reach it with his fingers; however, it started to slip away again. He tipped the chopper, and the helmet came close again, and he snatched it up from the floor and placed it onto the copilot seat. He unsnapped the chin strap and finally got it onto his head, snapping the visor down over his eyes. It was as he corrected the helicopter to line with the horizon that he saw it, a helicopter heading back through the light of the sun like a fly against a lamp. It was nearly a half mile off to his right. He wanted to continue, wondering if it was just another chopper, but he had to know. He needed to get closer to see the numbers, so he turned the chopper to intercept them, the sun burning now to his left.

———◈◈◈———

"What are they saying back on base?" Hanson asked.

"Still a firefight going on. They've moved from an office to an inner room, the hall is getting plastered from what I can tell," the pilot replied. "ETA two minutes." The pilot changed the subject, and Agent Matthews responded.

"Any word on casualties?"

"A couple of our guys have gone down, one dead, the rest wounded. We got one of them too, though. They say that there are three more."

"No other news?" Hanson asked, wondering why the bomber was just putting up a fire fight.

"No, sir, just a whole lot of the same."

"Joe!" the copilot exclaimed. "Look at this." He pointed down to the radar, a green dot seemed to be moving its way along with them, and it was starting to close in.

"A plane maybe, support chopper, you think?" the pilot asked.

"No, too small but not fast enough to be a plane."

"All right, ping 'em." Then the copilot looked back to his right.

"Unknown helo, please identify yourself, over." No answer came. "Unknown helo bearing southwest, we are at your ten o'clock, please identify yourself. This is the United States Air Force, over." Still no answer came. Hanson leaned over to try and see it, finally finding its glint back behind them; it was moving for them fast. "Sir, he's not answering."

"Keep trying. I think it's an Apache, so it's one of ours."

"Yes, sir." The co-pilot spoke again, "Unidentified helo bearing southwest toward Camp Bastion, this is Runner three, please identify yourself." The radio phased out for a moment, white noise growing in their ears until it went quiet. "Sir, I think he just cut the signal. He's deliberately not responding."

"I don't like this," the pilot remarked. Then he spoke again, "Agent Matthews, sir, do you know anything about this chopper?"

"No, not in the slightest. Pull back. See if you can't get him to signal with his hands." Hanson looked out his window; Camp Bastion was still about a mile and a half away.

The Black Hawk slowed up, then the decrease in speed tugging on Hanson in his harness. The chopper outside neared as they slowed, but it seemed to slow down as well, finally, it reached them, but instead of pulling alongside, it sagged backward and pulled in behind them. All of a sudden, loud beeping sounds rang throughout the helicopter.

"Captain, he's locking on! He's locking on!"

"Drive this thing, Captain!" Matthews asked.

Drive, the words resounded in Hanson's mind as if a cannon had gone off; he swore he could hear ringing. *Drive,* he remembered what Agent Windburg had whispered through his pain as he died, something about a drive. *Driver, that's what he meant!* Hanson thought, *He was trying to warn me about the driver! The driver of that Humvee!*

"Matthews!" Hanson shouted. "That helicopter, I think that's him!"

"Who, Corporal?"

"Zahid!"

Suddenly the helicopter started to lurch back and forth as the pilots tried to evade the shooter. Bullets pelted the side of the chopper, tearing large holes through the armor and a couple bounced around inside. The copilot tried to unclip himself from the harness, but then more rounds tore through the aircraft and one hit him after bouncing off the ceiling. He sank back into his chair, gasping for air as he gripped his chest. Hanson could hear his heavy breathing through the speaker, then it slowed and finally came to a stop.

"We gotta land this thing right now 'cause we aint makin' it to the camp!" He jerked his head forward toward the rapidly approaching walls of Camp Bastion.

"Do it, Captain!" the chopper lurched forward; it was heading toward the ground when the rotors were torn up by the machine gun. Hanson watched out the window as the ground below flashed by. It seemed like forever that they glided over the sand, getting ever closer but not touching, not yet. Hanson knew it would hit though, so he braced himself as the chopper slammed into the ground and bounced so that its nose tipped ever so slightly forward and then it hit again; this time it bounced and flipped. Sand tore its way through the glass window, and the world dimmed and then flashed out.

CALM BEFORE STORMS

0730 hours, July 21, Camp Bastion
Helmand Province, Afghanistan

Celia felt like she was holding a grenade in her hand; luckily for her, no one had pulled the pin as of yet. In her hands rested a long, three-page list of names and locations of three people who had worked with Agent Matthews—although "worked *for*" would be more accurate—while he was in Kandahar in the late nineties. The first one was a man, and by his bio, he was somewhat of a high-roller in his area. He had connections galore, a business that gave him access to higher-level faction leaders within the province or individuals in the growing government; however, it appeared that his only use was for locations on enemy deposits—nothing more.

The woman, who though she had very little by ways of a bio still had a role to play in the asset's realm. Her connections and value seemed to lie in her relationship with women in the area, most of whom are now dead—as she read in the other file about an anti-militant group that comprised of nearly fifty other women—including her. However, she died prematurely, and none of her connections were used. Instead, it seemed that her only use was her in-out relationship with a local Sheik who had plenty of connections as well—in the black market.

Then there was the boy, no more than eighteen and still very low when it came to having enemy-intel worth; in fact there was almost no information on him other than the fact that he was dead. From what the sheet she read told her, he was important to "the apprehension of several suspects." From there, the bio went on about how he was very useful in determining enemy supply lines and funding banks (which is a nice way of saying he was a terrorist with access to loads of money and artifacts and this "Agent Matthews" flipped him).

The issue wasn't that they seemed to be being used in an unorthodox fashion, and it wasn't even that they all died (most of the other assets in fact met the chopping block after their work with the CIA). Instead it was how they died, which according to the files was in a firefight at a home by town militia. Rather, the strange coincidence was the fact that they all died in the same place, even though the files mentioned no connections with each other. Most importantly, however, was that the woman who died in the firefight, without even a mention as to why it happened, had a last name that rung a bell in Celia's ears, so eagerly she tried to remember where she had heard it. It was when she turned to her computer and typed the name "al Khatri" into the search bar that it scared her to death. She wasn't supposed to have that name on her computer after the old files were lost; it was because that last name belonged to the crazed Afghan bomber Zahid al Khatri.

—⟨⟨⟩⟩—

Agent Black walked into the CID building, his mask in his pocket and his black billed hat pulled low over his eyes. The MPs to his right paid little attention, though they did notice the dark character, one they hadn't seen before, walk up and punch in the code to the computer room without even pausing to remember like most others did; strange but not a big deal to them. As he walked in, he scanned the room quickly, found her sitting facing away from him at one of the computer cubicles lining the wall, and walked over to her.

"Excuse me, miss," he said, pretending he didn't know her. "Can you tell me where I can find the team in charge of the CIA inquiry?"

"You're standing right in the middle of it." She didn't even look up from her page; she was taking notes on. He grew impatient.

"Miss, I need to talk to whoever is in charge of it, as some information in the files they gave you has been deemed extremely hazardous." He straightened himself. "I'm here to collect that hazardous material."

"Listen, whatever you're looking for it's in CID hands now, and the CIA gave it to us. You can't recollect anything. Now I'm extremely busy so…" she gestured her hand to the door.

He knew she wasn't the mole, even though a lot of the signs actually pointed to her. Agent Black was there under orders from the director himself, and his orders were not actually to recollect information but rather to find and remove the mole that Agent Matthews had placed inside CID. Whoever it was protecting Matthews from something in these files, all Black had to do was find them. He checked the list of names, crossed off the first four and read the next one. The mole had been placed by Agent Matthews after sending his liaison, Agent Windburg, to work the assets in Helmand. Whoever it was would try to get rid of the hazardous material, and what better way than for it to get buried in a CIA vault, right under assassination files that would never see the light of day. So he stood, reading off the names and dangling the bait as he asked the potential moles to hand over the "hazard."

The next person on the list was another miss-fire, and things were starting to look like it really wouldn't work, until after he set down his book, took out his phone, and quickly glanced around him; only one person was looking over at him, and he figured he'd give it a shot. Besides, he only had two names left and only one was a guy. Quickly he looked up, the man in front of him was trying to appear as if he weren't looking.

"Excuse me," the man still tried to ignore him. "I need to talk with you for a moment, I'm from the CIA."

"I know know, you've been flashing your name around to everyone in the room, Agent Black."

"Then you must know what I'm here for. Do you?"

"Yeah, but that doesn't mean I feel like talking to you."

"Listen"—Agent Black held up the file in his hands—"I already have some of the information I was sent to collect, however not everyone here is being very forth coming about it. If you would be so kind, mister?"

"Haley, Chris Haley." He seemed almost upset the agent didn't know his name.

"Right," bingo, last name. "Mr. Haley, if you would be so kind as to help me with some of this gathering, I would be obliged to pay you."

"You are trying to bribe me now?"

"You know what, never mind." Agent Black turned and grabbed his leather book and went to walk out the door, but after he reached the door he remembered that he left the folder with Haley and so he walked back.

"Here you go," the man said, looking strangely angry as he gazed over toward the girl he had spoken to first. "Wouldn't want to forget this now would you spook?"

"Thank you for your time." As he left, Agent Black opened the file, inside were all the fake papers he'd planted from the agency, but near the middle was a new piece. It was three pages long and three different biographies stapled to it. He found his mole, and the mole gave him the pieces he needed to get the investigation into full swing. If his instincts were right, those names had something to do with the bombings, Agent Windburg's death, and the message Matthews received a few days earlier. The mole was quick though, he gave him that.

Celia grabbed the file from her desk again and flipped it open, still mesmerized with what she had found, at least until she opened the file and found the bios were gone. At first she thought she left them at the computer, but when she checked, they were nowhere to be seen. She rechecked the file, checked her other files, and even opened her drawers—still nothing turned up. Then she remembered the agent, who she didn't even look up to see. She wanted to smack herself for being so naïve, for just leaving it out for him to take, but it was too late now. The notes on the pages, the bio's the pictures, everything she had on them was gone except for what she had in her head. She was upset, understandably so, and no one else seemed to notice that she had lost her most important piece of information to the guys she was investigating. At least that's what she thought until a hand touched her shoulder.

"Celia, why so pissed?" Chris stood to her side and looked sorrowfully down at her.

"Why? Because I'm an idiot, Chris, I messed up and I can't fix it."

"Come on, it can't be that bad."

"Just leave me alone, Chris, I have to think about some stuff, all right."

Chris really wanted to make her feel better; he didn't really care that he had put her that that situation, but he did want to be there for her. He thought desperately on how to fix it, but wasn't really thinking about much more than the way her dark hair curled over her shoulders when he started speaking again.

"Listen, you can't beat yourself up over that file, it wasn't your fault. These CIA guys are trained to—" he watched her face change suddenly, became angry but looked at him in disbelief. "What?"

"I didn't say anything about a file, Chris." She stood and searched his eyes, guilt strikingly apparent on his face. "You gave it to him, didn't you? Tell me!" she demanded.

"Celia, I didn't, I just wanted…" he paused, barely able to think. "I just—" she cut him off.

"What did he pay you or something? Huh?!" she started to back away, reaching down and grabbing her files. "You know what?" She turned around to her boss, who was still standing with others at the other side of the computer room "Major, sir?" she called out.

"Celia, wait." He tried to grab her, but she turned and hooked his arm under hers then twisted until he bent over, then she used her heel kick him in the head. He collapsed, holding his head, and she stepped away as everyone turned to look.

"Agent Salviana, would you like to tell me what the *hell* you are doing?" The Major had started over to them; MPs were already rushing by people to get to the scene.

"Sir." She stood straighter, still panting a little as he walked up to her. "I don't know why but Chris gave that Agent Black the Kandahar file."

"Agent Black?"

"The CIA, he gave him back a file they wanted to cover up, and now it's gone." She felt like kicking him again, but she restrained herself.

"Is this true?" The major looked down at Chris, who was just starting to stand.

"Uh…" he looked up at her and cleaned off some of the blood that had formed above his lip. "I…um." He looked around, smiled, and attempted an evasion. "No, sir, she and I are just having a little dispute over a date. No big deal, sir."

"What the hell!?" she went to hit him again but the MPs behind her gripped her arms and kept her at bay.

"I hope you realized she accused you of paid espionage, most couples don't do that."

"I know, just a falling out." He looked at her with disdain but hid it relatively well.

"Major, that's not true! He's lying!" the room was silent, then she looked at the major, but his face was unbelieving. But when she looked at Chris, he looked worried; he was staring at something behind the Major.

"Excuse me, Major Blake," a voice rang out of the silence and he turned to acknowledge.

"Can I help you?"

"No, probably not. But I can help you." Then he looked over at Celia, his eyes still shrouded but his devious smile perfectly visible. "Well, I can help *her*." He lifted a file from in his hand and handed it to the major. He took it and opened it up.

"What is all this?"

"Major, that file is full of fake information, a ruse I used to find if someone takes the bate." He looked over at Chris, whose face was now a ghostly white.

"And how does this help?"

"Well, sir, none of that information has to do with the case, I set it up that way, but when I left the file with this man"—he pointed to Chris—"and came back to get it, there was an extra packet of information. Three pages long, center of the file with names and biographies of three persons. Your man, Mr. Chris Haley, removed that from Agent Salviana's files and placed it in there, assuming I would take what I had and burry it in the CIA archives."

"Why would you do this?" the Major asked Chris, but he was speechless, so Agent Black filled in the blanks.

"We at the CIA knew that Agent Matthews, the man whose past you happen to be investigating, had a mole in your little outfit. So we, wanting to make sure that truth came to our attention and yours, decided to get rid of the mole, just in case something were to happen to some information key to the case."

"The CIA wanted truth?" someone asked from the back.

"Believe it or not, we are on your side, we're the good guys, and we *do* want the truth. It's just in our business sometimes our men confuse fact with fiction and then try to keep it that way. We dislike cheats as much as the next guy, so we decided to help."

"That's pretty nice of you, guys. Why haven't you done that before?"

"Mostly because when it comes to information, we're the best, and a lot of other agencies are jealous of that. Makes it hard to make friends." He smiled and turned around, about to walk out when he said, "You should keep her on the case, and you should get back to work." He turned and backed out of the office. "You're welcome." And he was gone.

"Sir, what do we do with him?" the MP asked as he grabbed hold of Chris.

"What do you think? Just put him in the stockade." He turned around. "Everyone else get back to work, I want to nail this Agent Matthews to the wall." Then he turned back to Celia, handed her the file, and said, "If we can't nail him on this file, we can at least nail him to Chris. Nice kick by the way." Then he went back over to the computers.

Celia exhaled, her heart rushing a mile-a-minute in her chest, and her hands shaking with adrenaline. She sat down and laid the file down next to her then rested her head on her hands. She was so caught up in what just happened, in fact, that she barely noticed the sirens fill the room until someone came up and told her.

"Celia, someone is having a shootout at the CIA office."

PINNACLE

0827 hours, July 21, Outside Camp Bastion
Helmand Province, Afghanistan

First there were noises; muffled shuffling and what he thought could have been voices. Sound resonated like an echo in a cave, barely understandable and impossible to tell where it came from, only that it was there. Finally his vision returned, at least for a moment, and he was able to see through what appeared to be broken glass a wave of smoke and sky of sand. Hanson's mind cringed at its sight, flashing images of bodies and craters through his mind until it peaked at the moving picture in front of him, his sight locked on the smoke as it drifted by. He felt heat, beads of sweat forming and dropping off his hands and ears as he gazed at something moving in the smoke. A silhouette, a person, walking quickly behind the curtain. At first he thought it was Billy, coming through to pull him out of the monstrous dream that he had been locked in, but he remembered Billy was gone. He thought it was another soldier, someone from his dreams who he had only seen lying dead on a battlefield, but it wasn't. His heart pounded like a heavy drum, his mind screaming some warning that he still couldn't understand until it was too late. The man coming through the smoke was Zahid.

The name caused his heart to pump faster, pure rage building in him as he strived for control over his failing body. He watched in a blur as Zahid reached in and pulled some man out of the other side of the chopper. *Matthews,* his mind whispered; he remembered his name. He reached up and unplugged the safety harness, dropping to the ground as his world spun over and he regained his balance, slowly moving himself out of the chopper. The sounds of the sand and the wind become more and more clear until everything had gone from the dull haze to the crisp nightmare of the crash.

He looked around, striving to see where they had gone until he saw the tracks moving up and away from the crash site, a dragging stripe of sand left by the body Zahid grabbed. He stood and followed, trying desperately to see through the smoke until he reached the top of the small dune, but still the tracks went on. He followed them, his hands in front as he tried to see the tracks without losing his balance. Then the dragging track ended, and he looked around for the body, trying to find him or the one who took him. Then, just a few feet away, he saw Matthews lying in the sand, he went to go grab him, to see if he was still breathing or if he could help but before he could a massive pain struck in his back. He turned to see what had happened and felt as second pain in his abdomen. He looked down and watched as the blade was pulled slowly out of his stomach, his blood covering some of the glint that reflected off of the blade. He fell back, stumbling until he landed next to Matthews. He looked up at his assailant, and his eyes locked on the cold hard stare of Zahid, the blade still dripping crimson in his hand.

Hanson was in shock, barely understanding that he'd been stabbed as he panted, searching for an easier breath to pull into his wheezing lungs. He tried to push himself up on his hands, trying to only use his arms, but his abdomen roared its disapproval with a grimacing pain that climbed up his spine. He looked to his left; Matthews was just moving himself up from the ground when Zahid came and kicked him with the heel of his foot, knocking him back onto his side. Hanson tried to move, blood saturating his shirt as he strained upward, his hand caked with mud from his wound above his kidney, but he couldn't find the strength at first, and he collapsed back onto his knees. In front of him Matthews had started speaking, but Hanson could only hear part.

"...you doing this!? What are you after, huh?!" He could see Matthews sliding away from Zahid as he walked toward him, the knife still dripping with Hanson's blood. He dropped it into the sand, letting it stick.

"You want to know what I'm after. You want to know why?!" the man sounded mad in his anger. Hanson watched as a strange shiver ran up his muscular back. He kicked at Matthews again, and Matthews rolled himself with the strike and grabbed the knife, stepping hard into the sand while thrusting the knife's wide point up at Zahid. However, Zahid sidestepped the blade, using his forearm to push against Matthews's wrist as he grabbed the bottom of his hand, twisting upward and then pulling down ward as he turned, striking the now over extended agent in the chest with his left; the knife came out and flew as if thrown. Agent Matthews stumbled back but regained his balance, grasping his chest as he kept his other hand in front of him, watching through squinted eyes and sweat.

"Are you gonna tell me, boy, or we gonna circle?" The agent joked, bringing his hands into a stronger position as he staggered his feet, slowly closing in on the dark man in the gray work uniform. Zahid didn't wait for a second question, stepping quickly forward and thrusting his clenched fist in an uppercut, followed by a full salvo of elbows after the first strike missed. Matthews dodged one, but the second elbow stuck him just below the mouth, square on the chin. He staggered back, but Zahid had turned again and leaped into the air, crashing with a third elbow Matthews's clavicle; the snapping bone sounded sickeningly crisp in Hanson mind. He winced, heard a scream from the agent, and opened his eyes again just as Zahid had spun and smacked Matthews in the side of the head with the back of his fist; the agent crumpled to the ground, pushing himself away again with the arm that still worked. It was then that in Hanson's mind one image, the picture of him with his friend.

He stood straight, and started toward the bomb maker, but collapsed as his muscles gave out in his core, and he staggered to the side, holding himself up by the over turned chopper he had walked around earlier. The smoke started to clear around them, the sun finally breaking through to reveal the crash site, and now he could see perfectly as he approached the two men. Zahid seemed to be listening to the older man, Hanson could tell, though, that there would be no negotiating with him. Hanson went for his pistol strapped to his leg as he approached them, but it was gone. He looked back for a moment, trying to see if he'd dropped it, but again someone took him from behind, strong arms across his shoulders as he pulled him back and threw Hanson a few feet away from Matthews; Hanson watched as Zahid took out a pistol, his pistol, and aimed it at Matthews.

"You know why I'm here? One cannot forget murders like yours."

"What are you talking about?" Hanson could see a strange look of fear come across Matthew's face.

"The people, a whole family that you murdered and then burned their home to the ground. I was there." Matthews stayed silent "I remember the money they made you, the things they stole for you because you promised them safety, you promised us a better life, but we didn't know what you would really do."

"I ran out of time, it wasn't my fault. They were calling me back and if I left evidence—"

"You mean if you left my family alive someone would find out what you had done besides your job. So you killed them all."

"I didn't want to. I just—"

"Silence!" the bomber screamed "Shut your mouth! Your time for speaking is over." He clicked the hammer of the gun in his hand's back. "You killed my mother as she crawled away from the death trap you turned my home into. No matter what you think you did it for, I don't care, I have had my fill of waiting, and now that you are here, I will end you."

CLEARING

0830 hours, July 21, Camp Bastion
Helmand Province, Afghanistan

Agent Black walked through the broken window nearly awestruck with the destruction inside. Massive holes had been ripped into dry wall, and several bodies strewn the inside of the hall; only two were of the enemy. As he walked through the hall, he could still smell the gunpowder, the smoke from the guns, and one or two grenades still drifting through the hall like a terrible fog. Around the corner, another couple bodies, one more of the enemy who was wearing US military garb, several holes of blossom red scattered over the torn uniform. He knelt down next to it, tore off the American flag, and laid it atop the body of a true US soldier toward the end of the room. Then he heard it, a low but certainly audible whooshing, like the white noise of a radio. He kept walking, following the noise to the door of Matthews's office, where the final stand of the last two had taken place. Inside, he found four bodies, two of the enemy, two of his fallen soldiers, all dead strewn with papers and book that had fallen from the walls during the struggle. One of the enemies still had a bayonet in his abdomen, the man who stuck him a few feet away holding and empty pistol in his hand, the clip lying down near his feet.

The white noise was still calling indefinitely from one of the radios, and as he looked the room over he found it was the one still attached to the last enemy, who was sitting up against a wall, several bullet holes in his chest and legs. Matthews reached over and turned it off, silence followed quickly after, but just for a moment when the man stirred, opened his eyes, and tried to bring up his gun; Agent Black just rested his heavy hand on the rifle and gave the man a stare.

"What's your name?" he asked the dying man.

"Has…" he wheezed, blood bubbling in the back of his mouth. "Hassan." He finished.

"Why are you here?" he asked, maybe learning which of these men would be the bomber everyone had been searching for.

"To protect him."

"To protect who? Zahid?" Hassan's eyes started to close but Agent Black straightened his head. "Come on. Is it Zahid who you protected? Which one is he?" The dying man chuckled a little but winced at the movement.

"He is not here, American, he is not one of the dead." He pushed himself up a little as he looked around the room. "Strange," his voice was beginning to waver. "We fought with death to protect the dealer of it. He will finish what he started, your beloved devil Matthews will die." Blood started to poor down his cheek, and Agent Black's mind registered what he's just heard.

"I'm sorry, but Matthews isn't here, your men are dead, and he is safe. You failed."

"No, he is not safe; soon you will see." With that, the dying Hassan's eyes rolled to the back of his head and his breath finally came out; none went back in.

Agent Black stood, thinking intently on what he'd just heard. He tore off the radio from Hassan's chest and turned it back on, switching to the right frequency. "Chief, Chief, this is Agent Black, where is Agent Matthews?"

"He's on his way to Kandahar last I checked."

"Call his chopper, make sure they're still flying."

"Yes, sir, but why?"

"Because I don't think our bomber is in here, and one of his boys seems pretty confident that he is on his way to kill him."

"Yes, sir." The radio went silent.

———◆———

Celia couldn't believe her eyes. Right in the heart of a US base, a firefight went on and nearly destroyed the entire building. She had seen battle in the field, and it didn't phase her really, but she had never expected it so close to the place that had been home for such a long time; it was like someone had broken in to her house. She didn't feel safe. It seemed like hundreds of people had collected around the building, many of whom were making their way back and forth with stretchers for the wounded and body bags for the dead. She walked over to one of the men on the stretchers, his eyes closed and his mouth covered with an oxygen mask, but his chest moved slowly up and down as he held onto his breath. Blood, what seemed like only a small amount, had collected on the side of his leg and soot caked with sweat had matted around his face except for where his sunglasses had been. She moved away from him, watching the others move by her as she looked for someone she could talk to, learn more about what happened in there. Finally she reached a man who was lying up against a short crate, a white wrapping around his head and covering his left eye.

"Hey." She put her hand on his shoulder and he nearly jumped at the touch. "You want to tell me what happened?"

"Um." His hands were shaking, "I...uh, well, my partner and I had cornered a couple guys, a nurse said had drugged her or something. Uh...it all happened so fast."

"It's okay, take your time." She dropped one of her knees to the ground.

"Well, uh, one of them pulled out his gun and was pointing at Stan."

"Your partner?"

"Yeah. And then somebody else fired out at us, I think from the building and then..." His hands shook more and his lip quivered.

"And then they hit him. I got hit in the leg then, when I fell one of Stan's shells landed on my eye and…" he whimpered a little.

"Okay, okay, don't worry about it. Just rest, buddy, you did good." She stood and went to walk away.

"Ma'am?" he called out.

"Yes?" she turned back to him.

"After I fell, I remember seeing the other guy, the one who pulled his gun after." He waited for her to acknowledge she understood; she nodded her head. "Well, after I fell, I saw him running over to a chopper on the other side of the building. I think it took off. It was strange, I first saw one helo go up then he went up too. It was like he was chasin' somethin'."

"You're sure, soldier?"

"Yes, ma'am, I'm sure." He looked away then, off toward one of the body bags, which she presumed had Stan's body resting inside.

"Private!" she called to one of the men heading in. "Who's in charge here?"

"The chief, I mean, Chief Walters, ma'am, but he left to check on something for Agent Black."

"Then where is Agent Black?"

"Inside, ma'am." Then the private kept on walking.

She walked in, stepping into the now dimly lit interior of the hall and made her way down the hall, asking for Agent Black as she went. One of the men told her he was on his way back from the offices, and so that's where she went. She caught him just before he rounded a corner.

"Agent Black!" she called out. He turned to see who called him.

"You can thank me later, Agent, I'm pretty busy with other things."

"I'm not here to thank you, Black, I think I know where the bomber went."

"What!?" he immediately jogged over to her.

"I was talking to one of the men that cornered him and one of his men, he said he saw him jump in some chopper and take off like he was after one that had left earlier." She looked at his face and was surprised with the knowing look in his eye. "*Was* he after something?"

"Agent Black." The radio buzzed to life.

"Yes," he acknowledged, holding his finger to the radio for her to listen.

"Hey, your Agent Matthews isn't responding, I pinged his chopper several times."

"Well, did you track it?"

"Yes, sir, and I think our computer might be on the fritz."

"Why do you say that?"

"Because it says he's right outside, and there's another chopper right next to him."

"Outside the camp?!" he yelled.

"Yes, sir, and I think Corporal Hanson went with him."

"Hanson?" Celia asked, remembering the man she'd met, the same one she told to go to hell. She realized what that other chopper was there for; everything came together in her head. "We need to get our men out there right now." She turned and started to the door.

RECKONING

**0840 hours, July 21, Outside Camp Bastion
Helmand Province, Afghanistan**

Hanson watched, half with horror and the other half with rage. In front of him, Zahid had pulled back the hammer and fired into Matthews's leg, blood spattered over his face and sand kicked up from underneath; the bullet went through and through. Hanson looked over and saw it, still resting in Matthews holster was his .45, it was just in reach, but Zahid was still watching.

He looked up at Matthews, whose face was cringed in pain as he gritted his teeth, holding onto his bullet wound. Hanson looked up at Zahid, looking right at the monster he had hunted for weeks that now stood with a gun in his hand, holding his own life again in his hands. Then it came to him, like a strike of lighting in a dark forest of thought he realized how to get the gun, and how to get behind Zahid. He positioned his legs beneath him, his back and stomach feeling as if a blade ran all the way through, but he pushed the pain aside, lurching himself over Matthews to protect him, unsnapping the pistol with his left hand, and he started to pull, but Zahid knew too quickly. He threw himself downward, ramming the handle of his pistol into the back of Hanson's head. Dazed, Hanson's grip slipped just a little, and Zahid capitalized, ripping Hanson off Matthews and throwing him to the left. He pointed the gun at Hanson and prepared to fire when Hanson heard it, sand slipping beneath rapid steps behind him. Zahid noticed too.

Quickly he went to grab Matthews, pulling him up to act as a shield as several men moved in around the area where they stood. Zahid didn't notice the .45 fall out of the holster. Zahid went to back up, screaming for them to back away as he pressed the gun to the bleeding agent's head.

"Put the gun down, Zahid," a voice said from behind him, one that Hanson recognized but wasn't prepared to hear. In front of him, pointing a rifle at Zahid's head was the man who Matthews had called Agent Black but the voice was different, a strange deepness to it reminded him of... Daniil?

"I will not," Zahid spoke quietly, his resolve to death apparent in his voice.

"Listen, we know what he did to you, we can handle him. Just put the gun down and both of you can walk away from this."

"I do not want him to walk away!" Zahid screamed, pulling himself closer to the side of chopper and resting his back against it.

"Zahid, you don't want to do this."

"Don't tell me what I want, you have no idea," he said, his voice lowering again. "But you soon will see." He clicked the hammer back again, the sound as cold and metallic as his eyes as he looked at Daniil.

"If you pull that trigger, you will have had only a small part of your revenge." He glanced over at Matthews, who was now looking less afraid than guilty, eying Daniil with disdain.

"What are you telling me?" Zahid smirked. "That you will try him for his crimes, and he'll pay for them." He laughed. "Your justice is a mockery. You allow your criminals to live for free with more accommodations than children in my own country."

"He'll be tried by an international court and whatever they decide goes. If you let him go, and let the people exact their revenge on him as well, then maybe you will not have to die. I cannot promise..." he stopped talking when Zahid started to laugh again.

"Do you think my men died in your camp so that I could fail? I do not fear death, and neither did they! This conversation is over." When he was about to pull the trigger, a shot rang out. Matthews cringed, not crying but pulling himself to the ground. Daniil drew his pistol and aimed at Zahid, but he noticed that he hadn't fired, and then he saw the blood in his side. He looked right and Hanson had picked up the .45 and fired into Zahid's side. He fired again, and Zahid fell to the ground. Agent Black tried to stop him, but he pushed him away.

The world seemed to slow again, pictures in Hanson's mind of a distant battlefield, a picture with him and a friend, the smell of burning flesh and rifle fire filling the air. He stood over Zahid, their eyes connecting truly for the first time. In his mind, he heard his own voice as if it weren't him, calling Billy's name, pleading for him not to be dead. He remembered the flags over coffins, he remembered the man in the medical center breathing hard in his sleep as he lay on the bed. All the images of death that plagued his mind had built up in his mind's eye as he gazed into the dark eyes of his enemy. He raised the gun, the images in his mind locking onto the white dot at the tip of the pistol.

"This one's for Bill," he said and then pulled the trigger.

Everyone stood in silence around then, the sound resounding around them like a shout in a cavern. Agent Black was the first to move, picking up Agent Matthews and handing him off to a man behind him, who immediately called for the medic who was behind the chopper to come around with a stretcher. Another pair of Navy corpsman pulled the body of the pilot out of the wreck, laying him next to his fallen bird. Several soldiers crowded around Hanson, pulling him away as he dropped the gun and sat him next to a medic, who immediately ordered he be taken to the camp hospital. Agent Black turned back around, finding Agent

Celia kneeling next to the body of Zahid, looking down at his left hand. As he walked over, he noticed she had pulled a folded piece of white paper, but when she unfolded it, she realized it was a picture. She looked at it for a moment and then stood to show it to Daniil. "Agent Black," she said, still only knowing him by his alias. "Is this of his wife and son?" She handed him the picture, a woman holding the hand of a child.

"I don't know, just put it back with him." And so she took it and placed the picture of his mother and him into his pocket then stood and walked away.

"I'm gonna go see how the corporal's doin'," she said, and she followed after the medic with Hanson, sat in the side of the Humvee, and closed the door. As it pulled away, a second one pulled up and they began loading Matthews into the back. Daniil walked over to him.

AWAKE

0950 hours, July 21, Camp Bastion
Helmand Province, Afghanistan

"Agent Richard C. Matthews," Brish said as he walked into the small white room, bullet holes still riddled the walls around where Matthews was seated, a desk set in front of him.

"Don't talk to me like some suspect," Matthews snapped. "I know the routines freshees like you go for, Agent Black." His cuffed hands were tied, his leg was wrapped and the doctor had said he was stable for interrogation.

"Agent Matthews, I hope you don't see yourself as a suspect. No, you were a suspect after we found discrepancies in your files over a month ago. You became more after that message Zahid sent to your phone. You remember, after we lost Agent Windburg."

"Circumstantial, any of what you think you know is circumstantial. I'm clean, Agent Black, at least according to your books."

"Yes, but not according to what Corporal Hanson told us." Matthews went completely silent, not even breathing. "Yes, from what he said, not only did Zahid, who just so happened to be related to your old contacts, know who you were, but he did all of this, everything that happened to our soldiers, to bring you back here. Apparently his vendetta against you was more than just hate." He sat down at the desk in front of Matthews and slid a picture over to him wrapped in a plastic bag. It was the one Zahid had in his hands. "The woman in the picture, as our computers told us, is the same one who worked for you years back. Her husband and elder son too. The strange thing is, they all died, same day, just before you packed up to your big office in Denver." He stared at the white-haired agent, his face seeming to grow older by the moment as his strength slipped away. "So do you want to tell me what really happened to them, and why? Because, circumstantial or not, our evidence plus Hanson's testimony is enough to put you down, big man. Do you have anything to say in defense?"

"No." The old man went quiet.

"Good, you come quietly, and we can send you back to the States, where we can prosecute you, and well, I'm sure you know the rest." He wasn't sure if that was exactly what Windburg had said to Jakub, but he had to give it a shot; last time it worked.

"All right, but I want a lawyer." It worked this time too. Daniil felt like saying "good boy," but he thought one good line was good enough.

Light alternated from dim to brilliant above the lids of his eyes. He knew it was there, but when he tried to move to cover them, he found his hands would not respond. He felt nothing, heard only dim sounds of voices, clanking of medal, and some strange ringing that refused to move from his mind. He tried to reach out, tried to turn off any of the sound or block the lights but still his arms were caught, still his hands would not move; he felt paralyzed. Then a touch, a small bit of warmth on his leg, then his arm, growing higher up his body until it seemed to vibrate over his skin.

The light started to grow dark, the sounds started to die away except for the ringing. Instead it grew, multiplying in intensity until it clouded everything else around him. An image flashed— too fast for him to see at first, but then it returned from the darkness, again and again with greater speed until he could see it. Like a movie, his mind showed him his hands on a gun, the feeling of cold steel on his fingertips. Then another picture, another image growing in his mind and trying to push the gun away. Fire grew on the other side, the pistol growing black like a silhouette against a spotlight, but the other picture still pushed until he could see it. She was there, Billy was, too—both still together and both still smiling like he'd never left her for the war.

He saw himself, his arm around Billy's neck as they smiled, and his wife pressed close to him, still laughing. He wanted to say something, wanted to yell to them not to go, but still he couldn't move. The fire grew again, the pistol locking itself into firing position, the ringing drowning everything out as if he were still lying on that broken battlefield, smoke and sand concealing the bodies beyond, but his mind told them they were there. The gun was in his hand, the picture in the other, and they seemed to be intertwined, caught together as if they were the same.

Then the ringing started to slow, started to fade along with the fire, the smoke and sand pulling back as it grew quiet; someone walked through the smoke in front of him. His voice was barely audible, or was it a she, he couldn't tell. But it was asking him something, wanting him to do something. He closed his eyes, everything but the voice gone and he could hear it. A single phrase, reverberating louder and louder with each time it was spoken. *Let go.* His hands tensed, he felt himself under control and so he clenched, tightly holding onto the gun and picture; he couldn't let go. *Let go.* It repeated, it was only a whisper, not pleading, not begging, just suggesting, as if it were a small choice. He tried to say he couldn't, wanted to explain what he had to do, why he held fast to the gun and picture, but the voice didn't care.

Let go, it asked, once more. Silence followed and he was there, standing in the sand with his gun in his hand, his picture in the other. Then he started, little by little opening his fingers and starting to let go. It was his mind that tried to hold on, forcing him to grip harder, but he resisted and finally prevailed. The gun dropped into the sand and was consumed. In his hands, he held the picture. He took one last look, his friend still smiling, his life still reflected as a single moment. He let go, and it fell into the sand. He could hear his breath, his heart beat taking the place of the ringing. Darkness flowed like water over the scene in his mind, the sand and smoke steadily drifted away. The curtain lifted into shadow, and then his eyes opened.

Above him, a bright light shined down but then turned dull as his eyes adjusted. He could see tiles, white walls surrounding him. On the wall, a small clock ticked away, it was nearly six O'clock at night. He looked around again, the door was shut, the window was open, and a sliver of light that was cast onto the ceiling flowed down the wall to his left and over the door. He was back in the hospital. He felt something, a small brushing sound accompanying a warm movement on his arm. He turned and found someone was squeezing it lightly, a man with his head bent before the bed as if he were trying to rest, but his lips were moving.

"Hi," Hanson said, trying to see who it was. Daniil Brish immediately jerked his head up, grinned, and stood, sticking his hands into his pockets. He was still wearing mostly black.

"Hey, how those little cuts doin'?" he joked.

"Cuts... I can't say it's any worse than getting blown up, but it still hurts." Hanson closed his eyes for a second, took a deep breath, and then turned again. "Hey, were you praying?"

Brish smiled. "Yeah, was a little worried you'd wake up with amnesia or something."

"Wow, I didn't take you as a prayer."

"My parents raised me Christian in Russia, I just sort of stepped away for a while, thought I'd find my own way. As you can see, though, I couldn't stay away long, I couldn't help but pray."

"Well, I'm still here, so I can't say it didn't help."

"That's what I've found." He smiled and looked away, eyeing the room with a small piece of nostalgia in his eye. "Looks like you had the same experience with this hospital just couldn't stay away, huh?" Hanson laughed, still under pain killers so the jerking didn't hurt as much.

"Yeah, liked it so much I just had to bring a piece with me last time." He remembered his fall out with Celia and immediately remembered why. "Now here's my question, why on earth did you tell Cel—" he corrected himself—"Agent Salviana about me, and how did you know?"

"Hanson." A knowing look had crept onto his face, his steely blue eyes as kind as ever. "I just knew that you couldn't start a relationship on lies. I did it for you. To protect you." He tried to hold back his smile.

"Really?" Hanson was almost floored, but then Daniil lost his control and smiled. "I knew it, you didn't do that for honesty." They both laughed.

"Well, part of it was, the other part was something I shouldn't talk too much about. Had to know who had been taking some things that really weren't theirs. Turns out some of that was you, bud."

"And that's another thing. I've known you for almost a year and you're not even a soldier, you're CIA?"

"All right, seeing as you know too much already this won't be too much of a shock." He sat back down and began to explain, "I was sent here to be, basically, internal affairs for the CIA. They found something in Agent Matthews's past they didn't like, which had something to do with a large amount of money that trickled into his account from the Cayman Islands. Langley wanted to know why he had it, and so we started digging. Halfway through, Agent Matthews started digging into some more things about Helmand that had to do with attacks. We checked into it, a month later, I'm sitting in Afghanistan showing drill instructors a few moves while waiting for more information. It was when that third attack, the one you were in, that I received information that a mole had been placed. From there I had to go hunting with Agent Matthews, searching for a mole in CID and tryin' to figure out where all the money popped up. I got swamped, and so I got myself a new name, new clothing, and had to avoid people for a while. From there you know the rest."

"So you telling Celia, that was to find a mole?"

"Yes, first, I thought it was her, but it wasn't, however I came up with finding that she would be the one to figure out the part I couldn't get. Told Langley to give it to CID... they agreed—which I got to say they don't do often—but it worked out. Found the mole after Celia figured out the last parts of what we needed to know and now all that's left is for you to sign off on that record you told to us after you heard what the bomber said to Matthews."

He laid back in his chair and looked up at the ceiling. "It's sad really, one guy's greed and fear of getting caught sets the spark for something twenty years down the line and hundreds of soldiers pay the price. That's why I pray, I guess, because people are too fickle to pray to, and half the time they do it all for themselves. God don't have those problems."

"Yeah," Hanson said, still taking everything in. "So what happens next?"

"Well, we take Matthews to court, the money he stole goes back to Afghanistan, and the world court decides what to do with him. I'm sure your testimony will be helpful."

"And what about me, though, I mean, I did shoot Zahid."

"What!?" Daniil asked sarcastically. "From what our men remember, he resisted arrest, and threatened you. Self-defense presides over your case." Daniil stood, walked around the bed, and shook his hand. "Besides, it's a warzone out there, sometimes it's hard to see through the smoke." He smiled, winked, and left, leaving the door opened as he returned his hat to the top of his head.

Hanson rested his head on his pillow, his mind finally slowing, his heart finally at a resting pace. Thumping its approval with his calm against his chest. He sighed, oblivious that someone else had made their way into the room.

"What's up, doc?" she asked. Hanson immediately knew who it was. He turned to see her, she was smiling, her hair still up in her hat, but her posture far softer.

"Hey, I'm good." He remembered what she called him. "And it's not, doc. It's Damian."

"Yeah, I know. We went over this a while ago." She smiled at him, her face still a little sarcastic.

"Yeah," he said. "Yes, I remember. Listen, I'm sorry about all this, I shouldn't have lied to you. I should have just asked you for what you could give me."

"Did you have that prepared?"

"Why? Did it work? 'Cause if it did, then no, I'm just that good." He attempted a joke; she smiled a little—that was enough for him

"It was good. So how do you feel, did you get what you were looking for?"

"Honestly, I don't know, I mean, I think so, but I still feel like…" He hesitated. He didn't know what else to say. "I'm just not sure."

"Oh." She walked into the room, walking around the chair and came near the edge of the bed. "Do you know what else you're looking for then?" he closed his eyes, a certain woman in his mind, a picture of her smiling. He wondered if she was still smiling; he hoped she was.

"Actually, I think I do." He looked back up at Celia, he didn't know how to read her then; he didn't know if he wanted to. "Did you want to stay for a while, unless you still don't want to see me?" She shook her head, looked at him like he was a little too daring; he thought he was, but he didn't care. He just wanted one more shot. She turned around, grabbed a chair from near the wall and pushed it up near him, the back of the chair to him as she rested her forearms on the top.

"All right, Damian, we can talk." He smiled, she smiled; he almost said bingo.

SECTION FOUR

CINDERS

OOH-RAH

12:03 hours, August 2, Arlington National Cemetery
Virginia, USA

The day was typical for Virginia in August; bright sunlight, birds song's carrying through a light breeze, and grass an emerald green. As always, the grounds of Arlington were well-kept, grass cut in perfect lines, and the headstones kept brilliantly white. Everything rested in perfect order, each stone, each field, the trees even kept back so that light still rested upon every slice of open ground. Along the one side of the plots ran a road, long and straight like the places around it, at least for the stretch along the field closest to a line of dark trees, their green leaves shining against the light of the perfect sky.

It was on this road that a car, a small blue one kept cool under the shade of the trees that lined on side of the road. In the car, the radio was on, a young talk show host was still ranting about some American being tried on the world court; Kristine Tompkey didn't wait to hear what sentencing was passed; she just turned the radio off. She slowed the car, parking it to the side and stepping out the driver's seat she turned and opened the back door. A young boy, carefully balancing a bouquet of flowers; he handed it to her once out and then flicked his bangs to the side. The pair walked along the road to the end, stepping onto the grass and slowly making their way toward the other side of the wide open field. Her blond hair was down to the side, and she was wearing a blue summer dress that came down to her knees. Eventually they made it around the last set of stones till they came to one at the end of the field, looking out to the trees. The two stared at the stone for a moment, quiet, the young man surprisingly still.

"Hey, Billy," She said. "We're here." She smiled, staring down at the stone as if he were staring back. "Jed wanted to give you something?" She blinked a little, trying to keep the water from building in her eyes. "Honey." She pressed against Jed's back, and he walked forward, taking a box out of his pocket.

"It's, uh, it's the tank you got me for Christmas last year. I sorta figured you'd want something for the road." He placed it at the base of the grave, just below the inscriptions. "Aunt Kris?" he asked.

"Yes?"

"Should I have brought something else? Maybe he would have wanted something else, like a car or a plane or something."

"Oh no, Jed, he loved those things, and I think that one was his favorite. He gave it to you because you told him it was your favorite too." She knelt down and put her hand on his shoulder "You brought just what he wanted, Jed." He stepped back again and waited, staying quiet as he watched her place her flowers at the base.

"I think he liked your flowers too, Aunt Kris," he said, trying to make her feel better that she hadn't brought his favorite thing. She just smiled and said thank you.

"Hey, Jed," a voice came from behind them. "You think he'd like mine?" the pair turned around, Jed's face immediately glowing with a smile.

"Dom!" he said, running over to talk to him; however, he kept a little distance, as he believed he'd outgrown hugs. "I thought your tour ended in October."

"Got home on good behavior, buddy, now you gonna answer my question." Hanson pulled out a set of keys, the letters "Stang" etched into the plastic base.

"Oh, he'll love it." He went for it but then restrained himself. "May I?" he asked.

"Sure, take it to him." The boy took it eagerly, running back over to the stone, slowing himself down so that he could walk the rest of the way. As he went, Kristine went to Hanson and hugged him.

"It's really good to see you, Dom," she said as she let go. "I wish you could have seen the service, everyone was there."

"I heard it was great, I knew you wouldn't let it be anything less." She nodded in thanks.

"How long have you been home?"

"I landed this morning, took me a while to get here as I had to figure out what to bring him."

"Well, he would have liked anything."

"Yeah, but I knew he loved that car." He pointed out to the stone; Jed was just making his way back.

"Hey," she started, "how long until you do see your folks?"

"A couple days, they said I could use some time to think, although I *think* they were renting out my trailer so it was probably too soon anyways." She laughed, her eyes still watering.

"God, we missed you, guys," she said, holding back tears making her voice quiver.

"I know, I'm sorry, I didn't"—he paused—"I'm sorry I didn't bring him home." He looked into her eyes, wondering, fearing, and hoping she wouldn't hate him. She didn't.

"Don't, Dom. What happed out there isn't on you." She started to walk, calling Jed to come with her. "That wasn't on you. I'll see you at the house, all right?"

"Yeah," he said, watching as the two made their way to their car. As it drove away, he turned to the grave, straightened himself up, and walked to the grave. His uniform, the gold shining out from the blue under the sun, seemed like it wasn't appropriate; but it wasn't like Billy ever cared about clothes.

"Serge." He removed his cap and set it on the ground. "Billy, I don't know if you care about this, I know that I probably cared too much but..." from his pocket, he took out a small box and opened it, showing the content to the grave. "Can you believe they gave me a medal? There wasn't a big ceremony or anything, just the chief walking up and handing it too me before the plane took off." He looked at it for a moment, blurring in his eyes was pushed back when he squeezed his eyes closed. "It's for bravery. I don't like it, though; I just don't think it fits me." He closed the case again and laid it at the base, just below the flowers. "It suits you, though." He stood, looking down at the grave. "Yeah, looks good on you, bud." He backed away from the gravestone, holding his hands straight down as he stepped into attention. He took his hat up and placed it on his head. Above him the sun was shining down, its warmth against his shoulders, carrying a feeling of strange calm over him. He raised his hand to his head and saluted, holding himself in perfect standstill for what seemed only a moment. He brought his hands down, turned on his heels, and slowly walked away, feeling as though he still needed to do something, like the salute wasn't enough but he pressed on. His tan car sat still underneath the trees, and as he entered, he started thinking about what he would do, where he would go. He looked back once more at the grave, the white and yellow flowers shining bright before the stone looking majestic. He started the car, slowly pulling forward as he made his way to the gate. As he passed the graves he remembered what Brish said about people not being good enough, that was why he prayed. He didn't really know what to say at first, feeling as though he were running in a library, as if he wasn't supposed to. As he drove, however, he saw the picture of his friend and him and his wife, and the words just flowed into his mind. As the gates opened to let him out, the sun in front and the trees casting light shadows over his dash he mouthed out the words in silence. He ended with "ooh-rah."